The Last Call

The Last Call

A Novel

PHILIP JAMES JOHNSTON

iUniverse, Inc.

New York Lincoln Shanghai

The Last Call

iUniverse books may be ordered through booksellers or by contacting:

iUniverse
2021 Pine Lake Road, Suite 100
Lincoln, NE 68512
www.iuniverse.com
1-800-Authors (1-800-288-4677)

This is a work of fiction. All of the characters, names, incidents, organizations and dialogue in this novel are either the products of the author's imagination or are used fictitiously.

ISBN-13: 978-0-595-38952-0 (pbk)
ISBN-13: 978-0-595-83336-8 (ebk)
ISBN-10: 0-595-38952-X (pbk)
ISBN-10: 0-595-83336-5 (ebk)

Printed in the United States of America

CHAPTER 1

▼

The tavern closed at two o'clock, but Vincent usually let his friends stay until three. The digital clock, hanging on the red brick wall behind the bar, read 2:52 AM. The top-shelf liquor glowed deep hues of amber and gold, filtered through a smoky haze, in the dim bar light. Two men sat side by side along the business end of the counter, at the extreme end of the bar. The counter was long, with enough room for about twenty chairs, but the doorway was drafty; it was a clear shot for a gust of wind to run down the length of the room when the door was open.

It had been another long night of drinking, and as was customary at the end of a long night of drinking, Meridian started with his usual shit.

"I'm going to kill her, Vincent."

"You're not going to kill her. You're just loaded." Vincent gave Meridian that baleful stare that he usually reserved for last call, which for him should have been several hours ago.

"Vincent, I am going to rip her goddamn head off. I mean it this time. I am going to take my shotgun and hollow out that miserable bitch." Meridian slouched over the bar. The weight of the night was starting to creep up on him, and his shoulders sagged toward his chest. He rested his head on the polished wood banister, the touch cool to his skin. Suddenly, he sat up. "You know, I could get away with it. I really could. No one would find out."

James, seated next to Meridian, looked up from his beer. "You need to find her first."

Meridian let out a large burp.

"Yeah," Vincent chuckled. "Anyway, you'd be the first person the cops came looking for."

James nodded. "Vin's right, Meridian. Come on, man. You have to get over this. She left two months ago. She's probably far away by now. You can't change the fact that she's gone."

"She's probably living two towns away," Meridian replied.

James leaned into the bar and rested his chin on his hand. "I still don't get it. Why did she leave? You're telling me everything was going fine, and then one day, she just up and leaves?"

"No. Everything was going good. She had started talking about marriage, and I didn't say no, but I wasn't saying yes either. But that's no reason to leave."

James shook his head. "I don't know, Meridian. There had to be something going on with you two."

"I'm telling you no. And there was no warning. No note. And she took all of my goddamn money."

James chuckled. "Hey, she worked, too. But I do agree that you were responsible for most of what you guys had saved."

"That was my money!" Meridian snapped.

"But you weren't even married! Why in God's name would you open a joint account? That's just stupid."

"I didn't know it was a joint account."

"How could you not know? You went to the fucking bank with her and opened the account!"

"She's the one who worked at the bank. I trusted her. I don't know. Why are you bothering me about that? I'm not the one who went to college." Meridian glared pointedly at James. "I work for a living. Besides, I'm not good with that high-finance shit."

"Dude, don't bullshit me. You knew what a joint account was."

Meridian frowned. "I just didn't think."

"Well, you should have thought. She'd been dropping hints about getting out for years. And as soon as she took your money and split, you should have gotten a good lawyer."

"I did get a lawyer!" Meridian spat.

"Bullshit. You waited a month before you even tried to get a lawyer. And look—calling every lawyer in the phone book and then hiring the guy with the lowest hourly rate is not what I would call hiring a good lawyer. You know what? That doesn't even matter. By the time you actually got around to doing something about it, it didn't make a difference anyway. She was long gone." James sat up straight and sipped his beer. "What you need now is a private detective to find her, *plus* a good lawyer."

"Well, she took all of my money. How the hell am I supposed to pay for a private detective and a lawyer?"

"How much did she take you for again?" Vincent asked.

"Almost forty grand," Meridian sighed.

Joe Meridian was your average, single, working-class stiff. He'd been working as a technician at James' father's company since high school. His once thin and muscular frame had grown thick and barrel-chested, making him a tank of a man. Now pushing thirty, his dark brown hair was graying on the edges and thinning out on top. Joe's face was big, round, and kind; he could make people laugh with just a glance from his gray eyes.

Working at Cameron Voice and Data was what you would call a roll-up-your-sleeves-and-get-your-hands-dirty type of job. The company sold and installed the telephone and data systems that all companies needed but didn't want to think about.

The best compliment for those who were in this line of work was an absence of criticism or complaint. The job required long hours and came with untold frustrations. Everyone chipped in and wore as many hats as needed, including the technicians. In his years at Cameron, Meridian had pulled cable, physically installed the telephone systems, learned how to program them, and eventually learned to fix them when they broke. The work was tedious, but it paid well for a union job. And Meridian was good at it, so he stayed with it.

Vincent and James looked at each other, sharing a moment of pity for their old friend. James shrugged and looked down into his beer. Vincent turned to read the time on the clock. Then they looked over at Meridian and burst out laughing.

Meridian tipped his mug and swallowed the remaining third of his beer in one gulp. "I did love her, you know. I may not have told her, but I loved her."

"Well, you fucked that one up royally," Vincent said.

James was in mid-drink when his sudden laughter caused him to spit out his beer onto the bar.

"You guys really suck. Give me another beer, Vin," Meridian slurred.

"No."

"Give me a shot, then."

"No."

"Come on, man. It's the end of the night."

Vincent gave Meridian a pensive once-over. "What do you think, James?"

"I guess it's all right. Can't you see the man is wallowing in the mire? Line one up for all of us, Vin."

Vincent grabbed a bottle of whiskey, then lined up three shot glasses on top of the bar and very slowly poured three clean shots of whiskey.

"Cheers, big ears," James saluted.

"I love you guys," Meridian burped.

With one movement, the three of them drained their glasses.

Vincent motioned them towards the door. "Look, guys, I'm beat. I'm going to close up. I'll see you later."

"Okay, we're out of here." James stood up, his drunken frame wobbling a bit as he grabbed his coat off the adjacent bar stool.

The cold, crisp winter air hit James and Meridian immediately as they walked outside. It was one of those bright winter nights where the snow seemed to glow, reflected by the moonlight. Putting his arm around Meridian's shoulder, James turned to stare at the soft neon light radiating from the sign over the door of the Bell Lap Tavern. The Bell Lap—their bar.

Years ago, when this part of New Jersey was still mostly farmland, there was a dog-racing track in the lot across from the Bell Lap. This was back when gambling in New Jersey was mostly unregulated, and people would come from New York City to wager at one of many various dog- and horse-racing tracks that were scattered around the northeastern part of the state.

The "bell lap" was the final lap the dogs would run in their respective races. It alerted the gamblers to pay attention. The bellman would ring the bell, and the gamblers would come out from the bar and walk across the street to stand in front of the small wooden fence that separated the spectators from the track. They would bring their drinks, hold their tickets, and watch the dogs finish. Then they would go to the betting booths to collect their winnings—if there were any—and place wagers on the next race. They would then return to the tavern, stand at the bar, munch on hot pickled-peppers and sweet Italian sausage, and listen to the radio, waiting for the announcer to signal the start of the next race.

Appropriately enough, the bar across the street from the dog track was named the Bell Lap Tavern. Eventually, gambling was regulated, and the dog track went out of business and was ripped down. As the area became more populated, it was replaced by typical suburban fixtures: convenience stores, donut shops, and gas stations. The tavern itself changed owners half a dozen times over the years, fell into increasingly greater disrepair, and was now the property of one Al Capalba, managed by Mr. Vincent Ferrara.

The neighborhood had fallen into disrepair as well. Originally, it was one of a great number of growing commuter suburbs, full of life and energy, that had sprouted like weeds all along the length of the Hudson River on the Jersey side. Young and vibrant, the community had provided the American Dream for the increasing number of middle-class families who moved into the area. Now, it had become tired, worn, and faded. Most people of means had moved west into newer and more spacious suburbs, traveling the highways that had given rise to the sprawl that society today held in contempt but coveted without reservation.

The decaying neighborhood around the Bell Lap was like many of the other once-thriving suburbs in New Jersey. It was now composed of a mix of the young, the working class, the immigrant families, the elderly, and the "lifers" (those people who stayed because it was all they knew). Collectively, they had not been able to muster the impetus necessary for urban renewal; no grand plans had been conceived, and maintaining what they had was all they could do.

This is not to say that people didn't care. Streets were still swept; people still repaired their roofs when they leaked and replaced their house siding when it started to rot out; and they made a living, working and shopping at the neighborhood stores. But there was a general sense that the status quo could not be preserved forever. Soon, things would change, for better or worse—and everyone knew which way the smart money was betting.

But the Bell Lap Tavern remained, and the name stuck, and half of the regulars now didn't even know the story behind their favorite bar's name. What they did know was that the beers were cheap, and the buy-backs were frequent. And the Bell Lap still had pretty good hot pickled-peppers, and every one of the Bell Lap's owners, over the years, had taken pride in upholding the hot pickled-pepper tradition, never deviating from the original recipe. And the peppers still were free for customers.

James and Meridian swayed down the street, arm in arm. Their vehicles were parked around the corner in a vacant lot owned by James' father. They thought it best to walk past them.

James Patrick Cameron was the son of James Cameron, Sr., founder and owner of Cameron Voice and Data. James was of good height and build, blue-eyed, with dirty blonde hair. He had grown up in town, like the rest, but went to college in Florida, majoring in journalism—he was good at it and had hoped for a promising career. But after college, he returned home to work for the summer at the family concern, which turned into a year, which turned into a full-time job selling the very solutions that Meridian worked to install. Home he had come and home he had stayed, and the promising career remained just that: a promise.

"I think I'm sleeping over," Meridian said.

"Sure, c'mon. We'll walk it. It'll sober us up a little."

"I'm getting too fat to walk that far."

"It's only about ten blocks. The exercise will do us good."

"Maybe we should get a Freddy pie."

James began to salivate. "That's the best idea I've heard tonight."

To most of the local citizenry, Fred owned the world's best pizzeria. Fred was an off-the-boat Italian who barely spoke a word of English. He spoke with his pizza. He was a night owl and rarely opened before five o'clock. And his pizza joint was always hopping. On a good night, Fred took his two-line phone off the hook around ten o'clock because he had more orders than he could fill by closing time. His closing time was a moving target. Sometimes he would close at midnight; sometimes, if he was in a good mood, he would stay open until the last hungry straggler rolled in. And he absolutely never delivered. In fact, he didn't even write the names of the customers on the boxes. He would simply tell them when to come to get their pie. When someone walked in the door, he would simply take one of the pizzas off of a stack that was warming on top of the double oven and ring it up.

The official name of the place wasn't very original: Pizzaland. People in the know called it "Freddy's."

Nobody in town seemed to know or care what Fred's real name was. The story goes that when Fred first opened his pizzeria, a man stumbled in for a pie after a night of drinking (it wouldn't be the last time). Fred tried to explain his name to the man, but Fred's English was too poor, and the guy was too drunk to follow him. "You're name is Fred!" the man declared. And it has stayed Fred ever since.

The local boys were always able to walk in off the street and weasel a pizza off of old Freddy. Fred would give them a look, and then waggle his finger and say, "You shoulda call." He'd shrug and ring them up for one of the fresh pies.

A pizza right now sounded good. James and Meridian decided to take a shot and see if Fred was still open. Comfort food was always the thing that made things better, no matter how bad a situation was.

They made off in the direction of Pizzaland.

The warming aroma of Fred's efforts permeated the air as they walked into the small, narrow room. An old man sat smoking a cigarette at one of the two two-person tables that butted up against the right wall. As usual, Fred was dressed in a white T-shirt and white pants. His white apron was covered in flour. Fred smoked a cigarette as he leaned against the left-side counter. At least twenty pizzas were piled up on top of the double ovens right behind him, and the phone hanging on the wall, adjacent to the ovens, was, as usual, off the hook.

James and Meridian leaned across the counter, feeling the heat coming from the oven. "Fred, thank God you're still open," James said. "We need two pies."

Fred's pizzas were not large, about twelve inches in diameter, so one person could eat a whole pie if he were hungry enough.

Fred took a long drag on his cigarette and rubbed his considerable belly. What hair he had left at the sides of his wrinkled head was white. "You-a lucky I stay open. I still have-a some pie, but they-a going fast and then I close."

James reached into his pocket and pulled out fifteen bucks. "Thanks, Fred."

Fred leaned over the counter and took a drag on his cigarette. "You-a guys-a drinking too much. You should be home!" Fred scolded.

James grabbed the pizzas and felt the heat coming through the bottom of the box. A small wisp of steam flowed out from a space between the lid top, giving off a faint hint of garlic.

"We're on our way home now."

Meridian grabbed two sodas out of the small refrigerator standing against the wall and slapped a dollar down on the counter. "You're a lifesaver, Fred."

Fred smiled. "You two shoulda save your own life. What ten, fifteen years you come in here? And still at three in the morning? At least I'm-a making some money. You no get married, huh?" Fred pushed the butt of his cigarette into an ashtray on the countertop. "A woman would change your life, that's for sure! Now, get outta here!"

As they walked down the two-step entrance to the street, a younger group of late-night revelers approached the doorway. "You better hurry," James said. "There ain't a-many left, and they a-goin' fast."

James and Meridian continued down the street, each holding a pizza.

"Remember when we were that young," Meridian asked, breathing heavily in the cold air.

"No." They went on a few blocks farther in silence. "Don't worry, Meridian. She'll turn up. You'll see."

Meridian didn't answer. All James heard in response was the soft crunch of their footsteps in the snow.

CHAPTER 2

▼

The restaurant door blew in with a gust of wintry wind. Two men stepped into the dark interior, which was almost as cold as the day outside. Through watery eyes, they surveyed the carnage around them.

"This place is an absolute disaster!" Mike exclaimed. He scanned the wall for a light switch and flicked it on.

Mike Munro was Cameron Voice and Data's high-strung executive vice president and the confidante of James Cameron, Sr. He was also the voice of reason— although some would say he was only reasonable when he wasn't snorting cocaine or drinking booze, which wasn't often. He was a local kid who made good. He hadn't attended college, so Mike felt that any lack of knowledge was a slight against his character, and it must be immediately corrected. He began working for Cameron Voice and Data when the company was being run out of the basement of James, Sr.'s house. They both worked relentlessly to build the company, to make something happen with it. They also both drank like fish when they weren't working, but in those days that wasn't often.

By the time he was in his early forties, after twenty years with Cameron Voice and Data and some measure of success, Mike had promoted himself to executive vice president. The fact that there was only one vice president in the company didn't factor into his decision. He always wanted to be an executive, and he thought "executive vice president" had a nice ring to it. He was very proud of that achievement, just as proud as he was of the Mercedes he drove.

He was tall, with brown-black eyes and thick, jet-black hair that covered his large, square head. He was constantly moving, constantly on guard, as if he thought a predator were on the verge of attack. His appearance was always impeccable: custom suits, Italian shoes, and silk ties. Nothing less than the best would do for Mike.

He was a total piece of work.

"Mike, are you sure my father wants us to do this?" James asked.

"Don't be stupid. He owns the property now. He just wants us to check it out," Mike snapped.

"What the hell are we supposed to be looking at? I don't know anything about the restaurant business, except how to order from a menu. Shouldn't he have hired a consultant or something to do a proper audit?"

"Your father, hire a consultant? That would require him to spend some money," Mike smirked. "Let's just give it a once-over and get out of here."

The restaurant used to be an Italian place called A Taste of Italy. It had been a popular place for many years and served good, affordable food. Then the owner won the lottery and decided to make major changes to the restaurant. He ripped out half the tables and put in a bar, the prefab kind, like you can buy at Home Depot—the kind that are meant to go in a basement or sit on a deck. He just stuck it in the middle of the room, put half a dozen chairs around it, and stocked it up. No one really knew why.

A Taste of Italy's business very quickly faded after that. People talked about parties that went on all night. The rumor was that the owner left town with one of the college girls who started hanging around the place after he put the bar in.

The restaurant was in exactly the same condition as the owner had left it. There was still a faint odor of beer in the air, and the floor was a mess. The rug was ripped in several places, and two broken tables lay in a heap in the back corner. There was garbage everywhere.

James stepped around the scattered debris. "I can't believe he left it like this. You think he would have at least cleaned it up before he sold it."

They made their way to the kitchen. The stench of rotten tomatoes hit them as soon as they opened the door.

"Will you look at this mess!" Mike yelled.

The sinks and cabinets were covered in tomato sauce. The sauce was caked on just about every visible surface, along with various bits and pieces of food stuff. There were empty industrial-sized cans of tomato purée scattered around the floor. A large keg of beer was sitting in one of the deep sinks by the stove. It appeared that someone had vandalized the kitchen with reckless abandon. If it hadn't been for the fact that it was the dead of winter and the temperature in the place was barely above freezing, the stench would have been unbearable. As it was, it was bad enough.

"What the hell happened in here?" James asked.

Mike took a few tentative steps farther into the kitchen. He took care to not the get muck on his expensive shoes.

James followed. "Whatever made my father interested in a place like this?"

Mike opened the refrigerator door. The sight was worse than he expected, and it was accompanied by a terrible stench. "Maybe Booby needs a place for you to work. Didn't you bartend in college?" Booby was James Cameron, Sr.'s nickname. Mike grimaced, shutting the refrigerator door and glancing at James. "The guy just wanted out—and quick. Booby was drinking with his attorney at the Iberia House and happened to run into the owner. When Booby found out it was for sale, he and the owner came over here, but the asshole had forgotten his keys so they couldn't get in. Booby bought it anyway, right on the spot. Cash deal." Mike opened one of the cabinets next to the refrigerator. "He only saw it from the outside, but Booby felt he could turn the building around and make a nice profit. Your dad got it for about half its commercial value."

James reflected on this. It didn't even faze him that alcohol was involved in the latest major business decision. "It's funny; he hasn't even mentioned it to me. He must have made the deal more than a few weeks ago. It's done, right? He actually owns it? I mean, they had to do a title search and have it clear before he actually wrote a check, right?"

"Yes, I told you. He owns it. The title's clean. And he probably didn't mention it to you because it's none of your business what he invests in. He doesn't answer to you."

James gave Mike a dirty look. "I bet if he'd come in here, he wouldn't have been so quick to buy it."

Mike nodded his head in agreement. "Maybe so. But the property is in a good location. It will sell—after it's cleaned up first."

"Cleaned up! It needs to be fumigated." James kicked one of the tomato cans. "While we're at it, get a priest, because I think we also need to perform an exorcism." James turned toward Mike. "Who do you think my father will try to recruit for clean-up crew?"

"As late as you've been coming in recently, I think a little hard work would do you some good. It's not like you're setting the world on fire with your sales."

"Do you always have to be such an asshole?" James asked.

Mike glowered at James. "Just remember who the boss is."

"Gee, like I could ever forget." James gave the kitchen a final once-over. "This place sucks."

"Look, it is what it is. Let's get back and fill Booby in."

They walked out of the kitchen, through the restaurant, and back toward the door.

As they locked up the restaurant and got in Mike's car, James could think only how absurd this whole situation was. Here they were, his father's executive vice president and his sales manager, evaluating a trashed restaurant that had been bought sight unseen from a deranged millionaire ex-cook, instead of doing what they normally did this time of the day—drinking at happy hour.

James stared out the passenger window as they drove away, watching the drab brown, gray, and red buildings pass by. "Do you think my father would want to actually do something with the building, instead of sell it?" He watched an old lady, bundled warmly against the cold, hugged herself as she walked down the street. "This neighborhood could use something new."

Mike frowned. "I really have no idea. I hope to God not."

*   *   *   *

"Let's open a steakhouse!" Booby exclaimed. The excitement broke across his face like a tidal wave. He opened his arms as if to hug the entire room. "A big, fancy, old-fashioned, bourbon-and-fine-wine-drinking, aged-beef-eating steakhouse. It will be great! We can even have a dress code on Friday and Saturday nights. Jacket and tie required. We can renovate the dining room and put in big fireplaces at each end and have tables with overstuffed chairs. We can build a huge oak bar for cocktails. It will be the nicest place in town."

James Cameron, Sr., was a smallish man in his mid-fifties. Once thin and wiry, he had grown paunchy with age. Not one to actively work out, his weight fluctuated with the seasons, and the holiday weight he was now wearing clearly showed. He dressed neatly but not sharply, preferring off-the-rack suits and print ties. Today, he wore an older brown suit and yellow tie with martini-glass patterns. He was bald and round-faced and had dark blue eyes that still possessed a devilish glint. He was, however, a heavy smoker, and his eyes creased at the corners and sagged into his cheeks from years of squinting.

Booby, James, and Mike stood in the middle of Booby's office. The room was simply appointed. At one end stood a large, black granite table-top desk with matching high-back leather chair. Two smaller black leather chairs were pushed out in front of the desk. Behind the table-top desk was a black credenza. The only other item of note was a painting on the wall: It depicted a young woman, standing on a cliff in a storm, wrapped in a thin slip and a shawl, with one breast exposed.

James eyed the painting and smirked, as he had done many times before. He turned to his attention to his father. "Dad, that's a great idea!"

Mike turned beet red. "Great idea? That's a horrible idea." He pointed a finger at Booby. "You said you were going to flip it. Now you're *not* going to flip it?"

James rubbed his chin, reconsidering. "You know what, though? This is kind of a blue-collar town. Do you really think people would appreciate that kind of fine dining?"

Booby nodded. "I grew up in this town. I know the people in this town. I think they will love it." Booby smiled at Mike. "Come on, booby, have a little faith."

Booby was not only James Cameron, Sr.'s, nickname; it was his nickname for just about everybody he met. Cameron, Sr., was notoriously bad at remembering names. And when he was drinking, alcohol had the side effect of making him forget even the names of people he knew very well. After many years of having these memory lapses and causing himself no small embarrassment, he resigned himself to calling everyone "booby." And everyone called him Booby right back.

The great mystery was where he got the name "Booby" in the first place. A more common salutation might have been buddy, pal, friend, fella, or any one of a dozen others. But he'd settled on Booby. Cameron, Sr., couldn't remember where he picked up the name, either, so he told people it was something his grandmother from England had called the grandkids.

"Booby, you barely come to work now!" Mike yelled. "What's going to happen after you open up a steakhouse? Do you really think you'll be sober enough at the end of night to close it up? People will steal money out of the register right out in front of you, and you won't even know it. It will turn into a money pit. And how much is it going to cost to get this thing off the ground? Some big, grand, steakhouse? Oak everywhere and fireplaces? What? Two hundred grand?" Mike paced across the office. "There goes my bonus money."

"I'm not going to manage it. I'm going to have Russell manage it." Booby smiled.

"Russell?" James and Mike blurted simultaneously.

Russell Davis was one of Booby's best friends and social companions. He was a little younger than Booby, with thinning blonde hair and a perpetual suntan. They belonged to the local civic organization, ate lunch together, and entertained with their wives together. Russell had recently become Cameron Voice and Data's newest employee, assigned to the sales department. The fact that Russell knew nothing about the business or was even capable of learning the business didn't matter. It was a great hire, Booby thought. Plus, Russell desperately needed the job.

Russell had worked his entire career on Wall Street. He'd started as a retail trader and worked his way up. He was really starting to do well when he hooked up with Ivan Mandelbaum, or "Ivan the Terrible," as he was called on the street. Ivan was a high-profile, high-risk investor who was hugely successful. Ivan wanted to expand and was hiring brokers to trade on his account, as well as their own. It was a way to better leverage his investment strategy, he said. "We're all going to get filthy, stinking rich!" he said. Ivan had already made millions and seemed to have the magic touch. Russell invested everything he ever owned with Ivan.

For a while, everything was great. Russell and Ivan ate at the best restaurants, had the best tickets to the most popular shows, and were VIPs just about everywhere they went. Hell, Russell was even on a first-name basis with the mayor. And the money poured in.

When the FBI arrested Ivan, and the SEC closed the office and stripped Russell of his trading license, he didn't need to ask why.

"Insider trading," they said.

"That's the way the game is played," Ivan said.

Either way, Ivan went to jail, and Russell lost just about everything.

Russell occasionally received letters from Ivan. In his last letter, Ivan said things were pretty tough: They were redesigning the eighth hole on the prison golf course and the green was going to be closed for the whole season, so the warden was making them play the ninth hole twice. He complained that his official USGA handicap was going to be invalidated.

Russell didn't do so well after Ivan went to jail. Some people said he had a nervous breakdown; others said he just lost the will to live. But sometimes people just burn out.

Russell was in a pretty tight spot. He still was putting his youngest kid through school, and he was determined to see it through. It was a culinary institute, and it had to be the most expensive culinary institute on the planet. The fact that Russell's son was thirty and had never had a full-time job didn't faze Russell. The fact that this was his son's third full-time college-level endeavor didn't enter his mind either. He needed to put his kids through school, and he was going to do it.

Because Booby and Russell had been friends for a long time, and because Booby was always willing to help a guy down on his luck, Russell got the break that he needed: He was hired.

After a few days of training Russell, James realized that Russell wasn't going to be able to help with the business. So he showed him how to play solitaire on the computer, and Russell loved it. A few days later, James showed him how to play Tetris and Russell loved that, too.

"Booby, Russell has never managed a restaurant," Mike argued. "There's more to running a restaurant than just being a good host. You need to hire cooks and waiters, manage the books, the whole thing. This is ridiculous!"

"Relax, Mike. He can learn. I'm sure he'll do fine if he puts his mind to it. Besides, I could really use a great tax shelter." Booby smiled.

James rolled his eyes. "What are you planning to call it?"

Booby paced across his office. "I haven't really decided on anything. I've been tossing a few names around in my head. Let me bounce my favorite off you. How about 'The Mad Cow'?"

James' jaw dropped in amazement. The Mad Cow. Somehow, it seemed perfect.

Mike was beside himself. "What? Mad fucking cow? What are you? Fucking nuts? First, you tell me you're opening a restaurant. Then you tell me your stockbroker buddy is going to run it, and now you tell me you're going to name if after a disease! I haven't worked my ass off here for twenty years to make money for you to piss it all down the drain! You're going to sink hundreds of thousands of dollars into this whim, and it's going to be a disaster! Why don't you pay me another hundred thousand? At least I'll do something productive with it."

"Yeah, like put it up your nose," James muttered.

The more Mike ranted, the more enraged he became. Spit gathered at the sides of his mouth, and his eyes bulged. "You said you were going to flip the property! This makes no sense. I know you. In a few months you're going to get bored with the whole idea, and then it will be too late." Mike's face was beet red, and he shook with anger as he stared at Booby.

"Settle down, Mike," Booby said calmly. "This isn't a whim, and I'm not going to quit on it. I've been looking to do something different, and I think the timing is right on this. My gut tells me that the timing is right. I think it's going to be great."

"I think you've lost your mind," Mike snapped.

An uneasy silence followed. At last, James said, "You know, Dad, I kind of like it. When do we start?"

CHAPTER 3

▼

It was one of those nights again. James and Meridian slouched against the bar, each gripping a pint of beer. The Bell Lap Tavern was fairly empty for a Thursday, which was Ladies Night. Tonight, like most nights, the women the Bell Lap might have attracted were not to be seen. The women who would come in were typically young and poor, out looking for a few hours of fun or to meet some guys. They usually traveled in packs of three or four and didn't stay long.

James and Meridian had just stopped in for a few beers for happy hour, but one thing led to another and now here it was, going on eleven o'clock. Again. The jukebox blared, its sound filling up the smoky space of the room. Vincent was at the other end of the long counter, cleaning glasses and pressing empty beer bottles through an upright disposal unit.

The grinding noise of bottles being destroyed, coupled with the volume of the jukebox, was giving Meridian a headache. "Vin, please turn this shit down. And who played this disco dance crap anyway? Put on some rock and roll." He stared through a full pint of beer. Playing a game with himself, Meridian shut one eye and looked through the amber liquid, trying to focus on Vincent as he went about his work. Vincent appeared lost in a foamy, carbonated vision.

Vincent made his way down the counter, wiping the wood surface as he moved. "Okay, okay, I'll turn it down." He reached under the counter and adjusted the volume-control knob. Vincent turned to Meridian, "I thought your New Year's resolution was that you weren't going to drink anymore."

"I'm *not* drinking any more." Meridian gave Vincent a wink. "But I'm not drinking any less, either."

James burst out laughing, then asked, "Hey, Vincent, when do you think Big Al is going to sell you the bar?"

Vincent seemed to contemplate something off in the distance. "I hope soon. I've been bartending here, going on—what? Ten years? And I've always been the most reliable guy he's got. Hell, I'm the only reliable guy he's got. He leaves the day-to-day management up to me now, too. He really only comes in a few times a week to collect. His health isn't too good anymore. I think it would be a relief for him to get rid of the place." Vincent looked around the bar, at the aging lights hanging from the green, paint-chipped ceiling, at the smoke-stained wood paneling that covered the walls. "The old Bell Lap could use a facelift, too." Vincent continued his way past the men, wiping down the counter. "I think Big Al just wants to be sure he leaves it in good hands."

"Winding up owning the mighty Bell Lap Tavern is far cry from being an architect, right, Vincent?" Meridian chided. He was almost glad to be talking about someone else's failures instead of remembering his own.

Vincent's face grew sullen. "Yeah. That was a long time ago, Meridian. Do you really have to be such an asshole, considering all the free beer I let you drink?" Vincent threw his dishrag at Meridian's face. "At least I didn't let my girlfriend steal forty large from me and get away with it."

Meridian scowled. "I didn't let her get away with it. I'm still trying to find her."

"You are?" Vincent asked. He became animated. "Well, let me help. Maybe she's under the bar? Kelly, are you there?" He ducked down behind the counter for a few seconds and made a few muffled noises. Then he stood up, hopped over the bar, and ran to the ladies room. He opened the door and yelled in, "Kelly Chippendale! You in there? Kelly?" He slammed the door shut, jumped up on a table in the open area adjacent to the ladies room entrance, and signaled with his hands. "Excuse me! All Bell Lap Tavern patrons! May I have your attention?"

The few people in the place glanced in Vincent's direction, somewhat bemused.

Vincent continued, "Has anyone in this bar seen or heard from Meridian's ex-girlfriend, Kelly Chippendale? Has any one seen the lovely lady who stole forty thousand dollars from this man, his entire life's savings? Has anyone seen or heard from Kelly Chippendale in the last two months?"

A few people shouted no, a few people laughed, and one person yelled, "Loser!"

Then the room went quiet.

"Meridian, I don't think she's here, man. So why don't you go out and look for her?" Vincent walked back to the bar, lifted a hinged wooden section that served as the gate, and took up his usual station. Meridian had placed the rag back on the counter, and Vincent returned to wiping down the countertop.

"Sorry, Vin, I was only joking," Meridian said.

Vincent's face softened. "So was I, Meridian. So was I." He sighed as he took three shot glasses from a shelf behind the counter and placed them on the bar. "How about a round of shots on the house?"

James burst out in song. "I'll tell you a story of whiskey and mystics and men. I'll tell you a story about how the whole thing began." He stopped singing suddenly and stared at the shot glasses. "I don't remember how it all began. But maybe someday I'll figure out how it's all going to end."

Meridian gave James a withering look. "Uh-oh. Make way for the philosopher."

James studied Meridian. "Seriously, haven't you ever wondered if you've made the right choices in life? Haven't you ever wondered how different your life would be if you could go back to just one pivotal moment and make a different choice?"

Meridian wondered where James was going with all of this. "Like what?"

"Like…what if you'd joined the Marines after high school instead of taking a job humping cable? Where would you be now?" James took a sip of beer. "Or if I'd gone to that Ivy League school. And then what if I'd taken that job in Alaska instead of coming back here? Where would I be at this point?"

"Drunk. Just like you are right now." Meridian laughed at his perceived cleverness. "C'mon, James. Who gives a shit? The past is the past. You can't change it, and it's a waste of energy to even think about it. All we have is the present."

Vincent poured the whiskey. "Let's just drink for today, boys, and concentrate on the here and now."

"Here, here! Here, here!" they all chorused, raising their shot glasses to their lips.

"Hey, Vin," James said, staring pensively into his now-empty shot glass. "Still, do you still ever think about it? About not becoming an architect, I mean?"

Vincent scuffed a toe against the floor. "Yeah, sometimes. You know, it is what it is. I try not to dwell on it." Vincent filled the whiskey glasses again. "One more for the road."

Vincent Ferrara's name was very Italian but in fact, he was only half-Italian; his mother was Irish. His mother always said that Vin had his father's Italian good looks on an Irish fighter's body.

When Vincent was a boy, he was good at math, particularly geometry. At all the parent/teacher conferences, his teachers spoke very highly of his abilities: "He's an excellent student," they said. "He has such promise," they said. "College material," they said.

Vincent's parents were very proud. "Honey, someday, we want you to go to college," Vincent's mother would say. "We will pay for it, regardless of what it costs. No one in our family has ever gone to college. It would be an amazing accomplishment."

When Vincent was in the seventh grade, his parents got a divorce. The following year, his mom married a guy who was not that fond of Vincent, to put it mildly. The guy had a couple of kids from a previous marriage, and having more kids to care for was the last thing he wanted or needed. He did think, however, that Vincent's mom had a really nice ass.

Vincent's mother and stepfather started taking really nice, expensive vacations. Vincent thought it funny that his mother never took fancy vacations before the divorce. Of course, Vincent didn't get to join them on the nice, expensive vacations. "You're old enough to take care of the house," his stepfather would say, giving Vincent a wink. "No wild parties, okay?"

After the divorce, Vincent's biological father gradually had less and less contact with his son. Eventually, he remarried, started a new family, and lost contact for good.

Vincent's new stepfather didn't make enough money to support his lifestyle and his new extended family. Vincent's mother went to work part-time at the bakery, just to make end's meet. It soon became clear that they weren't saving for Vincent's education.

Vincent continued to be a good student through high school. He took a few mechanical-drawing classes and fell in love with architecture. He would design buildings, malls, schools, hospitals—anything that would allow him to manipulate form, style, and substance into something tangible and permanent.

When Vincent graduated high school and showed his mom his acceptance to State, his mother was very happy. But happiness doesn't pay tuition, and Vincent was told that if he wanted to go to college, he would have to pay for it himself.

He worked a few odd jobs and eventually wound up working at the Bell Lap Tavern. But going to school during the day and bartending at night took its toll; Vincent's grades started to slip. After two years, his grades were barely good enough to get him into the architectural program.

Vincent was tired, and he resented his stepfather—after all, if the man hadn't blown all Vincent's education fund on fancy vacations, Vincent wouldn't be in such a state. His resentment grew into hatred, and eventually, the cold silence that he reserved for his stepfather turned to confrontation, first verbal and then, ultimately, physical.

The end result was inevitable. Vincent was kicked out of the house, but not without first disowning his mother and cursing his stepfather. His stepfather told Vincent to never to come back; his mother had stood motionless and mute.

The added expense of an apartment, even one he shared with a roommate, was too much to bear. Vincent dropped out of college and took up a full-time career in "personal alcohol distribution management."

James scratched mindlessly on the rim of his beer mug. Suddenly, he sat up straight. "Guys, I almost forgot! This Sunday is the final game of the season, and I got four invites to the Jeff Lewis luxury box down in Philly. It's going to be cool. All the food and booze you can eat and drink, and we get to watch New York play Philadelphia for the division in the comfort of a heated room. Maybe we'll even meet some hot chicks."

"When were you going to tell us about this?" Meridian asked. "This sounds great!"

"I know. I'm sorry. I just found out a few days ago, and it completely slipped my mind until now."

"How did you get tickets to a luxury box in Philadelphia?" Vincent asked.

"This guy, Jeff Lewis, is a part-owner. He was involved with the Boys and Girls Club organization down in the Philly area. Last summer, they had a charity golf tournament, and we bought a foursome and sponsored a hole. I guess this guy remembered that we were from North Jersey. He called a few days ago with complimentary tickets to his box. Awfully nice of him." James took another sip of beer. "I'll reserve us a couple of rooms at the Holiday Inn down in Cherry Hill so we can stay the night. It's a four o'clock game, and there's a huge sports bar right there where we can watch the one o'clock games."

Vincent frowned. "I don't know if I can make it. Sunday is a big day here. I get good tips on Sunday."

"C'mon, Vincent! Don't be a sissy. How often do you get to see New York and Philly play from the comfort of your very own luxury box? It's the biggest football game of the year. And it's for the division! Look, I'll even pick up the rooms. You can afford to miss one day. Call Kevin; he can cover for you."

"All right, all right. It does sound like fun. Let me work on it. I'll let you know by tomorrow night."

James looked at the clock and grimaced. He had an early meeting in the morning to go over the new Federated Wines and Liquors project. "Vin, I got to get out of here. By the way, did you hear about my old man buying A Taste of Italy? He wants to convert it into an old-fashioned steakhouse, with a dress code and everything."

"No shit," Vincent said.

"No shit," James replied. "What do you think?"

"I don't know. I'm not sure about the dress code. I don't think that's going to fly around here. But it sounds interesting. What's he thinking of calling it?"

"The Mad Cow."

Meridian spit out his beer. "What? The Mad Cow? Like the disease? Is he out of his mind?"

Vincent chuckled. "That definitely sounds like Booby. You know, I bet people around here will get the joke. The people who know Booby will definitely get the joke."

"How about 'A Taste of Booby'?" Meridian volunteered.

"Now that's classic," Vincent laughed.

"Yeah, A Taste of Booby!" James agreed.

A couple of guys down the bar were waving for refills.

"Okay, guys. I have to go take care of the paying customers."

"Are you staying, Meridian?"

"One more."

"I'm out of here," James said. "See you in the morning." James stood, adjusted his tie, put on his coat, and left the warmth of the Bell Lap Tavern for the cold of night. A light snow was falling, and James dug his hands into the pockets of his wool coat. "Damn winter. Got another three months of this." He walked down the street in the direction of his apartment.

CHAPTER 4

▼

When James arrived at work the next morning, the office was empty; it was not yet eight o'clock. He turned on the coffee maker, watching the black liquid slowly fill the pot. *Not too hung over today,* he thought as he poured a cup of coffee. He opened the refrigerator door, looking for milk. There was none. "Damn it," James muttered, pouring some of the dry coffee creamer, which he hated, into his mug and adding too much sugar. He carried his coffee back into his office and sat at his desk.

James had dressed this morning in his best suit—a custom-made blue pin stripe—and wore a royal-blue striped silk tie, which complemented his eyes. His white dress shirt was freshly starched. He had even polished his shoes.

He gazed down at the floor plans covering his desk. *This is going to be a good job,* he thought. He forced himself to focus on all the details, making sure none of them were overlooked. James had not made a big sale in months and the commission from this project would pay off what he had run up in credit-card bills, as well as allow him to set aside a fair amount for a rainy day. He was even thinking about taking a Caribbean vacation.

After making the appropriate mental notes, James rolled up the floor plans and secured them with a few rubber bands. He organized his contracts and equipment schedules, and then placed them in his black portfolio.

He turned on his computer, logged on, and began checking his e-mail.

Soon, the office began to hum with activity, first from his sales team, then from the rest of the office staff.

James looked up from reading an e-mail when Mike walked into his office.

"What time is your kick-off meeting?" Mike asked.

"Ten," James replied, returning to his e-mail.

Mike sat down.

James looked up again. "Is there something you need? I'm kind of busy."

Mike smiled. "There's been a change of plans."

James eyed Mike suspiciously. Mike was dressed sharply, as usual, but this morning his eyes looked glassy, and the skin under his nose was red. "What do you mean, a change of plans?"

"Work is slow, so I had to change some crews around."

"What do you mean? I'm subcontracting the physical plant installation on this. I'm using Triad Communications. They're the best. I already sent them the purchase order."

"I pulled it."

"You pulled it?"

Mike smirked. "I pulled it."

"Okay, who's starting the job this morning? I have a ten o'clock kick-off meeting with whoever it is."

"You're getting in-house resources."

James could hardly contain his frustration. He glared at Mike. "Who?"

"You're getting Gray Mason's crew."

James clenched the arms of his chair, his face reddening. "No. No fucking way. Mason is green field. New construction only. He can't have customer interaction." James tried to control his anger. "This is a rewire. A rewire! There are live customers here, Mike. We're going to be working in a production facility. You know how Mason is. He's a loose cannon." James smashed his fist into his desk. "You don't have to do this. You're doing this to me on purpose."

Mike stood and pointed his finger at James. "Don't tell me what I do and why I do it. This is not your decision. This is a business decision. We're slow, so we can't use outside contractors. We need to keep our own people busy." He moved closer, leaning over James' desk. "Maybe if you worked a little harder, and maybe if you managed these candy-ass salespeople of yours a little better, you would have more sales, and we wouldn't be in this situation."

"That's bullshit, Mike, and you know it."

"If you're so worried about Mason, why don't you go down there and manage the project? Every day. Make sure it goes right."

James rolled his eyes. "I sell. That's what I do. You're telling me I'm not selling enough as it is. How can I sell and baby-sit a job at the same time?"

"I'm telling you to do some project management!" Mike yelled.

James stood up. "That's what project managers are for. Not me!"

Mike stood rigid and stared at James for a full minute. "Don't use words with me," he finally said.

James looked blank-faced at Mike. He shook his head and laughed. "Okay, Mike, you win. I will never use words to communicate with you ever again."

Mike started to say something, then turned around and walked to the door. He paused. "By the way, tonight is that trade-show cocktail party over in the city. There are going to be a lot of good banking and financial services companies there. Good prospects. I just wanted to remind you because I'm sure you forgot. We're going." His eyes bored into James. "And don't forget your business cards like you did last time."

Mike stormed out of the office.

James sat back down and stared dejectedly at his office door. He took a sip of coffee, and coughed. He dumped what remained of his coffee in a wastepaper basket under his desk. *Mason,* he thought. *This is going to be super. And Mike's right—I did forget about the party tonight.*

Brian, a salesperson, walked into James' office. "Who was he calling a candy-ass?"

James grabbed his coat, scarf, and gloves, and collected his paperwork. "Don't worry about it, Brian. It's not even worth discussing."

✳   ✳   ✳   ✳

Vincent was at the Bell Lap Tavern early. He had decided to go to Philadelphia with his friends on Sunday, so the weekly cleaning and organizing that he normally did on Sunday morning had to be done today.

The bar stools had been stacked in a row, upside-down, on top of the bar. An industrial mop-and-bucket combination sat in the middle of the floor. Vincent stood, leaning on a mop, taking a break. Most of the floor had been scrubbed, and he contemplated wiping the down the top-shelf liquor bottles to remove the smokers grit and grime that perpetually collected there.

Vincent eyed the ancient smoke-eater hanging from the ceiling. The machine grumbled, and the fans whirled grudgingly. *Big Al has got to spring for a new unit soon,* Vincent thought. *I'm going to get lung cancer if this place doesn't get ventilated better.*

The door to the Bell Lap Tavern opened, and a man entered.

"Yo, dude," Vincent called to him. "We're not open yet." He looked at the clock. "Dude, it's barely after nine."

The man approached, shuffling across the floor. He smelled unwashed and of brandy. His green army coat was ripped in places, and his black pants were wrinkled. Vincent couldn't tell how old the man was, only that he looked slightly ill because he was so thin. His hair was slicked back from his craggy face, revealing dull, sunken eyes. He gave a toothless smile. "It's cold out today. Can I sit at the bar?"

Vincent sighed. "Look, I said I'm not open yet." He considered the man. "Do you have any money?"

"I have a few dollars."

Vincent hesitated. "Okay. But I don't want any trouble."

"I won't be any trouble."

Vincent walked over to the end of the bar, took a stool off the top of the counter, and turned it right-side up. "Sit," he commanded. "I've got a lot to do this morning. Just sit here and be quiet. Do you have somewhere to go?"

The man sat. "I'm going to the shelter, but they won't let me in until eleven."

Vincent bent behind the counter and took out a glass. He poured the man a beer, and placed it in front of him. "You can stay here until eleven, then."

"Thank you."

Vincent returned to mopping the floor. The man sat at the bar, huddling over his beer.

Momentarily, the door opened. A tall, heavyset man in his late sixties entered the bar. "Vincent, it's cold as hell out today."

Vincent stopped mopping. "Hey, Big Al. I didn't expect you so early."

Big Al removed his gloves and wool hat and patted Vincent on the back. "Good to see you here early, getting the place cleaned up. We're going to have a busy weekend." He unbuttoned his coat and took a deep breath. "Feels good to get warm." Big Al moved behind the counter. "You're a hard worker, Vincent."

Vincent grinned. "Just doing my job, boss."

Big Al reached took out a small metal safe from behind the counter. He noticed the man at the end of the bar. "I see you already have a customer." He tilted his head in the direction of the man at the bar.

Vincent looked up. "He's all right. Just down on his luck."

"You've got to watch that soft spot. It could get you in trouble, especially in this business." Big Al turned the away from the man and fiddled with the safe's lock. He found the right combination. "How'd we do?"

"Not too bad. A little light, but the weather's been keeping people away."

Big Al took the money out of the safe, locked it, and placed it back under the counter. "You've been a good manager, Vincent, for a long time. And I think you've kept the stealing to a minimum." He chuckled. "I know you've wanted to talk to me about buying the bar. I think it's time."

Vincent stopped mopping.

Big Al continued. "I just bought a condo down in Boca Raton, where it's nice and warm. Brand new unit. You should see it, Vincent; it's beautiful. I'm retiring to Florida, Vincent. Leaving in March. That is, provided we can come to terms on a price for the old Bell Lap."

Vincent smiled. "That's great news, Big Al. I've been looking forward to this." He leaned the mop against the wall and moved over to the counter. "I'm going to need some help with the bank. Getting a loan and stuff. Provided we can agree on a price," Vincent teased.

"Don't worry. I not going to take advantage of you. You've been good to me, Vincent. I'm going to return the favor." Big Al put the money in a brown paper bag and stuffed it into a pocket on the inside of his coat. "Don't worry about the loan. I'll talk to the bank. You'll get the loan." He looked around the bar. "This place may be a dump, but it still makes money."

"That's true," Vincent agreed. "I've actually got a few good ideas for fixing it up. If things work out, I may be able to turn it into the local hot spot."

"That's my boy!" Big Al cheered. He buttoned up his coat and put his hat and gloves back on. "We'll talk more next week and start the ball rolling." He walked to the door. "Of course, after I'm gone, feel free to visit me in Florida. Anytime."

"Thanks, Big Al."

Big Al walked out the door of the Bell Lap Tavern.

Vincent turned to the man at the bar. "Did you hear that, fella? You just witnessed a momentous event in the life of Vincent Ferrara. I'm going to be the new owner of the Bell Lap Tavern. Drinks are on the house."

The man eyed Vincent coldly. "Very kind of you." He saluted and drank his beer.

*   *   *   *

James stood in the parking lot of Federated Wines and Liquors. He looked at his watch. It was a quarter to ten. A stream of frozen mist escaped his mouth with every breath.

"C'mon, Mason. Where are you?" he sighed.

A trio of large commercial vans screeched into the parking lot. They were all white except for blue block letters on each side that read "Cameron Voice and Data." The vans pulled up next to James.

The driver's door of the first van flew open and out jumped Gray Mason.

"Hiya, handsome!" he announced.

Gray Mason was average height, stocky, with frizzy brown hair that exploded out in every direction. He wore an old Iron Maiden T-shirt, blue jeans, and work boots. His eyes darted around wildly. "I hear this is some job you got here, James. You hit the big one. Don't worry; you're in good hands with Gray Mason. We'll wire this bitch up from here to China," Mason said excitedly. He grabbed James in a headlock. "Look at you, handsome, the big businessman in his fancy suit."

James put his arms up and stepped back. "Settle down, Mason. We got a meeting in about fifteen minutes." He gave Mason the once-over. "Where the hell is your coat? It's freezing out here."

"I don't need a coat, handsome. I just keep moving. I didn't need a coat in the war."

"Which war is that?"

"Vietnam!"

"Vietnam?" James asked incredulously. "How could you have been in Vietnam? You can't be older than thirty."

"I was in 'Nam, handsome. I shot the shit out of everything. Men, women, children. I killed everything that moved."

"Whatever, Mason." James said.

Mason bent over and touched a spot on the side of his head. "Feel that right there, handsome. I got a metal plate. I got a metal plate in my skull."

James felt the spot on Mason's head. He tapped with his knuckles and felt something hard. "No shit. You do have a metal plate in your head. How did you get that?"

"Land mine. Fucking gook land mine. Blew half my brains right out the side of my skull."

"Whatever, Mason." James shivered. "Not for nothing, didn't they tell you this is a kick-off meeting? Why aren't you dressed appropriately?"

Mason looked puzzled. "This is how I dress. How should have I dressed?"

"Never mind," James sighed. He pointed at the vans. "Who's your crew?"

Mason's eyes lit up. "I only work with one crew, handsome. The McGirk brothers. All five of 'em. We're the best."

The five McGirk brothers looked almost exactly alike. They ranged in age from mid-twenties to mid-thirties. They all were thin and tall, with blue eyes, and wore their long, straggly brown hair in ponytails. The only real way to tell them apart was to look at their piercings and tattoos.

Mason walked over and banged on the sides of the vans. "Let's go, you copper jockeys. We got a job to do."

The doors of two vans opened, and a huge cloud of smoke billowed out from inside the vehicles.

James recognized the sweet, pungent odor. Not tobacco. He eyed Mason, exasperated. "Christ, man. These guys are totally stoned. Mason, don't do this to me. Not today."

The oldest McGirk brother got out of the van and approached James. "Well, well. If it isn't Junior. Don't see you out where the work happens too often."

"I'm here to get things off on the right foot," James replied. "But it looks like you guys aren't going to make this easy on me."

"Relax, dude. We're just getting our heads together." He wiped his nose with the sleeve of his jacket. "We need to be in the right frame of mind to do our thing." His voice was sluggish.

The other McGirk brothers spilled out of the vans.

"Wow, that shit was the shit. Totally crypto. That shit would get Superman high," the youngest brother said.

James attempted to get control of the situation. "Okay, look. Mason and I are going to go in and have a meeting. I want you guys to get back in your vans." James pointed at the Federated entrance. "Do not, and I repeat, do not go into that building until either Mason or I come out and get you. Understand?"

All five McGirk brothers nodded.

"In fact," James continued. "Go get some coffee or something to eat. Get out of here. Come back in an hour."

One of the middle brothers grinned. "I could go for some pancakes. A big stack of pancakes." He smacked his lips lazily. "Let's go to the diner."

They all nodded in agreement.

The McGirk brothers got back in their vans and drove away, the exhaust leaving a smoky cloud that expanded rapidly in the cold air.

James turned back to Mason. "Look, Mason. I need this job to go right. I need this commission. This is important to me. You and I are going to go in there and instill some confidence. I need you to be cool."

"What do you want me to do, handsome? Do you want me to do back flips for them?"

"Just be normal. In other words, don't be yourself."

"Don't worry, handsome. We'll wire this bitch from here to China."

"That's what I'm afraid of," James said.

*   *   *   *

The technician service line began to ring. Dennis Galright, comfortably leaning back in his desk chair, glanced over the newspaper he'd been reading and stared at the his telephone. *Who can that be?* he wondered. It was just barely eleven o'clock. It wasn't yet time for any technicians to be closing out for lunch.

He put down his half-read copy of *The New York Times.* Dennis was of medium height in his early forties. He wore wire-rimmed glasses and was in complete denial of his thinning hair. As the Service Manager for Cameron Voice and Data, Dennis had his job down to a routine. He dispatched from eight to nine, closed out from eleven-thirty to twelve, dispatched from one to two, and closed out again from five to five-thirty. In between, he read *The New York Times,* cover to cover, and listened to classical music through the speakers of his computer monitor.

He was a man of arts and of letters, having graduated college with a degree in eighteenth-century literature. His cultured, if somewhat affected, mannerisms were reminiscent, Dennis felt, of an English lord—although to most people, he more closely resembled an English butler, with his detached, condescending attitude.

Dennis continued to watch the telephone ring. "Persistent little bugger," he muttered. Reluctantly, Dennis answered the telephone. "Hello?" He drew out the last vowel in an exaggerated drawl.

"Dennis, it's James. I need to talk to you."

"Ticket number?" Dennis pronounced the words deliberately.

"Hello, Dennis? This is James."

"Ticket number, please?"

"Ticket number? Dennis, it's James. James Cameron."

"Ticket number, please?"

"Dennis, damn it! It's James. We've got a problem at Federated Wines and Liquors. We got Mason working here, and he's already making the customer nervous."

Dennis paused briefly, then informed James, "This line is reserved for the technicians who have ticket numbers."

"Dennis, I tried calling upstairs. I can't get anybody. Booby is not around and neither is Mike. I'm calling just to give you a heads-up, okay?"

"Oh, all right," Dennis sighed. "What customer are you having a problem with?"

"Federated Wines and Liquors. The really big one I just sold. Ring any bells?"

"Oh, yes. Federated Wines and Liquors. Very appropriate project for this company, don't you think? How may I help you?"

"Just please tell my father we've got a situation brewing here, and I just want him to be aware of it. Mason's nuts, and the McGirk brothers are high. And Mike is trying to sandbag me, and I don't understand why."

"I know why Mike is trying to 'sandbag' you," Dennis said imperiously. "He doesn't like you."

"Thanks, Dennis. Can you please just tell Booby when you see him? I need him to be aware of the situation."

"I will do my best."

"Dennis, I got to get back and deal with the customer. I've got a lot of work to do this afternoon, because the guys are going to be working pulling cable all weekend, and then I got this business thing tonight so I'm not going to see my father today. I need you to please tell him, just in case something happens over the weekend."

"Did I not just state that I will do my best?"

"Okay, please? This is important."

"May I make a suggestion?"

"Please do."

"You should suggest to your father that it would behoove him to fire all the drug addicts that he employs—oh, wait. That would include the executive vice president and half of the company."

"Right, Dennis."

"Perhaps you should also suggest that he fire all the drunks. Oh, no. That would include him, you, and the other half of the company."

"Thanks, Dennis."

"Perhaps if you suggested to him that he fire everyone, there wouldn't be these problems."

"I'll make sure I do that first thing, the next time I see him."

"Very well. Have a splendid day."

Dennis picked up *The New York Times* and resumed his reading.

CHAPTER 5

▼

James' day passed quickly. He coordinated with Mason and the customer on the work that needed to be done over the weekend, got the McGirk brothers busy, and made sure that Mason didn't speak to anyone unless James himself was present.

When James returned to the office at the end of the day, he found Mike waiting for him in the parking lot. James exhaled a couple of cold breaths, opened the passenger door of Mike's black Mercedes, and got in.

"I heard you were causing trouble today," Mike snapped without preamble.

"What do you mean?"

"I heard you gave Dennis an earful and told him to get Booby involved with Federated."

"All I wanted was for my father to be aware that we have a potentially negative situation on our hands concerning a very large project that his company is starting."

"You're supposed to run these things through me, not go around me to Booby."

"You're the one who put me in this situation."

"I told you. That was a business decision. You're going to have to deal with it." Mike glared at James. "Do you really think I would do something to hurt the company?"

James' eyes held Mike's glare. "Look, I don't want to argue about this. You know what you did. And this thing had better not blow up. That's all I'm saying. Just forget it for tonight, and let's just focus on making it through this cocktail party."

They didn't speak to each other during the drive to Manhattan. James stared out the window at the series of ugly, dilapidated towns lining each side of the highway that led to the tunnel to the City.

The annual New York City Voice and Data Technologies Expo was held in the Marriott's convention hall, and most of the major industry manufacturers, software developers, and large area integrators were exhibiting. For the companies that found the exhibitors' fee prohibitive, a large cocktail reception was provided in the hotel's revolving bar overlooking Times Square.

James and Mike walked to registration booth, filled out guest tags, and took the elevator to the top floor. The elevator doors opened onto the bar.

The room had the capacity to hold several hundred people, and it was just about full. The cacophony of dozens of simultaneous conversations filled the air. James' pace quickened in excitement.

Mike grabbed his arm. "James, I have to go to the bathroom. Stay right here."

James shrugged, observing the elegant room. An immense crystal chandelier hung from the middle of the thirty-foot ceiling. Surrounding it were four smaller crystal chandeliers. A large, circular bar slowly rotated in the center of the room. Its copper and mahogany finish was waxed and gleaming, and hundreds of liquor bottles rose up in a pyramid. James' eyes sparkled.

At the far end of the room, windows rose from floor to ceiling and covered the entire length of the room. White linen-covered tables were arranged, offset from the windows, to offer patrons a stunning view of the skyline.

Food stations occupied each corner, and a line of people spilled out from each one. In the tiled open space between the bar and tables, people milled in groups, drinking beer and cocktails. Waitresses carrying trays of hors d'oeuvres weaved throughout the crowd.

Mike returned from the bathroom, rubbing his nose. "This party looks crowded," he said, seeming agitated. "We should be able to make some good contacts. Why don't I go left and you go right. Let's meet at that center bar in one hour."

James watched him disappear into the crowd. He hesitated slightly, then grabbed a waitress who was carrying food, wolfed down some finger sandwiches, and made his way to the bar. "Fuck Mike," he muttered.

Groups of people crowded the bar, all engaged in conversation. James looked for an open spot. The bartenders were moving frantically back and forth, trying to keep up with the drink orders. James leaned on the polished counter and was finally acknowledged. "I'll have an apple martini," he said. James eyed the large drink appreciatively, fiddled with the cherry, and took a sip.

"Isn't that a girly drink?"

James turned toward the voice. A redhead was perched on a stool, staring at him, her mouth turned up in a smile. She also sipped an apple martini.

James adjusted his tie. "I figured since I was at this frou-frou party, I should have a frou-frou drink. Besides, I already had beer for breakfast." He took an exaggerated sip of the martini.

The woman laughed. "You're funny. Most guys in this business immediately get defensive when I bust their balls." Her smile broadened, and she held out her hand. "I'm Shannon O'Rourke."

James took her hand; it was soft and carried with it a faint scent of perfume. "James Cameron," he said.

"Well, what brings you to this gala event?"

"I sell voice and data network systems. I'm here with my VP, trying to make contacts," James replied.

"Did you make any?"

"Yes." James grinned. "You."

Shannon laughed. "Where's your VP?"

"He's around here somewhere. I'm supposed to meet him here at the bar after an hour of 'networking.'" James made air quotes with his fingers.

"When is that?"

"In an hour. I just got here."

They both laughed.

"What brings you here?" James asked.

"I worked the booth at our exhibit. My company makes traffic-analysis software for large multi-site companies. I work in sales, too."

"Sounds about as much fun as what I do."

Shannon acknowledged him with a slight nod. They were silent a few moments, sipping their martinis, each looking watching the crowd. James motioned for the bartender. He ordered two more of the same.

"Do you live here in the city?" James asked.

"Yes. Down in Battery Park City. Just south of the World Trade Center...well, just south of Ground Zero."

"Do you like living in Manhattan?"

"I like it well enough. There's actually an interesting quote inscribed in the pavement in the esplanade that I think sums it up—'A hundred times I have thought: New York is a catastrophe, and fifty times: It is a beautiful catastrophe.'"

"I like that. How long have you lived there?"

"I bought the place in March 2001. I moved there in May."

"Wow. You lived there through the terrorist attacks." James stared down into the bottom of his martini.

"Yeah. It was a real mess. My office is in Midtown, and I was uptown on an appointment when the first plane hit. Nobody knew what was going on. I ran outside and just saw all this smoke and fire coming from the north tower. I ran back to my office, but everybody was leaving the building, running into the street, trying to see what was happening." Shannon paused and sipped her martini. "We were all standing in the street when the second plane hit. At that point, people just went into shock. I went across the street to a bar and just stood there, watching TV for the next ten hours. I got drunk." She ran a slender finger around the rim of her glass. "I finally got the nerve to try to go home around eight. I remember that night. It was a beautiful, late-summer night. There wasn't a cloud in the sky. The weather was perfect. The sunset was that deep orange that you only get that time of year—you know, right before fall starts. But then when you looked south toward the World Trade Center, all you could see was this huge plume of smoke.

"You couldn't get a taxi, and the subway had stopped running, so I just started walking. Walking toward the smoke. I eventually made it down to Canal Street, but that was as far as I could get. There were cops everywhere, and firemen. They had cordoned off everything. I couldn't go home."

"What happened?" James whispered.

"I turned around and walked all the way back to my office. I went to my desk and just sat and cried. I finally remembered to call my parents in Rockland, to let them know I was okay, because you couldn't make a damn cell phone call all day. That first night, I slept on the floor next to my desk.

"The following day I managed to get out of the City, and I went home to stay with my parents. I had nothing, just the clothes on my back. My parents took good care of me. My mother even took me to the mall to buy new clothes, just like we used to do when I was a kid, right before school started. She bought me a whole new wardrobe; wouldn't let me pay a dime of it. If it wasn't for my parents during that time, I don't know what I would have done." Shannon looked off into the distance toward at the Manhattan skyline. "It was three weeks before I could get back into my apartment. And getting there was a royal pain in the ass. The train wouldn't run south of Canal, and there were army guys with machine guns on every fucking corner checking IDs. For the next six months, I think it took me an hour to get home from work every day. And my apartment was a disaster. There was an inch of soot and dust on everything. And I mean everything. It took me weeks to clean it. One room at a time. Thank God the apartment is only three rooms."

They both finished their second drink, and James ordered two more. He was starting to get that warm, alcohol-induced feeling. He gazed at Shannon; she was flushed and sweating a little. Her eyes were teary.

"I'm sorry," James said. "That must have been a really difficult time."

Shannon wiped a tear from her cheek and composed herself. "Don't be sorry. It's not your fault. It was hard, and it sucked, but it wasn't me in those towers. And I don't mean to sound cruel."

"I understand exactly what you mean," James replied. "I was supposed to have had an appointment at the World Trade Center on September 11. It was scheduled for nine o'clock in the morning on the ninety-second floor of the north tower. My customer canceled the appointment the day before."

"What happened to your customer?" Shannon asked.

"He was there. He didn't make it." Two new martinis appeared, and they stopped talking for a few minutes. Then James said, "Wife and three children. Three daughters. I remember, because he had this big framed picture of his wife and kids hanging on the wall next to his desk. He would always tell me how hot his wife was and how beautiful his daughters were. But he mostly talked about his wife. He would show me pictures of her and tell me she was the hottest thing going and ask me if I thought his wife was hot, too."

"Well, was she hot?" Shannon asked.

"Yeah," James answered quietly. "She was really hot." James shook his head, as if to clear the image. "I haven't thought about that guy in a long time. I used to wonder what happened to his wife and his daughters." He took another sip of his drink. "And to think that could have been me as well. If my meeting with him hadn't been canceled, my ticket would have been punched. I used to wake up in the middle of the night in a cold sweat, dreaming about that guy, and then I'd get this amazing sense of euphoria—you know, just glad I'm waking up in my apartment." He locked eyes with Shannon. "So yeah, I know what you mean. Having those feelings is not being insensitive. I think that's just a normal, human reaction to a very emotional situation."

Shannon took a deep breath. "So…what's your story, James?"

"I live in Jersey. I live in an apartment in a dumpy little town called North Harrison. It's about two square miles. I'm sure you've never heard of it. I work for my father's company selling this exciting shit." He waved an arm through the air, taking in the people in the room. "And I hang out with my high-school friend at my other high-school friend's bar. I drink a lot. That's it."

Shannon batted her eyes at him. "You really know how to sweep a girl off her feet; do you know that?"

"I try really hard."

"Give me your cell phone," Shannon demanded.

"What?"

"Give me your cell phone."

James pulled his cell phone from his suit pocket and handed it to her.

She flipped it open. "It's not even on."

"I hate the damn thing. I only leave it on when I have to."

"You work in communications, but you don't like communication devices?"

"That's about it," James admitted.

She turned on the cell phone. "I don't even know why I'm doing this," she said. She punched in a string of numbers and pressed save. Then she entered in a short text description next to the number. She handed the phone back to James. "That's my cell number and name. See? I always have my cell phone on, James." She gazed into his eyes. "Look, I'm not trying to be forward, but I'm in the middle of our year-end, and I've been working every night until nine for the last month, and my social life has been a little on the slow side lately." She took a gulp of her martini. "I don't know you, James, but I know people, and I can see in your eyes that you're a nice guy. I feel this weird connection to you. So if you want to call me and ask me for a date, I won't say no."

James smiled shyly. "Shannon, I don't know you either. But you're right; I think it would be nice to try to get to know you." He grinned. "By the way, I think you're beautiful."

"That's the martini talking," she replied.

"No. I think you're beautiful. I really do. And I'm actually surprised that you find me interesting."

They both giggled and finished their third martinis.

"You know, you have the most amazing blue eyes," she commented.

"That's what all the boys tell me," James countered.

They ordered a fourth martini, and their continued conversation became a little slurred; that was how Mike found them.

"I've been looking all over for you!" Mike called out.

"Hiya, Mike!" James said breezily. "This is my new friend Shannon." He turned to Shannon. "Shannon, let me introduce Cameron Voice and Data's esteemed executive vice president, Mr. Michael Munro."

Shannon grinned and waggled her fingers in Mike's direction.

Mike glared at James. "I want to talk to you."

"'Scuse me, Shannon," James said, taking a few steps to his left. He leveled his eyes at Mike. "What's up?"

"What the fuck are you doing?" Mike snapped.

"Networking."

Mike's eyes were very glassy, and his upper lip was beet-red. Mike rubbed his nose and sniffled. "Bullshit. You're talking to that girl. How many people have you talked to?"

James grew surly. "No one, Mike. Nobody, okay? I wasn't in the mood to socialize. I'm not real happy about today, and to be honest with you, I'm not real happy with you, either. So to hell with you, and to hell with this trade-show bullshit."

Mike's face twisted in anger, and his eyes bulged. *This privileged, lazy little shit is going to ruin all my hard work*, he thought. "All I've ever done is try to make something out of you!" he yelled. "All I've ever done is try to get you to work hard, like I do. I give you opportunities to succeed, and you blow them off. You have turned into a lazy, unmotivated, spoiled brat. You may have your father fooled, but you don't have me fooled."

James waved him off. "I really don't want to hear this today."

Mike got right up in James' face. "You are never going to get ahead by doing the bare minimum. That's what you do, the bare minimum. Bare Minimum Cameron." Mike shook with anger. "You are never going to be like me."

James' nostrils flared. "You're right Mike. I'm never going to be like you." With that, James turned on his heel and went back to the bar.

"What was that all about?" Shannon asked. "Lover's spat?"

"It's not important," James replied.

Shannon slid off her barstool. "I'm going to go home, James. I'm tired, and I'm a little drunk. It was nice meeting you."

James reached out for her hand. "I'm going to call you."

She smiled. "That would be nice, James. But don't kill yourself."

"I will call. I promise."

She nodded. "Good-bye, James."

Mike shoved his way through the crowd as Shannon disappeared into it. "Don't you turn your back on me," he fumed.

"Oh, settle down. Have a drink, Mike. Here we are, in this beautiful room, with this beautiful view, with all these wonderful people, and with the finest free food and booze money can buy. Just settle down and have a drink."

"Okay," Mike agreed, sniffing and wiping at his nose. "I'll have a drink."

"So," James began easily, "did you make some good contacts tonight, Mike?"

"A few." Mike sniffed again.

"Are you okay, Mike?" James asked.

Mike ignored James' question and ordered a double vodka and lime on the rocks. James ordered another martini. James took a sip of his drink, and Mike downed his entire glass. He slammed it on the bar and ordered another, finishing the second drink just as quickly.

"Get me another," he said to James. "I have to go to the bathroom." Mike rubbed his nose.

"This is going to be an interesting night," James said to no one in particular.

James and Mike stayed another three hours, and to James' surprise, he actually loosened up, initiated a few conversations, and got two fairly good potential leads out of the evening. By the time they were ready to go home, both men had consumed a prodigious amount of alcohol and were visibly drunk, although Mike was more so than James. Mike swayed and staggered, and his eyes seemed to lose focus every few minutes.

"Okay, Mike, I guess we'll take a taxi home, and you can get your car in the morning," James said.

"No. Not takin' a cab. Drivin'."

"You're not driving," James said.

"*Not* takin' a cab," Mike insisted. "*Drivin'*."

Mike stumbled for the elevators; James followed. Once in the lobby, Mike fumbled for his ticket for the valet. The valet eyeballed Mike, shook his head, and left to retrieve his car.

James grabbed Mike's shoulders. "This is a bad idea."

Mike pushed him away. "You can walk if y'want."

James sighed. "No, I'm with you."

The valet drove up in the car and handed Mike the keys, which slipped through Mike's fingers. Mike bent over three times before he was able to retrieve the keys.

"Sir," the valet began hesitantly, "do you really think you should be driving?"

"Fuck ya," Mike slurred.

James handed the valet five dollars. "For your trouble."

The two men got in the car, and Mike screeched away into the night. He drove south down Broadway, then turned west toward the West Side Highway. Mike's Mercedes swerved across the street as he quickly accelerated down the road.

James had been playing with the radio but now looked up to see the oncoming traffic. "Holy shit, Mike! You're going the wrong way! You're going the wrong way!"

"S'what?"

Mike accelerated faster. Oncoming cars veered out the way, honking their horns. Flashing lights appeared in Mike's rear view mirror. A siren began to wail.

"The cops, Mike. The cops," James said. "Dude, you are screwed now."

Mike cursed and pulled over to the left, across a lane, and up onto the sidewalk. He put the Mercedes in park and shut the motor off. The patrol car pulled up behind the Mercedes. The flashing lights seemed blinding.

A police officer approached the Mercedes. "Get out of the car, now. Both of you. Put your hands on the hood."

James and Mike stepped from the car and did as they'd been told. The officer lowered his gun and approached the men.

"What the hell are you doing?" he yelled. "You were going the wrong way down the street."

Mike struggled to speak coherently. "I di'n't know I's goin' the wrong way."

"How could you not know you were going the wrong way?" the officer demanded. "Didn't you see the arrows?"

Mike turned to face the officer, grabbing at the roof of his car to steady himself. "Arrows? Arrows?" He grinned stupidly. "I didn't even see the Indians."

The officer stared blankly at Mike. The alcohol smell was unmistakable. He shook his head disgustedly. "I'm not even going to go through the motions—you're drunk. I want to see your license and registration. You're under arrest."

Mike took out his wallet and searched for his license.

The officer looked over the hood at James. "Sir?" he asked.

"Yes, officer."

"I assume you must also be very drunk to be riding with this gentleman."

"Yes, officer."

"Well, you're going to have to find a new way home. I'm not letting you get back in that vehicle." He looked at Mike. "You can't leave your vehicle here, either. I'll call a truck to impound your car. You should be able to pick it up in about two or three days."

The officer was taking out his handcuffs out when his radio cracked: "All units, all units. We have a code two-one-nine. I repeat, a code two-one-nine. All units, please respond."

The officer spoke to his dispatcher for thirty seconds. He came back over to the car. "I have to go. I can't believe this, but I have to go. There is something worse happening right now than you two idiots. But I want you to stay here. I'm sending backup." He pointed at Mike. "You are not to leave. Understand?"

Mike nodded.

The officer ran over to his car, got in, turned his lights and sirens on, and quickly turned his patrol car around. He sped off to the north up the West Side Highway.

James and Mike looked at each other. Without speaking, they both got back in the Mercedes and slammed the doors. "Go, Mike, go!" James said excitedly.

Mike started the car, put it in drive, and roared off down the road, still going the wrong way. The left-turn entrance to the Holland Tunnel was a few hundred yards away. A police divider was blocking the street, funneling southbound vehicles into exit lanes.

"Punch it, Mike, punch it!"

The Mercedes crashed through the wooden police divider, smashing out the left headlight, and turned left into the outbound lanes toward New Jersey. The Mercedes sped through the Lincoln Tunnel and exited out the far side into the night.

Mike slowed down to the speed limit and got into the right lane. His vehicle swerved within the lane. Luckily, the traffic was light at this time of the night. Mike put a hand over one eye, attempting to correct his alcohol-induced double-vision He gripped the wheel tightly with his free hand, staring intently at the road.

They made it back to the parking lot of Cameron Voice and Data without further incident. Mike parked the car.

James got out of the car, kneeled, and kissed the ground. "Thank God. Thank God. Thank God," he repeated. Mike's wild driving had served to sober up James considerably, and he wondered if he'd lost his mind to have gotten in the car with Mike in the first place. "You are an asshole!" he yelled.

Mike got out of the car on wobbly legs. He inhaled deeply and then expelled his breath, watching the vapor cloud in the cold air. "Don't tell your father."

Yeah, like that's what's important, James thought. Still, he had no desire to bring his father into it. "Don't worry," he said. "This little adventure is between you and me."

"If you tell your father, I'm going to kick the shit out of you."

James shook his head, looked up, and raised his hands to the sky. "I am surrounded by crazy people." He looked back at Mike. "Go home, Mike."

Mike turned around and staggered off.

James looked up at the clouds passing over the moon. He stood in the parking lot, staring up at the sky, and thinking to himself that at this point in his life, things should have started to be different—to be better. He felt like he was turning into the very people he tried so hard to *not* be like. He sadly realized that he was a lot more like those people than he thought. And he didn't like that realization.

"I coulda been a contendah!" James yelled into the night sky.

On the way home, he stopped and picked up a Freddy pie and ate it as he walked.

CHAPTER 6

▼

James slowly opened one eye and waited for the room to stop spinning. He gradually gained focus, and his clock indicated it was almost noon. Gradually he got up, popped some aspirin, took a long shower, and then collapsed on his couch. His apartment was a mess—clothes thrown everywhere, dishes piled up in the sink, dusty furniture.

His refrigerator was in similar disarray. His search for something to eat produced assorted condiments, a six-pack of beer, one can of lime soda, and a box of a half-eaten Pizzaland pizza. Disgusted, James watched TV for a few hours, wrapped only in his bath towel, as he waited for his hangover to disappear.

Absently, he picked up his suit coat and took out his cell phone. He scrolled through the entries in his directory until he found Shannon's number. Hesitating for a few seconds, he finally pressed the call key. Shannon answered just as James was about to hang up.

"Hi, Shannon. It's James, from last night."

"James, I...." There was a pause. "I didn't expect to hear from you so soon. How did the rest of your night turn out?"

"Uneventful." James laughed nervously. "We stayed a few more hours and then left. I actually got a few decent leads."

"Well, that's good to hear. Sorry I left so soon. I was tired, and those martinis knocked me for a loop," she replied. "So what's up?"

"I told you I was going to call," he said, his nervous laughter bubbling from this throat once again. "So I'm calling. Seriously...I was wondering if you were interested in going somewhere with me tomorrow. Do you like football?"

"I like football."

"That's great. I have an invitation to a luxury box down in Philadelphia for the New York versus Philly game. It's a big game, for the division, and these luxury boxes are usually a lot of fun."

"That does sound like fun."

"I was…uh…also going to get a hotel room and stay over. I didn't want to party all day and then have to drive back. Is that all right with you?"

Shannon hesitated. She liked James, but she wasn't sure about spending the night with him.

"I'll be a perfect gentleman," James promised.

"I'm sure you will be," Shannon said.

"I also want you to know that I have two friends coming as well. Don't worry; you'll like them. I know you wanted me to ask you out on date, so why don't we just call this a quasi-date, and if things go well, we'll go on a real date next week."

Shannon pushed her reservations aside. "That's fine," she assured him. "I don't mind going with your friends. I'm sure we'll have fun."

James smiled. "Okay, great. It's settled. Why don't you take the train over to Jersey City tomorrow morning, and I'll pick you up about ten."

"Okay, then. It's a quasi-date," she responded.

"I'll leave my cell phone on today in case something happens."

"I'll see you tomorrow morning, James."

James closed his phone and tossed it onto his coffee table. He scanned his apartment. *Time to get some thing done*, he thought. He got dressed and spent the next few hours dusting, vacuuming, and washing dishes. He took his clothes and sheets to the Laundromat. While the dryers were running, he made a trip to the grocery store.

When he got home, he put the groceries away, folded his clothes and put them away, and made his bed. He called the hotel, made a reservation for two rooms, and then called Meridian and Vincent to confirm for the following day.

His cell phone didn't ring all day.

*   *   *   *

Meridian and Vincent showed up at James' apartment the next morning, wearing New York football colors—blue-and-red jackets, and jeans. James put on his New York football jersey and corresponding blue-and-red jacket.

"So you decided to bring some chick, too?" Meridian chided him.

"Her name is Shannon. I met her last night. She's feisty. I'm sure you'll get along with her, Meridian."

"I guess that means that I'm sleeping in the same room as this fat, snoring loser," Vincent said, pointing at Meridian.

James smiled.

They piled into James' silver four-door Ford Taurus and drove off to Jersey City to pick up Shannon. James pulled in front of the station, and they waited for the next wave of passengers from downtown Manhattan to arrive.

James easily picked her out in the crowd. Shannon had her hair up and was carrying an overnight bag. She wore blue jeans and an emerald-green jacket. She also wore a green scarf and gloves.

James beeped his car's horn and waved to her. Shannon opened the front passenger door and got in. James offered introductions.

"What's with the green?" Meridian asked.

"What?" Shannon asked. "What do you mean, 'what's with' it?"

"Green is the color of the Philadelphia team. You're supposed to be wearing blue and red," Meridian stated.

"Oh. Well, I didn't think of it. I like the color green. Sorry."

"Women." Meridian frowned and shook his head.

"Don't listen to him," James laughed, turning the car south, down the highway toward Philadelphia.

James had booked rooms at the Holiday Inn, from which they could clearly see the football stadium. After checking in and dropping off their bags, they made their way to the hotel's sports bar. Meridian ordered a round of beers and two sampler platters of chicken wings, chicken fingers, mozzarella sticks, poppers, and potato skins. Football food.

The bar was already crowded, and most of the fans were wearing green. A few of the opposing team's fans were already getting riled up, directing comments at the group.

"These are serious fans," Shannon commented.

"Yeah. You don't want to get them started," James said. "In fact, it's not even really smart to wear the visiting team's colors. But we have safety in numbers. And Meridian."

"Don't screw with me!" Meridian yelled to a few scrawny fans in green. "I'll rip your arms off and use 'em as clubs!" He was cascaded with boos. "I love this game!" he said.

They all stood at the bar, cracking jokes and watching a variety of games on of the various televisions scattered around the bar. They polished off several beers as the early game wore on.

Shannon touched James' arm. "Thank you for inviting me today," she said. "I'm having a great time. And you're friends are really nice."

"I'm glad you agreed to come," James responded. "And I promise, next week we'll do an official date. I will even bring you flowers and chocolate."

"I'm looking forward to that," she said. She leaned toward him and kissed him on the side of his mouth. They both smiled.

At around three o'clock, the group decided to head over to the luxury box. It was another cold day, overcast with snow flurries, and they walked quickly across the street, through the windswept parking lot, toward the stadium entrance.

A gang of children ran up to them as they approached the stadium entrance.

"Look, it's our welcoming committee," Vincent said.

The children surrounded the four, chanting, "New York sucks! New York sucks!"

"What a lovely group of children," Shannon commented, pushing through the stadium gate.

"Indeed," James agreed.

A security guard manned the entrance to the luxury box level. "Your names, please?" he said. He studied a monitor as he typed their names on a keyboard. "You're confirmed," he informed them, as a printer chirped behind him. He took four passes off the printer, put them in plastic covers, and handed them out. "Please wear these and keep them visible at all times."

The group hung the passes around their necks.

"May I give you some advice?" the guard asked.

"Sure," James said easily.

"If New York is winning at the end of the game," the guard cautioned, "I would leave early. These fans are bad before the game starts. They're even worse afterward, especially if they lose."

"We'll keep that in mind," James said.

"Mr. Lewis' box is number twenty-eight," the guard said. "Enjoy the game."

The luxury-box level was busy but not crowded, and Meridian and Vincent jumped up and down the hall, clowning around, pushing each other, and pushing James and Shannon as well.

Their excitement was palpable, but James suddenly put a damper on it. "Guys, hang on a minute," he shouted above the din. "I have to check my messages. This will only take a minute."

James quickly checked his cell phone for messages. The familiar envelope icon, denoting a message, was blinking. He pressed a button, and the message began to play: "Mr. Cameron, this is Carl Anderson from Federated Wines and

Liquors. Mr. Cameron, we have been trying to reach you all morning. We called your office and left an emergency message with your company. We got a call from a gentleman named Dennis." The message suddenly broke up, then became clear again. "Mr. Cameron, we have a problem. We have a big problem. When we came to the office this morning to let your staff in, we found your project manager, Mr. Mason, passed out in the back of his van. With his pants down. And I don't know quite how to say this, but we found something else." James could hear Anderson clearing his throat. "Mr. Mason had defecated in our parking lot, next to his van. Mr. Cameron, your employee defecated in our parking lot."

James' face grew ashen. He was almost afraid to listen to the remainder of the message. "Mr. Cameron, we are having serious reservations about continuing this project with your company. I think we may have made a mistake. I would like you at our office first thing tomorrow morning to discuss this situation. And I would appreciate it if you would bring your boss or your father as well. Please call me today if you receive this message. Thank you."

James deleted the message and closed his phone. "No, no, no, no!" James moaned, pressing his phone into his forehead with each "no."

Meridian, Shannon, and Vincent stared at him, concerned.

"What's going on?" Vincent asked.

"Everything, that's what. I cannot get a break. Ever." He sighed heavily. "Just give me one more minute." James scrolled through his cell phone directory until he found Dennis' number.

"Hello? Who is this?" Dennis asked, using his proper diction.

"Dennis, don't give me any of your bullshit right now. I know you have caller ID. I just got a message from Federated. I know you spoke to Carl Anderson, and I know you know that we've got a mess on our hands."

Dennis was silent.

"Here's what I want you to do," James continued. "I want you to call Two-Boy. Jimmy Metzler. I want him out at that job site first thing tomorrow morning. I don't care how much he wants. I want him there. Tell him I'll meet him at eight-thirty."

"I'm not authorized to do that," Dennis said.

"I'm authorizing you. If you're too chicken shit, then go find Mike or Booby and get them to do it. Otherwise, just call Two-Boy and get him out there for tomorrow morning."

"Very well, I'll do it...but if there are any repercussions, you'll have to answer for them."

"Listen, Dennis, we're already dealing with repercussions," James barked. "Just do what I asked." He ended his call to Dennis, then immediately called Mike. James was directed to Mike's voice mail, and he waited impatiently to leave his message: "Hey asshole, this is James. I warned you that Federated was going to blow up. And guess what? It just blew up. You're internal fucking resource just took a crap on my customer's property, and he's not happy about it. He wants a sit-down. First thing tomorrow morning. Be at the office at eight. And don't pretend you didn't get this message, you workaholic freak. You got me into this mess, and you are going to get me out. Asshole!"

James snapped his phone shut.

"Are you having a bad day now?" Shannon asked.

James smiled thinly. "It's just office stuff. There's nothing I can do about it right now. Let's just go and enjoy ourselves."

Meridian punched the air. "Do you want me to take that Mike Munro out for you? I'll hit him so hard his momma will cry!"

"Let's just forget about it. Who's ready for a drink?"

The group quickly found box number twenty-eight, which was spacious but not overly large. A bartender in a tuxedo stood at attention at the bar on at one end of the room, and at the other end, raised, hooded, silver-plated serving platters were being warmed by sternos. Sliding glass doors opened to a covered outdoor seating area that descended down at a slight angle. There was a table with chairs in the middle of the room, and a couch against the wall next to the sliding doors.

Half a dozen people, all dressed in jeans and green sweatshirts, sat at the table, and four very tall black men, dressed in fine silk suits, white scarves, fedoras, and gloves, stood next to the couch. Accompanying each man was a woman dressed just as finely.

A short, thin woman dressed in a green business suit came toward them, frowning. "I'm sorry; this is a private booth. You'll have to leave."

James smiled at the woman and held out his badge. "I'm James Cameron, with Cameron Voice and Data. We're guests today of Mr. Lewis. We were given four passes to today's game."

The woman checked their passes, then smiled. "Oh, yes. I'm Nancy Silverstein, Mr. Lewis' personal assistant. Mr. Lewis told me you would be coming. But I'm sorry; Mr. Lewis won't be joining us today. He's enjoying the game from the owner's box." Nancy beamed. "But he did instruct me to take good care of you." She looked at James, Meridian, and Vincent. "I didn't realize you would be New York fans."

"Well, you wouldn't expect us to root for this shit-hole city, would you?" Meridian asked.

Nancy smiled thinly. "Can I offer you anything?" she asked James.

"Just take me to the bar," he responded.

Shannon elbowed James in the ribs. "See? Who's smart for wearing green now?"

Nancy nodded toward the people behind them. "That's Mr. Lewis' family. And the rather tall people in the back are basketball players with New Jersey. They're personal friends of Mr. Lewis."

Meridian glanced over. "Looks like a couple of niggers to me."

Vincent smirked, but James and Shannon shot each other a wide-eyed look.

"Please don't use that kind of language here," Nancy scolded. "You are guests of Mr. Lewis."

James coughed pointedly. "Okay, then. How about four beers and four shots of whiskey?"

Without a word, the bartender took four pint glasses from beneath the bar and poured four draft beers.

"What about the whiskey?" James asked.

"Mr. Lewis does not serve hard liquor in his booth. I'm sorry," Nancy answered.

"Don't worry," Meridian said. "I got it all under control." He unbuttoned his coat and pulled out an unopened bottle of Johnnie Walker Black.

"Where the hell did you get that?" Vincent asked.

"When I walk, the walking man walks with me." Meridian placed the bottle on the table. The bartender shrugged, opened it, took four highball glasses out from under the bar, and poured four large shots of whiskey.

"Cheers!" they all said.

"Please be careful," Nancy pleaded.

"Oh, I think we're fine now," James winked.

They made themselves comfortable. Nancy moved back and forth between the three groups, being very polite and very attentive. James, Meridian, Shannon, and Vincent kept to the bar. They tried to strike up small talk with the Lewis family and the basketball players but were politely rejected. The other groups were interested in keeping to themselves.

"Wow, this is some friendly crowd," James commented.

"I know. These people are lame," Shannon agreed.

The game started at four. They stood at the bar drinking and watched the kick off on a large monitor suspended from the ceiling in the corner behind the bar. They were alternating between beers and shots. Shannon and Vincent paced themselves, but James and Meridian did not show any restraint.

They continued to watch the game on the monitor from the bar. James and Meridian drank more and more and got louder and louder. The more boisterous they became, the cruder their jokes became. By half time James and Meridian were well on their way. Everyone else in the booth was giving them dirty looks.

Nancy approached them. "Don't you think you've had enough to drink?" she asked.

James and Meridian looked at each other and shrugged. James held up the bottle of whiskey. "We only drank half the bottle," James replied.

"Why don't all of you watch the rest of the game outside?" Nancy suggested.

"No. It's cold outside. We like it in here."

"Mr. Cameron, it's not cold outside. The seating area is heated. See the heating coils in the roof?"

James peered out. "No shit. Look at that."

Meridian moved closer to Nancy. "So what does a personal assistant to a really rich guy do?" he asked.

Nancy stepped back. "Well, it's a very interesting job. I get to meet many interesting people. For example, last month I was privileged enough to have dinner with our former president Bill Clinton and Mr. Lewis. I even danced with him." She smiled broadly.

"Did you blow him?"

"Excuse me?"

Meridian burped. "I asked if you sucked his dick."

Nancy gave Meridian a disgusted look and walked away.

Shannon turned to Vincent. "Do you think we'll make it to the end of the game?"

"Probably not."

The group headed outside to watch the third quarter, where it was indeed warm. Meridian brought the bottle of whiskey outside, and they passed it back and forth. The game was exciting, all tied up at seventeen. They actually got interested in the action, yelling and cheering when New York made a big play. James and Meridian continued to drink furiously and became very drunk.

At the beginning of the fourth quarter, James stumbled up the stairs for two more pints. He was intercepted by Nancy.

"What do you think you're doing?"

"I'm getting another beer," James hiccupped.

"No, you are not. You have had enough to drink. You and your friends have been very rude today, and I have been very patient. This is not a bar. You are guests of Mr. Lewis, and if he was here, he would have cut you off a long time ago. I will not serve you one more beer."

James felt frustrated and grew defiant. "Look…I want another drink. And you're right; I'm a guest. All day long, all my friends and I have gotten from you and these people are dirty looks. I feel totally mistreated. In fact, I think I'm going to write Mr. Lewis a letter and let him know how poor the hospitality was."

Nancy considered the situation. "One more beer. You take your beer, you sit down, you watch the rest of the game, and then you and your friends leave. Okay?"

"Fine."

Nancy walked away, and James put his two pint glasses on the bar. "Fill 'em up!" he yelled.

"She said one," the bartender stated.

"Are you going to argue with me now?" James asked.

The bartender grabbed both glasses and filled them to the rim. "Enjoy," he said.

James walked back outside, spilling beer on his way back to his seat. He noticed that the basketball players had sat down directly in front of them. James took his seat, beer sloshing over the rims of the glasses.

One of the players turned around and glared at James. "Yo, Homes. You are about five seconds away from spilling that beer all over me. You better watch it." He turned around.

James continued to hold both pints. He drank out of one, and the other wobbled precariously in his hand.

"Be careful, James," Shannon warned.

James watched the game intently, drunk to the point where his world was in tunnel vision. Everything else was blocked out.

New York moved into Philadelphia territory. The New York quarterback dropped back and spied a receiver sprinting down the sideline. He launched the ball. The ball spiraled in the air, zeroing in on its target. The receiver leaped and caught it over the defending cornerback and ran into the end zone.

The crowd booed. James jumped up, and as he did, the pint in his left hand tilted forward. As if in slow motion, a fountain of beer arced out of the glass and through the air and washed over the basketball player. The beer ran over the brim of his cap, into his face and down his back.

He stood up and spun around. "Mother fucker! I knew you was gonna do that!" He grabbed James with both hands and lifted him out of his seat.

Meridian leaped up. "Go ahead and hit him, you black bastard. Go ahead! We could use a really big payday!" Meridian yelled. He jumped between James and the player. Everyone started yelling, and a few of the Lewises came down and got in between the players and James' group.

Nancy came out running down the stairs. "That's it. Out! All of you! Out!" She waved them towards the door.

Meridian picked the bottle of whiskey off the floor and handed it to her. There was very little left. "You're probably going to need a stiff drink," he offered.

"Go! Go! Go!" Vincent yelled. All four ran up the steps, through the sliding doors, and toward the exit.

A young man grabbed James' arm, laughing. "Let me tell you something. My father's had this box a long time and nothing exciting ever happens. You and your friends were a big pain in the ass today. But when you spilled your beer on that dude, that was the funniest thing I've ever seen. Thanks for coming." The young man patted James on the back.

James saluted and left. They ran down the hall around the perimeter of the stadium, stopping at each booth to listen through the door for signs of a party. A few times, they had to duck out of the way when a security detail made the rounds. As they continued along the concourse, they heard noises coming from down the hall.

Meridian waved. "Do you hear that? It sounds like a party? Let's crash it!"

They followed Meridian to the source of the noise and entered a luxury box about twice the size of the one they had just left. Everyone was cheering. To the left of the door was a small bar station.

"What happened?" James asked the crowd.

An older woman dressed in green was dancing in the middle of the floor. "We just scored twice in the last two minutes. We're up by a touchdown!"

They turned to the bartender, who handed each of them a freshly made Bloody Mary. Their noses burned from smell of fresh horseradish coupled with tomato juice.

"The fourth quarter is the Bloody Mary rally," the bartender said.

"Now *this* is my kind of box!" Meridian exclaimed.

This box was raucous. People were laughing, cheering, hugging, and dancing around. Music played in the background, but the noise from the stadium crowd overwhelmed it, coming in through the open sliding doors that led to the out-door seats. Everyone was drinking, and quite a few people were drunk.

James and Shannon got into the mood, grabbed each other, and started danc-ing. A few people commented to James, Vincent, and Meridian that were wear-ing New York colors, but they were so intent on having a good time, they shrugged off the comments. Vincent and Meridian grabbed a couple of the older ladies and danced as well. Meridian's partner, who was enjoying the attention, gave him big kisses on his cheek.

James finished his drink too quickly and stumbled over to the bartender to get another one.

"James, don't you think you should slow down?" Shannon whispered. She locked eyes with him. "Hey, are you okay? Is this about that phone call earlier?" She put her arms around him.

James put his drink down and hugged her. "I'll be all right," he whispered, trying to shift his focus to the beautiful woman in front of him. They stood in the middle of the room for several minutes, swaying and hugging.

James picked up his drink. "I might as well finish what I started," he said. Shannon bit her lip and looked away.

The game ended with a Philadelphia victory, and the party continued. At some point they found out the box was owned by Cox Communications, the local cable monopoly. No wonder everyone was in such a good mood. Wait staff came around with "pigs in a blanket." A cook wheeled in a grill and served hot dogs and burgers with the works.

Around nine o'clock, people began to leave and the party broke up. James and the gang headed back to the hotel.

"Well, that actually turned out well," Vincent commented.

The night was cold, and it was starting to snow. They huddled together as closely as they could, shivering as they walked. About halfway back, James stum-bled and fell. The group stopped. James got up on his hands and knees and started to vomit. He vomited violently for several minutes and then sat on the ground.

Shannon sat next to James and hugged him. "Oh, James," she sighed.

"I think I had too many Bloody Mary's. And whiskey. And beer...I actually feel much better now."

James wrapped his arms around his knees, shivering. He made an effort to col-lect himself.

Shannon reached into her coat, pulled out a pack of gum, and gave him a piece. Meridian and Vincent helped him up, and they continued on. At the hotel, streams of people were heading into the sports bar to watch the night game.

James turned to the group. "Guys, do what you want, but we need to leave at six in the morning. I'm sorry it's so early, but I have to get back."

Meridian and Vincent considered the situation. "Well, if we're going to be hung over, we might as well be tired and hung over," Vincent said. They headed off to the sports bar.

"What about you?" James asked Shannon.

"I'm with you," she replied.

When they got to the room, Shannon took a long shower, and then James did the same. Shannon, hair brushed back, wearing a hotel robe, lay on the bed watching television. James came out of the bathroom, also in a hotel robe, drying his hair with a towel and with a toothbrush sticking out of his mouth.

"Don't you clean up nice," Shannon said.

The room was typical of the hotel chain, with soft patterned wallpaper and a dark carpet. The thick, heavy curtains were drawn. The only light came from the television and the bathroom.

James lay down next to Shannon and put his head on her chest. He listened to her breathing. She smelled clean and of damp cotton. He looked up at her. "Did you have a good time today?"

"Yes, I had a good time. Did you?"

"I guess. I'm glad you were here. I'm glad you came. Sorry if I acted like such a jerk."

"Oh, James," she sighed. "You are such a tortured soul. You really need to tell me about yourself."

"I will. On our date."

"I'm going to hold you to that."

He lifted his head, and moved up closer to her so he could gaze into her eyes. They kissed slowly at first, then more urgently. His tongue parted her lips. He ran his hand up under her robe and felt her soft breast. After a while, James put his head on her chest again and fell fast asleep. Shannon stroked his hair as she listened to his breathing. She shut her eyes and soon was asleep.

CHAPTER 7

▼

James awoke at a quarter to six, feeling the effects of the day before. He roused Shannon, and they both got up and dressed quickly. He went next door to Meridian and Vincent's room and banged on the door.

"We're coming," Meridian's muffled voice replied.

The door opened, and out came a bedraggled-looking pair. They both reeked of beer and had dark rings under their eyes.

"I hate you," Meridian said.

James' car was freezing as they all piled inside. James turned the car on and cranked the up the heat. He reached into the back seat and grabbed his snow brush so he could brush the accumulation off of the windows. Shivering, he got back into his car and sped off down the highway. Meridian and Vincent slept in the back seat, leaning into each other, snoring. James and Shannon were silent during the ride north, except when they agreed to see each other this coming Friday night. The radio was tuned to an early-morning talk show. James kept his eyes on the road, scanning for state troopers. Shannon watched mile after mile of icy, snow-covered ground, dotted occasionally by a housing development, warehouse, or tall, pine-tree-decorated cell-phone tower that was intended to blend into the scenery but only stood out more against the bleak white landscape.

James made it back in record time and was lucky not to get pulled over by a state trooper for speeding. He dropped Shannon off at the train station and gave her a kiss before she got out.

"Good luck today," she said.

"I'll call you later. I'll see you on Friday."

She blew him a kiss.

James sped back to his apartment. He rushed in, wet his hair and combed it, dressed in suit and tie, and rushed back to his idling car. He drove over to the Bell Lap Tavern and kicked Meridian and Vincent out of the car.

They stood in the street, shivering in the cold morning. They waved to James as he drove off.

*   *   *   *

Mike Munro entered the office, just about running into one of the salespeople. Brian stepped back from Mike, trying not to spill the mug of coffee he had just poured.

"You're here early," Brian said.

"Got an early appointment," Mike replied. His face was ghost-white and clammy, like the belly of a freshly caught flounder. Sweat beaded on his forehead. The whites of his eyes were bright redder, and the skin under his nose was even redder. He sniffled.

"You're all sweaty," Brian said.

"I went running this morning," Mike lied.

"Yeah? From who? The cops?" Brian smirked and went to his cubicle.

Mike grabbed his briefcase and went outside. James pulled into the parking lot just as Mike was coming out. He motioned for Mike to get into the car.

"I didn't like that message you sent me yesterday," Mike complained.

"I don't give a shit, Mike. You'd better get me out of this mess." He glared at Mike and did a double-take. "What the hell is wrong with you?"

Mike sniffled. "Nothing."

James shook his head. He drove quickly to Federated Wines and Liquors. As James pulled into the parking lot, Mike bent over and put his nose into a bag that contained white powder. Mike snorted, then sat up, eyes wide, and rubbed the excess powder off his nose.

"Okay, I'm ready," Mike said.

James said nothing.

James and Mike walked toward the glass-fronted entrance, where Gray Mason and the McGirk brothers were waiting.

Mason approached James with his hands up. "I can explain, handsome—"

"Shut up, Mason," James growled.

A bright yellow Hummer pulled into the parking lot. The door swung open, and an extremely fat man got out. A cigar was stuck in the corner of his mouth. He strode over to the men.

"Two-Boy!" James shouted.

Jimmy Metzler put his hand out. "Good to see you, James." He shook hands with everyone. "I got a frantic call from Dennis yesterday. What? Do I have to bail out your sorry company from a disaster again?"

"That's about the situation," James agreed.

Jimmy Metzler, or "Two-Boy," as he was called, was one of the best project managers in the state for infrastructure work. He was a top-registered and-certified design and distribution specialist and was too expensive for any one company to retain full time, so he worked per diem as a hired gun. Two-Boy got the job done perfectly—and on time. The work was in his blood.

Two-Boy had a good thing going. When he worked, he made great money, which allowed him to take off as much time as he wanted. And when he didn't work, he enjoyed life to the fullest. Some would say he enjoyed life too much, as his size suggested. But he was the hardest-working fat man James ever met.

Two-Boy established his reputation—and nickname—many years ago. He didn't believe in wasting time, so he would have his laundry and dry cleaning delivered to whichever job site he was working, as he was accustomed to working late. He had purchased some new dress clothes and had to have them tailored. One day at the end of a shift, an old Chinese man showed up with Jimmy's dry cleaning and alterations.

The Chinese man, who spoke broken English, said he was looking for Two-Boy. Nobody knew what the hell he was talking about. Eventually, Jimmy Metzler saw him with the clothes and figured the guy was looking for him. When Jimmy went up to him, the guy nodded at Jimmy and laughed. The man said, "My wife do your alteration. She take out pants and use lots of material. She say, 'Go find man who big as two boy and give him pants.'" The man pointed at Jimmy. "She right. You are big as two boy. Next time we charge more for alteration." Jimmy blushed, grabbed his clothes, and paid the man his money. And the name stuck.

Two-Boy chewed on his cigar. "So what is the situation?"

"I need you to take charge of this job. This is your crew. My current foreman," he said, pointing at Mason, "took a dump in the parking lot yesterday. He needs to be straightened out. And these clowns," he said, indicating the McGirk brothers, "like to get high all the time. They need to be straightened out, too."

"No problem."

"Mike and I need to go in for a little meeting to try to save this account, and after that, I can go over the floor plans with you to get you caught up to speed."

James opened the front door. "And if you have any trouble with any of them, you have my permission to kick them off the job."

"No problem," Two-Boy said again. "You're going to owe me big after this one, Cameron." He grinned.

"I'll buy you dinner," James volunteered.

"That's sounds perfect." Two-Boy rubbed both hands around his expansive belly. "And you'd better bring your wallet, because you know I'm going to put a big dent in it."

James grinned at Two-Boy and nodded. Then he glared at Mike. "Let's go."

They walked into the lobby and announced themselves to the receptionist.

"I will let Mr. Anderson know you're here," she said. "Please have a seat in the large conference room."

"Thank you. I know the way," James replied.

Mike suddenly grabbed James' arm. "I didn't authorize you to use Two-Boy on this project!"

"Mike, you can take that up with my father." He barely looked at Mike as he brushed Mike's hand off his arm. "Right now, I need you go into that conference room with me and do some groveling."

Mike rubbed his nose. "I need to use the bathroom." He looked around the lobby for a men's restroom and then darted off.

When Mike returned, he and James proceeded to the large conference room. A steel oval conference table surrounded with six chairs occupied the center of the room. In the center of the table sat an old telephone, one that was slated to be replaced by Cameron Voice and Data. A star-shaped conference room phone sat next to the telephone. A flat screen television was mounted on the wall at the far end of the room.

James and Mike sat at the table as an employee came in, carrying a tray with a carafe of water, six glasses, and napkins. She quickly arranged everything on the table and then left the room without a word.

James filled a glass. "Please drink some water, Mike."

Mike rubbed his nose and sniffled but ignored James' request.

James was about to insist, when two men and two women, all dressed in sharp business attire, entered the room. "Good to see you again, Mr. Anderson," James said, extending his hand.

Mr. Anderson shook James' hand but did not smile. The other three people also shook James' hand but also did not smile. James introduced Mike to the executives, and Mike stood and shook hands, sniffling as he did so.

"Let's get right to it, Mr. Cameron," Anderson said. "We are not happy with your company. Your manager, if you can call him that, is totally unacceptable. His behavior is completely inappropriate. On Friday, he made rude comments to several of our female staff members, and I can't even begin to explain yesterday's incident."

James was confused. *I thought I was watching Mason pretty well on Friday,* James thought.

The other gentleman spoke. "That man is either insane or has a drug problem, or both. And I am certain that your other workers have been using marijuana since they got here. Now, I'm not sure what the quality of the work has been since you started, but I'm sure it can't be good. This whole situation is making us very uncomfortable."

Mr. Anderson looked at James and Mike. "Gentlemen, I would like to know what you are going to do about it."

"I have to use the bathroom," Mike said. He got up and left the room.

"Mr. Munro doesn't look well," one of the women commented.

"No, he doesn't," James agreed. "Well, I can speak for Mr. Munro, as well as for Mr. Cameron. We apologize for any unprofessional acts or comments committed by our employees. And I truly, deeply regret Mr. Mason's actions yesterday." James cleared him throat. "I want to assure you that we understand your concerns and are taking corrective action. Mr. Mason will no longer be managing the wiring component of this project. I have brought in another gentleman, Mr. Jim Metzler, to do that job. He is one of the best there is. Effective immediately, all workers here will report to him. And he has been instructed to remove any employee from the job who continues to demonstrate…unprofessional behavior."

Mike came back into the room and sat down. His breathing was erratic, and his sinuses were clogged. He was more focused on trying to breathe clearly than on the conversation in the room. When he breathed in through his nose, he made a sound like wood scratching across sandpaper, which was audible to the others. He pressed on his nostrils. Everyone at the table stared at him.

"Mr. Anderson," James said, trying to divert attention from Mike. "Please give us another chance. We are a good company. We do good work. The solution that we are offering you is from a top-tier manufacturer, and we are giving it to you at a good price—less than our competition would offer."

Anderson sat back in his chair and rubbed his chin but didn't respond.

"Mr. Anderson, I promise I will personally check up on the work daily. And I will make myself available any time to address any questions or comments that arise. Please, Mr. Anderson, I beg you. Please give us another chance."

Anderson sat silently for no more than thirty seconds, but to James it seemed like an eternity. Everyone in the room was quiet, the only sound being Mike's labored breathing.

"All right," Anderson agreed, "I'll give you one more chance. It's against my better judgment, but I will give you one more chance. That and the fact you have cashed a rather healthy deposit."

James smiled. "Thank you, Mr. Anderson. Thank you. I will make sure everything goes fine from here on out. And one word about Gray Mason—I know what he did was inexcusable, but with proper supervision, he can be an asset. The man works like a beast. Frankly, purely in productivity terms, he's the best man here. And you're right; I think there is something wrong with him. But it's not entirely his fault; he was in an accident." The faces around the room were beginning to soften. James took advantage of his opportunity. "Mr. Mason was suffered serious brain trauma. He had to have a metal plate inserted in his head. If you force me to remove him from the job, we're going to have to lay him off. Right now, we have no where else for him to go. All I'm asking is for you to give him another chance as well."

Anderson sighed. "All right, Mr. Cameron. We're not evil people here. I'm not looking to add another burden to society. I will let Mr. Mason continue to work here. But if I hear one more complaint, you are the one I will be calling."

"I will take full responsibility."

Anderson turned to Mike. "Mr. Munro, do you support what Mr. Cameron is saying?"

Mike's head was tilted back against the top of the chair, and his eyes had rolled into the back of his head. He didn't move.

"Mr. Munro," Anderson said, "Are you unwell?"

Mike leaned forward slightly and collapsed, face first, onto the conference table. His head knocked over his glass of water, and the empty glass rolled off the table and onto the floor. James gingerly poked Mike but got no response; Mike was unconscious.

"Should we call an ambulance?" Anderson asked.

James nodded. "That would probably be a good idea."

CHAPTER 8

▼

"He's in the hospital?" Booby asked. "Why is he in the hospital?"

"Well, Dad, he passed out at our meeting this morning," James replied.

"Why didn't you tell me right away?"

"Because it happened at nine o'clock on a Monday morning. You're never here that early. And because I was trying to save the biggest project that we have going right now. I had to spend some time with Two-Boy to get him up to speed."

"Two-Boy?" Booby grimaced. "Why—?"

"Let me finish. The ambulance came right away and took Mike to Hudson General. I called over there and spoke to a doctor. He's fine. They got him on an IV, and he's sleeping. I'll take you over there later to see him."

Booby paced back and forth across the his office. "Mike has been under a lot of stress. He's been putting in a lot of hours. The business has been a little slow lately, and he takes it personally. He really gets nervous when things aren't firing on all cylinders. He's probably exhausted."

James stared at his father. "Dad, Mike does work hard; I will never take that away from him." James took a deep breath, not really wanting to speak the words. "But he has a serious cocaine problem. You know that. I don't think the guy's slept in the last three days. That's why he passed out."

Booby frowned and shook his head. "He just dabbles with the stuff. I don't think he has a serious problem."

"Why don't we go to the hospital later and see what the doctor has to say about it."

Booby rubbed his forehead. "What the hell is Two-Boy doing at Federated Wines and Liquors? That guy costs me an arm and a leg every time we use him." James quickly explained the situation to his father. Booby nodded but still grumbled, "Well, that wasn't very smart of Mike putting Gray Mason over there. Mason should only be used on new construction projects."

"Dad, Mike did it on purpose. He did it on purpose to screw with me, and he potentially cost this company a project that we really can't afford to lose right now."

Booby put his arm around his son's shoulders. "I don't think Mike would ever intentionally do something to hurt this company. I think that's just the way you're seeing it."

"Whatever, Dad," James said, rolling his eyes.

Booby hugged his son. "Don't worry, booby; we'll get everything straightened out, and everything will be fine."

James shook his head, frowning "I don't know, Dad."

*　　　*　　　*　　　*

Later that day, James met with his salespeople to review their week's appointments and activities. He was productive but couldn't keep his mind off the marketing plan he'd drafted a few weeks ago. He hoped sales would really pick up, and he felt a little frustrated at not being able to do much more than keep the status quo.

Later in the afternoon, Russell called out to James, wanting to show him his high score at Tetris; he was very excited. James patted him on the back and told him to keep at it.

Booby stayed in the office all day, covering for Mike. He called the hospital a few times to check on Mike and was told that he was sleeping.

At the end of the day, James approached his father. "Dad, before we go to the hospital, I want to talk to you about the marketing proposal I gave you. Did you get a chance to look at it?"

Booby shuffled in his seat. "I just got to it today, booby. I just got to it today. You did a real nice job putting it together. It looks like you spent a lot of time on it."

"Well, what do you think?" James asked.

"I think it's great. I think it's really great."

"So, do you want to do it?"

Booby waved his hand airily. "Well, I'm still looking at it. I'm still reviewing it. It's a lot of money. You're asking me to spend a lot of money here."

"It's not a lot of money, relatively speaking," James replied quickly. "The business is slow. You said it yourself. What this business needs is a shot in the arm. We need some exposure. We need to generate some leads." James sat back in his chair. "Look, our salespeople and I are struggling. We're trying our best, but we need help. We make the cold calls, go on the appointments, but we need more activity. No one here is afraid of working, but we need help."

"Okay, booby, I hear you. None of this is your fault; I'm not blaming anybody. I know everybody's trying. The market is a little soft right now. It's just a little soft. Things will pick up." Booby shifted in his chair. "I'm not sure that now is the time to spend this kind of money on an expensive marketing campaign."

James sighed. "Well, don't you agree we need more business?"

"Absolutely, booby, we could use more business," Booby agreed.

"And to get that business, don't we need more leads?"

"That makes a lot of sense, booby. More leads will get us more business."

"So, wouldn't it make sense to invest in this marketing effort to generate more leads so we can close some more business and get this place busy again?" James looked plaintively at his father.

Booby shrugged. "What you are saying makes perfect sense. You do a good job, James, a real good job. You're asking me to spend a lot of money, though. This is a lot of money."

James stared at his father. "So, when do you think you might make a decision?"

"As soon as I can, James. As soon as I can. I'm going to review it, and talk to a few people and see what they think, but I need to take my time and make sure we make the right decision."

James grew exasperated. "Dad, I don't understand. You just spent all this money to buy a restaurant, and you're going to have to spend a lot more to get it off the ground, which I'm actually fine with; I think the restaurant is a good idea. But if you can spend the money to do that, why can't you spend some money reinvesting back into this company?"

Booby squirmed in his chair and held his hands up. "I told you, booby, I told you. I'm going to seriously consider your marketing plan. I think it's great. It looks like you put a lot of effort into it, and I'm going to give it a lot of thought. Okay?"

James sighed and looked dejected.

"Cheer up, booby, cheer up. You do a great job, James. A really great job."
Booby went to his closet and got his coat, scarf, and hat. "I'm glad we could talk.
I like it when we get a chance to talk about the business." He patted James on the
back. "Let's go see how Mike is doing."

*   *   *   *

Hudson General was a sprawling hospital that served the entire county. The
main entrance had two thick plate-glass doors that slid open as James and Booby
approached. The lobby was extremely busy, and they had to wend their way
through groups of people to reach the reception desk. "Mike Munro, please,"
James said.

"Room 303," the attendant said. "Sign in, please." She pointed to a registry on
the reception counter. "Visiting hours end at nine o'clock. Elevators are straight
ahead on the left."

As they reached Mike's room, a middle-aged Hispanic doctor in a white lab
coat came out of the room, concentrating intently on the screen of her PDA. The
doctor seemed harried. She looked up, startled. "Are you here to see Mr.
Munro?"

"Yes," Booby replied.

"Are you family?" the doctor asked.

"Yes, we're family," Booby said.

The doctor glanced back through the door. She pulled Booby and James aside.
"I'm very concerned about Mr. Munro."

"Is he okay?" Booby interrupted.

"Yes, he's fine. For now. Physically, he was dehydrated and suffering from
exhaustion when they brought him in. His heart rate and blood pressure were elevated. We gave him a sedative and rebalanced his electrolytes via an IV." The
doctor looked intently at Booby and James. "I also ordered a blood test. I won't
have the results for another few hours...but I know what I'm going to find. Mr.
Munro is suffering from severe drug intoxication, most probably from cocaine.
He's lucky he didn't give himself a heart attack, particularly at his age." The doctor waited for this information to sink in. When neither Booby nor James
responded, she continued, "I've seen the effects of drug use and drug abuse. Mr.
Munro had to have ingested a large quantity of drugs to cause such a strong reaction. I will tell you that I don't believe that he is a casual user. He is most likely a
heavy user, probably a daily user, and very likely an addict—at least, psychologically." She paused again for several seconds. "Unfortunately, there's nothing I can

do for him, other than treat his physical condition. We will observe him over-night, but tomorrow he'll be released. I would suggest that you speak to him now and strongly suggest that he enroll himself into a drug treatment program. Imme-diately. I would also suggest long-term drug counseling."

"We'll speak to him, Doctor," Booby said, his eyes misting over.

"I'll be back in later to check on him."

"Thank you, Doctor," Booby said.

The doctor moved off quickly down the corridor, and the two men entered Mike's room. It contained two beds, separated by a rolling cloth divider. In front of each bed, a television hung suspended from a metal arm bolted to the wall. The room contained a single bathroom.

The air had the faint antiseptic quality of a hospital room. The far bed was vacant; Mike rested in the one closest to the door. He held the TV's remote con-trol in one hand and was staring groggily at the television. Booby and James stood at the side of the bed, looking down at Mike. The color had returned to his face, but his eyes were heavy-lidded and glassy. Mike turned from the television as he slowly realized they had come into his room.

"Hey…guys…."

Booby touched his arm. "How are you feeling, booby?"

"I'm a little out of it. They gave me something…I've been sleeping all day. I just woke up a few minutes ago."

"We saw the doctor outside," Booby said. "She's very concerned about you."

Mike sat up a little and looked into Booby's face. "I'll be all right. I've just been pushing myself a little too hard lately. I just need a little rest, and I'll be all right."

Booby rubbed Mike's arm. "Mike…the doctor said that she thinks you should check yourself into a drug rehabilitation center. The doctor thinks you collapsed due to drugs."

"I don't need to go to rehab," Mike snapped. "That doctor doesn't know me. Rehab is for people who have drug problems. Rehab is for people who can't con-trol themselves. I've just been pushing myself too hard lately." Mike pushed his head back into his pillow and shut his eyes.

"Okay, Mike," Booby said. "I can see you're tired. Why don't you take the rest of the week off, and we'll talk about this more when you're feeling better?"

Eyes shut, Mike asked, "You didn't tell my parents?"

Booby turned to James, who shook his head. "No, I don't think anyone has mentioned anything to your parents."

Mike nodded his head slightly.

"Is there anything you need, Mike?" Booby asked.

"No. I just need to rest. Thanks." Mike half-opened his eyes and focused on James. "Is everything all right with Federated?"

James squirmed. "Yeah, Mike. Everything is under control. For now. Two-Boy doesn't screw around. He'll keep a lid on things."

"I was only trying to do what was best for the company," Mike mumbled.

"We'll talk about that another time. Just get some rest," James replied.

"Thanks for visiting."

The strain of the conversation had proven to be too much, and Mike trailed off into sleep. Booby and James watched him sleep for a few minutes and then left the room.

"Poor guy," Booby sighed.

James turned to his father. "Poor guy? Dad, that's bullshit. Mike needs help. Did you hear him in there? He's in denial. He thinks he doesn't have a drug problem."

"I'll talk to him when he's better. Try to get him to listen to reason," Booby responded.

"No. He's going to rest up for a week and when he's feeling better, he's going to tell you that everything is hunky-dory. And you're going to buy it."

Booby scowled. "Well, what the hell do you want me to do? I can't force him to go to rehab. He's a big boy. He's responsible for himself. I can't make him do something he doesn't want to do."

"Listen, Dad. Mike told once me that cocaine makes him 'complete.' He said that cocaine made him faster and smarter than everyone else, and he likes that. Does that sound like someone who is voluntarily going to do anything?"

"I don't think he's that bad. I don't think he'd say something like that."

"What? Do you think I made it all up?"

"I just don't know what you want me to do?"

"Dad, you've known him for twenty years. For Christ's sake, you're like a father to him. He'll listen to you if you force him to."

"I can't make him do something that he doesn't want to do!" Booby insisted.

James paced back and forth in the hallway. "I'm telling you right now, if he doesn't get help, this is going to end badly, and not just for him."

Booby forced a smile. "Don't worry, booby; everything will work out all right."

James stopped pacing and considered his father. "Dad, you keep saying that, but I'm not so sure I buy it anymore."

"C'mon, I'll buy you a drink," Booby volunteered.

"Not tonight, Dad. I just want to go home."

"Will you drop me off at the Iberia House then?"

"Sure, Dad. Whatever."

Booby tried to make light conversation on the way back, but James was not interested in talking. When he pulled up in front of the Iberia House, Booby quickly got out.

"Are you sure you don't want to come in for just one? It's been a hectic day."

James studied his father. "Dad. It's a Monday night. Most normal people go home on Monday night."

Booby was undeterred. "Okay, then, booby. I'll see you tomorrow."

James drove home, his thoughts dark and gloomy, like the sky above.

CHAPTER 9

▼

James made it a practice to go to Federated every day to check on the progress. As expected, Two-Boy had cracked the whip, and Gray Mason and the McGirk brothers were working diligently. Mason kept a low profile under Two-Boy's watchful eye.

Mike was released from the hospital but did not return to the office. Booby spoke to him a few times on the telephone to see how he was doing. There was no further talk of rehab.

Booby came into the office every day, which was unusual, and attempted to handle the tasks that were under Mike's purview. He was rusty at it, asked a lot of questions, and generally made life miserable for everyone. He also decided to get caught up with every other aspect of the business.

Brian, for one, didn't like it one bit, and he complained to James. "Booby is being a real pain in the ass. He's getting into everything, and wants to know what's going on with everything. What's with him?"

"Mike's sick," James explained, "so now Booby thinks he's in charge."

"How long is this going to last?"

"Not long. I've seen him go through these spurts before. I actually have coined a business term for it. I call it 'Seagull Management.'"

"What's that?" Brian asked.

"It's the management process by which a manager flies in, squawks and makes a lot of noise, shits on everything, and then flies away."

Brian laughed. "That's pretty good. Seagull Management. I think I'll use it."

＊   ＊   ＊   ＊

James started going to the gym after work. He had a membership at Frank's Fitness Center, which was cheaper than the larger and more expensive fitness franchises. Plus, he appreciated getting his balls busted by Frank, the owner. It was motivational.

When James entered the gym, Frank immediately would accost him, saying things like, "Hey Cameron, you're really a fitness maniac. One workout a month. At this rate you'll be in shape in about fifty years."

When James would appear in his workout clothes and sneakers, Frank would tease him unmercifully. "Turn around and let me look at you. Look at that gut. The only six pack you're sporting is the kind you keep in a fridge."

Now, James was committed to setting up a workout routine, and he asked Frank for help. Frank took James through a series of free weights, Nautilus, cardiovascular, and stretching exercises. The entire routine took about ninety minutes.

"If you do this three times a week," Frank explained, "in three months you'll drop ten pounds of fat and put on at least five in muscle. I guarantee it. I'll get you in great shape."

"That's super, Frank. I appreciate it," James said. "But I think I'm going to be sore tomorrow."

"No pain, no gain, dummy."

On Wednesday night, James called Shannon.

"I wanted to talk to you about our date on Friday. How about if we go to the Forest Hills Field Club?" The restaurant was excellent, and James thought Shannon would like the view of the Manhattan skyline.

"You belong to a country club?" Shannon asked.

"It's no big deal. We have a corporate membership. The company pays for it."

"Aren't you special?" she teased.

"It's a nice place. You should enjoy it. And it's members only, so it's usually not very crowded."

"That sounds romantic."

"After last Sunday, I'm taking the sweep-her-off-her-feet angle."

"I would say that's the smart choice. Pick me up at the station at six?"

"I'll see you then."

*   *   *   *

On Thursday night, after James worked out, he decided to stop by the Bell Lap Tavern for a couple of beers. He called Meridian, who met him there. Vincent was behind the bar.

"Well, well. Look who it is. Fancy seeing you two strangers," Vincent said.

"Vincent, we were just together on Sunday," James replied.

"Yeah, four days ago. You haven't spent any money in my fine establishment all week. I'm thinking about rescinding your buy-back privileges."

James and Meridian sat at the bar. Vincent took two icy pint glasses from a small cooler, filled each to the brim with beer, and placed them down in front of each man. The golden beer foamed, fresh and inviting.

"That brings a tear to my eye," Meridian said.

"On the house," Vincent grinned.

"You're in a good mood tonight. What's the deal?" James asked.

"Big Al and I went to the bank today to talk to them about the loan."

"And?" James asked.

"And I got it. I got the loan. It took a little work, because my net worth isn't exactly what you would call large, and I just wasn't borrowing the money for the bar but for the renovations, too. Big Al was a big help. It wouldn't have gotten done without him."

"That's fantastic!" James and Meridian both shouted.

They raised their beer glasses and toasted Vincent. Meridian got the other guys in the bar to cheer for Vincent. Vincent smiled, blushing.

"So you're happy with the price?" Meridian asked.

"I guess. Obviously, I would have preferred to pay as little as possible, but Big Al was fair. I hope I can pay off the loan in about ten years and then start saving for my own retirement condo in Florida."

"So what are you going to do with the place, Vin?" Meridian asked.

"First of all, I'm going to rip out this nasty old ceiling and floor and put in a new one, and refinish the bar." He pointed up at the sputtering machine on the ceiling. "And get a new smoke-eater."

Meridian finished his pint and Vincent poured him another.

"I was also thinking about gutting the room upstairs and putting in a few pool tables and a couple of dartboards. Maybe even a smaller bar, and have two levels going on the weekends," Vincent mused.

"Look at Trump over here," Meridian said.

"Sounds promising, Vin," James agreed.

Meridian reached across the bar for the hot peppers, took one, and scanned the room. He noticed a gaunt man with slicked-back hair who was hunched over a beer at the end of the bar. "Who's that guy?"

"Oh, him. He's staying at the shelter," Vincent explained. "He's all right. Keeps to himself."

James and Meridian observed the newcomer and then looked at Vincent with raised eyebrows.

"Don't worry; he's harmless," Vincent assured them. "Besides, you should have seen him when he first walked in here. At least he's cleaned himself up now."

James fed the jukebox and became lost in his thoughts as he listened to the music. The door opened, and four young women came in. That got James' attention, and he elbowed Meridian. "Look at that, killer. We finally got a few ladies to go with the 'Ladies Night.'"

Meridian glanced over at the girls and shrugged. "They're not that hot."

James laughed. "Yeah. And you're fat and ugly. C'mon, you're not going to do any better. You should go say hello."

"Why don't you go say hello?" Meridian countered.

"I've already got a little lady on my mind. I've got a big date tomorrow."

"That's right. Your new fancy Manhattan girlfriend."

"C'mon, Meridian. You met her. She's nice and down-to-earth. You like her."

"She's good for a guy like you," Meridian said flatly.

"So, go and talk to those girls over there."

"I'm not in the mood."

James frowned at his friend. "Meridian. Kelly's not coming back. She's gone. You really need to get over her, and get on with your life."

Meridian chugged his beer, turned, and burped in James' face.

The four girls came up to the bar, and one of them announced it was her twenty-first birthday. Vincent checked her driver's license, and then poured each of them a pint of beer. He laid out four shot glasses and poured four shots. "Shots are on the house," he said.

The girls giggled and drank their shots; Vincent poured them another one. He told the girls a few jokes, flirting with them in the process. He offered the hot peppers, daring them to try one. One brave soul ate a pepper, and her mouth exploding in fiery heat. She chugged half a beer to douse it. Everyone laughed.

James drank his first beer slowly and then had two more. He made small talk with the girls, teased them, and tried to get Meridian involved, but to no avail. After he finished his third beer, he got up to leave.

"Where the hell are you going?" Vincent asked.

"I'm going home. I'm calling it an early night," James answered.

Vincent gave James the evil eye.

"What? I'm turning over a new leaf."

Meridian and Vincent heckled him all the way out the door.

"That's not going to last," Vincent stated as a matter of fact.

"You said it," Meridian burped.

✳   ✳   ✳   ✳

Late Friday afternoon, James straightened up his desk as he got ready to leave. It had been a good week. Good, but not great. *We could still really use that marketing program*, James thought.

They had gotten a couple of solid call in leads, and James followed up with the contacts he had made at the cocktail party, which turned into a couple more. He gave most of the leads to Brian and the other sales people, but kept a few of the more substantial ones for himself.

Brian came running into his office. "Nailed it!" he exclaimed. He danced around singing, "You don't make friends with salad, you don't make friends with salad, you don't make friends with salad—"

"What did you close?" James broke in.

"I got that law firm in West Orange. I thought it was a long shot, but they just called and said they wanted to go with us."

"That's great, Brian. That's a pretty nice-sized deal. What a way to close out the week. I'd buy you a beer, but I have some place to be tonight."

"Raincheck!" Brian said, as he danced out of the office.

Booby came striding in at the same moment, looking perturbed.

"What the matter now?" James asked. "I was having a good week."

"I've got a problem with the restaurant, booby," his father said, settling himself in a chair. "Well, I'm not sure if it's a problem yet, but it's a potential problem."

"What?"

"When I bought A Taste of Italy, I purchased the property, but I didn't purchase the liquor license."

"Why didn't you purchase the liquor license?"

"The guy wanted way too much for it," Booby complained. "But I bought another one. Remember the old Terrace Tavern, booby? Well, it's been closed down for a while. I remembered reading that they were going to tear it down, so I contacted the owner to see if he still owned his license and if he was interested in selling it."

"Did he still own it?"

"The old man still owned it, booby. He still owned it!"

"So you bought it?"

"I bought it!" Booby said. "And I got it for half of what I should have paid for it!"

"Good for you. So what's the problem?"

"Remember that old office building across the street from A Taste of Italy?"

"What about it?"

"Well, it got sold to a synagogue…you know, a Jewish temple."

"Yes, Dad. I know what a synagogue is."

"Well, it's a funny thing. They had to change the zoning from commercial to religious, and before I was able to transfer the Terrace Tavern license to A Taste of Italy, the zoning on the building across the street changed."

"Go on."

"It seems there's a law in town that you can't have a bar or restaurant with a liquor license closer than five hundred feet from a place of worship. A Taste of Italy is closer than five hundred feet."

"That doesn't make sense. I know plenty of bars that are just about right next door to a place of worship."

"Those places have been there for years and years. They're all grandfathered."

"So what happens now?"

"I have to get a variance. And I have to get it approved—"

"Let me guess. By the synagogue."

"Bingo!" Booby exclaimed.

"Why do I feel like you're about to ask me to do something?" James asked suspiciously.

"You know your mother and I are going on vacation to Belize for three weeks?"

"Yeah…I forgot. When are you leaving?"

"Tomorrow afternoon."

"Tomorrow afternoon? So what was this week all about with your hands-on management and—"

"Just trying to stay on top of things, booby. You know, I've got to keep myself in the loop. Besides, with Mike not here—"

"Look. It's not important. What do you want me to do?"

"The next town meeting is in three weeks. I need that variance approved. I need you to go with Russell and convince that synagogue to approve my variance."

"How the hell do you expect me to do that?'

"I'm prepared to offer them a substantial cash donation."

"You want me to bribe them."

"You got it, booby."

"How am I supposed to do that? I don't even know who—"

"Russell's already contacted them. He's got everything all set for next Thursday night. You're going to meet the representatives from the congregation at their temple."

James rubbed his temples with his fingers. "I'll try my best, Dad. But I'm not going to promise you anything."

"Don't worry, booby. Everything's going to work out fine. Just go with Russell and give him any help if he needs it. It's all going to turn out great."

"You really are a broken record," James sighed.

Just then, Meridian burst into the office. "Hey, Booby. Whatever you pay me, you'd better double it. I save this company's ass on a daily basis."

"What did you do, booby?"

"We had a system down over in Carlstadt. They sent two of your other retards—oh, excuse me, *technicians*—over there to fix it, but they couldn't find their asses from their elbows. Dennis finally sent me."

"Did you fix it?"

"Of course I fixed it. What do you think?"

Booby smiled expansively. "Why don't you drive me down to the Iberia House and let me buy you a drink, and you can tell me all about it?"

"That sounds like a plan," Meridian agreed.

Meridian turned to James. "You coming, Romeo?"

"Not tonight, Meridian. I got to get ready for my date."

"Hey, Booby, you're son's getting laid tonight."

"You're a class act, Meridian," James laughed.

Booby stood up, put his arm around Meridian, and walked him out of James' office. "You do a great job, booby. You do a really great job. You're a real asset."

Meridian laughed. "So how about a raise?"

"A raise? Well, I don't know, booby, I don't know. We're a little slow right now, we got to watch the cash…."

"Have a nice vacation, Dad!" James yelled after them. "I'll see you when you get back."

CHAPTER 10

▼

James pulled up to the train station at six o'clock. Shannon walked out with a group of other passengers. She wore black dress pants, black shoes, and a white cashmere sweater under a red wool dress coat. Her hair and makeup were done perfectly—she looked beautiful. She waved when she saw him and walked briskly to the car.

"Don't you look handsome," Shannon said.

He wore tan dress pants, brown shoes, a black mock-turtleneck, and a navy blue blazer under his black wool dress coat. He had just gotten a haircut and an old-fashioned hot shave. The hot shave was an indulgence, but James enjoyed occasionally going to one of those old-time barbers who still used warm cream and a straight razor. They nicked you up pretty good, but the shave was closer than you could do at home.

"You don't look so bad yourself," James replied, leaning over to kiss her. He lingered on her lips.

"You smell good, too," she said, breathing in his cologne. "I told you that you clean up nice."

Forest Hills Country Club was a short ride from the train station. A Belgian stone retaining wall on each side of the road, which led to the entrance, matched the road's contour. Off to the right of the parking lot sat an expansive clubhouse that overlooked the golf course.

The parking lot was mostly empty, and James parked in a spot close to the club entrance. He reached into the back of the car and pulled out a small box that he had hidden under the passenger seat. "Before I forget, this is for you," he said.

Shannon opened the red-laced white box. "Chocolate truffles! How sweet of you, James." She leaned over and gave him a kiss.

James opened the car door for Shannon and led her through the double-door entrance of the club and into a carpeted foyer. A staircase with a thick oak banister led to a sitting area, where a fire roared in a stone fireplace. Past the fireplace was an oak bar nestled in the corner of the dining room. About twenty cherry-wood tables were situated around the room. Large bay windows provided a stunning view of the golf course and, off in the distance, the Manhattan skyline.

A dozen small chandeliers hung from the ceiling, each containing six small arms that curved up into a light. Wine-colored lampshades topped each light, warming the room.

A hostess greeted James and Shannon as they entered the dining room. "Good to see you again, Mr. Cameron. Your table is ready. Please follow me."

The hostess led them to a small table in the corner of the room, next to the window facing the Manhattan skyline. Two overstuffed cherry-wood chairs were next to the table, on which a candle burned. A single white rose in a thin crystal vase was next to the candle.

"This is very nice, James," Shannon said. "Very romantic."

"So, am I sweeping you off your feet yet?" James teased.

"You're coming along nicely."

A waiter brought a basket of warm bread and a dish of whipped butter. He inquired as to their drink orders.

"Would you care for some wine?" James asked.

"Absolutely," Shannon replied.

James ordered a bottle of Merlot; the waiter quickly returned with the bottle and poured a small amount in a glass for James.

James swirled the wine in the glass, making a show of it. He stuck his nose in the glass and breathed deeply. He tasted the wine, swishing it around in his mouth, and swallowed. He smiled and indicated to the waiter to pour.

Shannon sipped. "Hey, this is really good? What is it?"

"It's called St. Francis. From Sonoma Valley. It's a really nice Merlot. Full-bodied, a little spicy with vanilla overtones. Swirl it around in your glass, and let it breath," James suggested.

Shannon swirled the wine for a few seconds, held it up to her nose, and smelled. She took another sip and considered the flavor.

"Do you taste anything else?" James asked.

She hesitated. "Chocolate? Is that chocolate?"

"Very good. You have a good palate. It's very subtle, but there is definitely a chocolate undertone."

"My, my James. A wine connoisseur? You do continue to surprise."

James blushed. "Well, I wouldn't call myself a connoisseur. I like wine, and I've tasted enough to know what I like. Besides, a real wine connoisseur wouldn't be caught dead drinking Merlot."

James and Shannon ate some warm bread and sipped the Merlot as they read the menu.

"Do you like Caesar salad?" James asked. "They make the best Caesar salad here. They use real raw eggs, not egg substitutes, like ninety-nine percent of the restaurants use now. It's amazing how a few lawsuits resulting from food poisoning have ruined the entire experience for the Caesar salad-eating world."

"I love Caesar salad," Shannon said. "That sound great."

"The portions are fairly large here, especially with the salads. How about we split the salad and split an appetizer?" he asked.

Shannon nodded, and scanned the menu. "Okay, how about car—"

"—paccio?" James finished. "I love carpaccio. Wow, we really seem to have a lot in common. Food-wise that is." He placed the order with the waiter.

"I told you the first night we met that I thought we had a connection. I didn't realize it was going to extend to a love of raw eggs and beef," Shannon said with a grin.

The salad was a perfect complement to the beef, olive oil, and Parmesan flavor of the carpaccio. They finished the first bottle of wine with the appetizers and ordered another. The waiter returned with the new bottle and then took their dinner orders. James ordered a New York strip steak with garlic mashed potatoes and creamed spinach, and Shannon ordered the same.

"I see you're a meat-and-potatoes girl," James teased.

"I'm Irish. Meat and potatoes were staples for me, growing up. My father was a firefighter, though, so we really didn't get to eat aged beef and garlic mashies too often."

She swirled the wine in her glass, and her face seemed a little flushed. The faint scent of her perfume wafted across the table, and she looked at James, her bright green eyes locking with his. "So what's your story James? You promised to tell me over dinner. You seem so troubled, so unsettled. It makes me sad."

James sagged back into his chair, gripping the stem of his wine glass, staring down into the red-black liquid, searching for some hidden truth. "Where do I begin?"

"How about the beginning?" Shannon volunteered.

"Right. The beginning. Okay. So, I grew up in North Harrison. Hudson County. You know the kind of town. Kind of the old, run-down, working-class type. A bar on every corner."

"I know it well. My family is originally from the Bronx."

"So I'm sure you know those kind of people."

Shannon frowned. "They're not bad people, James. You could say most of my family were 'those kinds' of people."

"I didn't say they were bad people. Most of them just don't set very high expectations for themselves."

"Maybe they just try to find happiness where they can. But what does all this have to do with you, James?"

James started to speak, stopped, and frowned in concentration. He spoke carefully. "I'm just giving you some background. I'm trying to find the right way to explain this. It's just…I'm not like those people."

Shannon laughed. "No, James. You are nothing at all like those people."

"Thanks."

"I didn't mean it is as a compliment. You are different from the people you grew up with, just like I'm different from a lot of the people I grew up with. James, look. You are intelligent, good-looking, articulate, polite…when you want to be. But you're not a better person. You're more educated, more polished, maybe, but you're not better."

"I didn't say I was better."

"You didn't have to say it. It's all right, James, really. I understand."

James rubbed his temples. "I'm still not explaining this right."

"No, I get it. Growing up, all you wanted to do was to make something of yourself. Make your parents proud. You felt superior to the people around you, and even though I don't agree with that, I understand it. And now, here you are, rubbing elbows with them on a daily basis, and that's the last thing you wanted. Believe me, I get it." Shannon sunk back in her chair.

"It's not quite that simple."

"James, life is not that complicated."

James sighed. "Look, you're right. I was the kid who did really well in school, who really tried to break out of the mold. And I did. I went out of state. I went to college. I graduated. I even got pretty good grades. And…"

"And?"

"And I wound up right back here. And you're right, it's the last thing I wanted."

"Why did you come back, James?"

James toyed with his wine glass. "I studied journalism, you know? My professors told me I was pretty good. One of 'em told me I was the most promising writer he'd ever had."

That's interesting, Shannon thought. *He seems genuinely excited about journalism.* "So why did you come back here?"

"Could you imagine?" he scoffed. "Me, working at *The New York Times?*"

Shannon leaned forward. "Cut the shit, James. Talk to me. Just tell me why you came back."

"I don't know! Okay? I don't know...I guess I was afraid. I was afraid to try and make it on my own. My father owned a company. I had a job if I wanted it. My friends never left town. I took the shortcut. I made the easy choice."

"Is your job so bad?"

"No, it's not a bad job and I do apply myself to it, but that's not really the point. I guess what I'm saying is I came back to something that I never really wanted for myself."

"And...?"

"And I guess I've regretted it ever since."

"Well, whose fault is that?"

James paused. "Right," he sighed. "My fault."

Shannon's face softened. "James, look. I'm not trying to be hard, but everything you've told me has to do with the choices you made for yourself. It's not like you were forced to go work in a mine somewhere. You've had your opportunities. It sounds to me like you're just feeling sorry for yourself."

Their dinners were served. James nibbled on a cooked carrot as he stared at Shannon.

"So what is it you want, James?" Shannon asked.

"I just want to be happy."

"So make yourself happy."

"I'm not sure I know how to do that."

"James, I don't understand you," Shannon said, exasperated.

James shrugged. "I just can't take the last ten years and pretend they didn't happen. My job needs me. Meridian and Vincent need me. Somebody has to keep an eye on Booby. I can't just up and leave, just to find some cosmic happiness."

"Don't do this to yourself, James" Shannon whispered. "It's not fair. You can do anything you want with your life. You might feel boxed in, but you don't owe anybody anything."

"It's not that simple, Shannon."

"What you need to do," Shannon said, "is decide, right here, right now, what you want to do with your life. That's what's bothering you. And that's all you need to figure out."

He nodded in agreement.

"Life is about taking chances, James," Shannon pronounced. "Life is about risk. Ultimately, what's going to separate you from the people that you surround yourself with is the will to make your life what you want it to be."

"The people that I have to deal with every day are out of their minds," James complained. "Talk about Dysfunction Junction."

"That's my point, James. And the reason why you drink so much, just like every other barfly in North Harrison, is because it is the easiest thing for you to do. Every night that you go drinking is one more night when you get to hide from yourself. In a very real sense, you *are* just like them."

"Ouch."

"And all this nonsense about having to take care of everything...and every-body...is just another excuse for not taking a chance on yourself. If you become everyone's crutch, James, it ultimately doesn't help anyone. You need to let people sink or swim on their own. Including yourself." Shannon chuckled. "You're not that important, anyway."

James grimaced. "All right, Shannon. Enough. I get it. I promise to give my future careful consideration."

Shannon smiled.

James arched an eyebrow. "Boy, you are one tough broad. You don't have a problem speaking your mind, do you?"

"I just call 'em as I see 'em."

James nodded. "Anyway, I'm glad you listened to my bullshit...and tried to understand."

"I understand you better than you think. I really do. People like you can be so frustrating, James. It's like you try to put the whole weight of the world on your shoulders."

James' smile grew wider. "I'm really glad I met you."

Shannon chuckled softly. "I really like you, too. I think that's the problem. What am I going to do with you?"

James winked at her. "I hope you stick around to figure it out."

They sipped wine, and Shannon considered her uneaten dinner. "Look. Our dinners are cold now."

James seemed not to have heard her. He stared out the window, lost in his thoughts. Gradually, refocused his attention on Shannon. Her bright green eyes studied him as James reached across the table and took her hands.

"Make love to me, Shannon," he said simply.

Shannon nodded.

James called the waiter and asked to have their dinners wrapped. They finished the wine as James settled his account. Then they took their dinners, put on their coats, and walked out into the night.

*   *   *   *

Booby and Meridian burst into the Iberia House, where Jack the bartender waved to them. A dozen patrons at the bar recognized them and waved as well.

The Iberia House was a typical Portuguese restaurant. The entrance opened onto a well-appointed bar, and the main body of the restaurant sat behind it. The walls were stucco, painted beige. The bar area contained a square bar, a jukebox, and a cigarette machine. A large television sat on a shelf in a corner. A painting of a shore scene featuring a prominent lobster hung over the doorway that led to the restaurant. The place reeked of garlic shrimp, the cornerstone of Portuguese cuisine.

Booby and Meridian went to the middle of bar and found two chairs. Jack came over and wiped down the counter in front of them.

"How you doin', Booby?" he asked in heavily accented Portuguese.

"I'm doing great, Jack." Booby smiled expansively, his teeth gleaming. "I'm leaving for vacation tomorrow. Three weeks. I got a fantastic deal on this resort package in Belize. It's going to be great!"

"Good for you. Take a rest; you deserve it," Jack said. "The usual, Booby?"

"Sure. And buy everyone here a round on me," Booby replied.

Jack filled a large martini glass with gin, poured in a smidgen of vermouth, and plopped in a three-olive toothpick. He placed it in front of Booby.

Jack took a dozen shot glasses and walked around the bar, turning over the shot glass in front of every customer. An upside-down shot glass was standard bar protocol for free drink. "This is on Booby," Jack said to each patron.

Meridian ordered a pitcher of red sangria and asked for a menu.

Jack prepared the sangria and served it to Meridian, with fruit floating at the top of the blood-red mixture. He filled Meridian's glass to the rim.

Meridian toasted the bar. "Cheers, big ears!" he yelled.

Booby grabbed Meridian and rubbed his shoulders. "You do a great job, booby. You do a really great job. You're a good kid."

"Thanks, Dad." Meridian rolled his eyes.

"Order whatever you want. Dinner's on me."

"Now you're talking, Booby!" Meridian exclaimed. "Hey, Jack. Can you do lobster Iberia tonight?"

Lobster Iberia was an occasional dinner special. It consisted of two one-and-a-half-pound lobsters: One lobster was stuffed with garlic crabmeat, and one was stuffed with garlic shrimp. It was served with a pile of home-fried potato chips, yellow rice, and vegetables. It was a lot of food.

"Let me check for you," Jack replied. He picked up the phone and spoke to the chef. Nodding, he told Meridian, "Yeah, we can do it, but I can't give you the special price. You'll have to pay for two lobster dinners."

Meridian grinned at Booby. "I don't care. Booby's buying. Bring it on."

Booby ordered a small garlic-shrimp dinner.

"What? Not hungry?" Meridian asked.

"I can't eat like you, Booby."

Booby and Meridian sat at the bar, chit-chatting and drinking their respective drinks.

"So, James is out on a date tonight?" Booby asked.

"Yep," Meridian answered.

"Nice girl?"

"Yeah, she's nice."

"Is she pretty?"

"I wouldn't throw her out of bed."

"So what about you, booby?" Booby asked. "Any new girls in your life?"

"Nope."

"You know, booby, you can't let the situation with your ex-girlfriend continue to bother you. You've got to let it go. You're young, booby. There's plenty of fish in the sea."

"Look, Boss, I really don't want to talk about it."

"You got to get on with your life, booby," Booby pressed.

Meridian grimaced. "I said I don't want to talk about it. Put a sock in it, all right, Booby?"

They both sat in silence until someone got up and fed the jukebox, and an old Rolling Stones song began to play.

Booby finished his martini, ordered another, and drank the fresh martini down quickly. He ordered a third. "So, booby, you've been friends with James a long time."

Meridian slugged down another glass of Sangria; he was getting toward the bottom of the pitcher. "Yeah, since before high school. Almost twenty years, if you can believe that."

"That James is a good boy, booby. He's a real good boy."

"I don't have a problem with James." Meridian shrugged, not knowing where the conversation was going.

Booby paused. "Have you noticed that James has gotten kind of moody lately? He seems kind of down to me."

Meridian eyed Booby, eyebrows raised. "Look, retard. Do you want to know why James is moody?"

Booby held up his hands, palms outstretched. "Don't get testy, booby. We're just talking here."

Meridian sighed. "James is moody because he has tried for years to make something good happen with your company, and no one gives him any help. Every time he makes an effort to do something positive, he gets kicked in the nuts."

"What do you mean? Who kicks him in the nuts?"

"How about your executive vice president?"

"No, that's not true, booby. Mike has tried to help James. He's taught him a lot about the business."

"That may have been true at one time," Meridian said, "but now he treats him like a dick."

"Mike's a good asset. He's a hard worker. He's—"

"Mike's an asshole to everyone in this world, including you," Meridian interjected. "And he's a cokehead."

Booby started to reply, thought twice, and turned back to his drink. He gulped down his martini, slammed down his glass, and ordered another one. "Okay, booby, forget about Mike. Who else in James' life do you think kicks him in the nuts?"

"You do," Meridian said flatly.

"Me? Why would you think that?"

"Because every time he comes to you for help or to get something done, you ignore him."

"I do not ignore him, booby. That's a lie!" Booby fidgeted in his seat.

"That's bullshit," Meridian argued. "I'll give you an example: He was telling me about a marketing program that he asked you to approve. He said he didn't think you were going to approve it."

"I didn't tell him that. I told him I was reviewing it. I told him I was going to seriously consider his plan. He's asking me to spend a lot of money, you know."

"That's bullshit and you know it. That marketing plan, like everything else James ever suggested to you, is going to sit on your desk and collect dust until he gets tired of asking you about it. Then he's just going to give up."

Booby sipped his martini. "I told him I was seriously considering his marketing plan."

"Look, Booby. I don't give a shit. I'm union. I work for a living. I work forty hours and you pay me forty hours. I'm telling you how James sees it. He's working for a guy who's made his money, doesn't want to come to work anymore, and is only concerned about maintaining the status quo. That's how James sees it, and that's a frustrating situation."

"That's not fair," Booby insisted. "I still want to work. I'm still interested in growing the business."

"Actually, I give James a lot of credit. If that was me working in that office circus you run, I probably would have hanged myself by now."

"I don't understand why you're so negative," Booby growled, his face becoming redder by the second. "You have no idea what pressures I have to deal with, and what's involved in running a company. You make it seem like I don't do anything right at all."

"Hey, I didn't say that," Meridian insisted. "I work for you, remember? If I thought it sucked that bad, I'd quit. You asked me about James, and I'm giving you my opinion."

"Well, I don't agree with your opinion, booby."

"Fine, then; let's just drop it."

Jack entered the bar carrying a large tray with two large lobsters on a plate. The aroma of garlic-shrimp and lobster made Meridian's mouth water. Jack placed the dinners on the bar and set out plates for them.

Meridian looked down at his lobster, red and steaming, and overflowing with garlic crabmeat and shrimp stuffing. "Now this is living!" he exclaimed.

Jack ceremoniously placed a lobster bib around Meridian's neck and placed a big wooden bowl for the cracked shells next to his dinner plate.

Meridian dove in.

Booby finished his martini and ordered another one. He stabbed at his garlic shrimp, taking small bites. By the time Jack brought Booby another martini, Booby's mood had grown melancholy.

Meridian looked up from his feast. "C'mon, Booby. Don't take what I said to heart," Meridian said through his food. "Look, James loves you. For better or for worse." He got out of his seat and gave Booby a big bear hug. "And I love you, too." Meridian squeezed Booby relentlessly until the corner of Booby's mouth showed the beginning of a smile.

Booby stabbed a shrimp and then held up his glass. "To good food and even better drink!"

Meridian raised his glass and clinked it against Booby's. "Amen to that."

CHAPTER 11

▼

James rented the second-floor apartment of a two-story walk-up, a fact he offered to Shannon somewhat apologetically as they made their way up the stairs.

"There are nights," James said as they reached his apartment, "when I'd sell my soul for an elevator."

"I don't mind the climb," Shannon assured him, although the last glass of wine had left her rather breathless. She followed James into the apartment and surveyed the space. To the right of the front door was a spacious living area; to the left was a kitchen, separated from the living room by a long counter. In front of the kitchen was a dining area. It was all spotless. Shannon nodded approvingly. "I see you run a tight ship. I like a man who's not a slob."

"If you'd seen the state of this place a couple of weeks ago, you wouldn't be so quick to throw those compliments around." James put their wrapped dinners in the refrigerator and then took two glasses from the kitchen cabinet.

"This is a big apartment," Shannon said. "It's probably twice the size of my place in Battery Park City."

"One of few perks of living in Jersey. Twice the room for half the rent." James got some ice from the freezer, placed it in the glasses, and filled them with water. He was feeling a little buzzed from the wine and was sure Shannon must be feeling the same.

"I really like wine, but it makes me so dehydrated," she said.

James nodded. He took her glass and set it next to his on the coffee table. Then he wrapped his arms around her and kissed her, softly at first and then more intensely, until their breathing was hot and ragged. James guided her to his bedroom without taking his lips from hers. He stepped back and removed his clothes, fully aroused.

Shannon stepped out of her clothes, revealing a pair of cherry-red panties and bra. She unhooked her bra, her breasts spilling out, nipples erect. The bra fell to the floor. She took off her panties, revealing a patch of red hair.

"Red all over. I like that," James commented.

Their mouths locked in a passionate kiss.

When their orgasms subsided, James held Shannon close and placed his head on her chest. Her heart was beating rapidly. They cuddled quietly, listening to their own synchronized breaths.

Shannon caressed James' face. "So what are you going to do, James?"

"I really don't know, Shannon," he replied softly. "I wish I had an answer. I wish I had a way out."

"James, there's always an answer. There is always a way out. You just have to find it."

"I wish it were that simple."

Shannon felt a tear run down his face, and she stroked his hair as he rested on her chest. Her contact aroused him, and they made love again.

Afterward, James turned on the television, and they settled comfortably on propped-up pillows in his bed, watching late-night programs. They held hands and kissed.

"Are you hungry?" Shannon asked.

"I'm starving," he replied.

Shannon got up and pulled on her sweater. James watched her disappear into the kitchen, naked below the waist. He admired her from behind.

Shannon removed the steak from their dinners, heated it in the microwave, and placed the steak slices on the bread. The aroma of steak and melted butter filled the air, mixing with the musk of their lovemaking, as she carried a tray to the bedroom.

James sat up, salivating. "You are the best!"

After polishing off the open-face steak sandwiches, they made love a final time. James felt a contentment he hadn't felt since college.

*   *   *   *

By the end of the night, Booby was too drunk to talk, and he could barely stand; Meridian was not that far behind him. They supported each other, leaning against the bar. The Iberia House had emptied out, but the jukebox still blared in the background.

"Should I call you guys a taxi?" Jack asked.

Booby's eyes wobbled in his head as he tried to form a response.

"Don't worry about it. I'll walk him home," Meridian slurred.

"Can you make it?" Jack asked.

"I can't send him home like this—James' mother will kill me—but I think a walk will sober him up a little bit."

Jack smiled politely. "Good luck, guys."

They staggered to the exit, with Meridian holding Booby under his armpits. They swayed together down the street on rubber legs until they hit an icy patch on the sidewalk. Meridian stumbled; Booby fell forward into a line of garbage cans.

Meridian picked up Booby, and they continued to zigzag down the street. It took them the better part of an hour to reach Booby's house.

Bobby and Meridian stood in front of Booby's house, evaluating their next course of action. The house was a red-brick custom ranch. A concrete staircase and metal railing led up to the front door, cutting the front lawn in half.

"Shhh!" Booby whispered. "Don't wake up Jane."

"Let's just get you into the house, nice and quiet like," Meridian agreed.

Meridian guided Booby to the railing, and Booby grabbed it tightly, leaning into it, as if a great wind were about to blow him away. He slowly pulled himself up the steps.

Meridian started to laugh, his laughter gaining strength until tears ran down his cheeks. *I wish I had one of those damn camera phones*, he thought.

Booby slowly, painstakingly, pulled himself up the steps to the porch. He wobbled and fell against the front door, and then he leaned his back against it to steady himself. Two dim porch lights mounted on either side of the porch provided the only illumination.

Meridian followed Booby onto the porch. "Which pocket are your keys in?" he asked.

Booby rummaged around in his coat and pants pockets and fingered his keys through the material.

Meridian reached into his pocket and pulled out Booby's keys for him. "Almost home, Booby."

"Wait...wait...." Booby waved his hand at a control pad on the side of the porch. "We have...to turn off...the alarm." He reached for the keypad.

"Are you sure you can manage that?" Meridian asked. "If you tell me the code, I'll punch it in."

"Be quiet!" Booby slurred, louder than he'd intended, "You'll wake up Jane." Booby's fingers wavered over the digits. He pressed one, backed up his finger to aim at the keypad, and then pressed another. It was hard to tell if he was pressing what he was aiming for. He found the enter key. "Okay…open the door."

"Are you sure, Booby?" Meridian asked.

"Open the door," Booby slurred.

Meridian put the front door key into the lock, turned it, and opened the door. The alarm started to beep.

"Shit!" Booby cried. "We have…to disable it…before it goes off!"

"What's the code?" Meridian demanded. "Quick! Tell me the code!"

Booby fell against the alarm panel, punched some digits, and pressed the enter button. The alarm continued to beep. He tried again.

A siren began to wail. The halogen flood lights mounted under the roof and buried in the front lawn suddenly came on, lighting up the night like a stage at a rock concert. A recorded voice interrupted the siren: "Warning! Warning! Someone is attempting to enter this house! Warning! Warning!" The siren played for another fifteen seconds before repeating the message.

"Jesus Christ, that siren is louder than the hounds of hell!" Meridian yelled, putting his hands over his ears. "You're going to wake up the whole neighborhood!"

Booby continued to fumble with the alarm.

A petite middle-aged woman with perfectly coiffed black hair appeared at the door; she was dressed in a bathrobe. "What the hell is going on out here?"

Booby looked up slowly into the eyes of his wife. He moved backwards and lost his footing on the steps. Meridian reached out to grab him, but he was too late. Booby fell, and he rolled end over end down the steps.

He hit his forehead on one of the concrete steps, causing a nasty gash. He came to rest at the bottom of the steps, and he looked up, dazed, with blood streaming down his face.

Meridian ran down the steps; the siren was still blaring.

Mrs. Cameron entered the correct code on the alarm panel; the alarm stopped, and the lights shut off. She looked down the front steps at her husband. "Be careful, Joe," she cautioned Meridian. "Don't you hurt yourself, too."

She stood in the doorway, shivering in her light robe. "It serves him right. We're leaving for vacation tomorrow, and he goes out and gets drunk. And no phone call."

Meridian carried Booby up the steps and into the house. He sat Booby down at the kitchen table, and then grabbed a towel off the sink to attend to the gash on Booby's forehead.

Jane Cameron went to the kitchen, following the trail of blood from the entry hall. "Is he all right? He's bleeding all over my carpets. Where the hell were you tonight?"

"The Iberia House," Meridian answered.

"Figures." Mrs. Cameron went to the sink, retrieved a wet cloth, and began to wipe the blood off her husband's face.

"This gash needs stitches," Meridian said. "You'd better call 9-1-1 and have them send the paramedics."

Booby squinted through dazed eyes at his wife. "Did you change the alarm code, honey?"

CHAPTER 12

▼

Meridian called James to fill him in on what had happened to Booby—eight stitches to his forehead—and to let James know that Booby and Jane had left for vacation the following day as planned.

On Monday morning, James was sitting as his desk, sipping coffee, and scanning his e-mail messages. Mike entered, dressed sharply as usual. He looked fresh-faced and rested. His eyes were clear. He held a mug of coffee.

James looked up from his computer.

"I just wanted to let you know that I'm back," Mike said.

"How are you feeling?"

Mike narrowed his eyes. "I'm fine. Don't you worry," he snapped. "I also wanted you to know that since your father is gone for the next few weeks, I'm in charge."

James shrugged.

"Don't think that…recent events have changed anything. Everything is business as usual. There aren't any angles to play here. I'm totally in control."

"Look, Mike, I'm not looking to play any angles, whatever that means. You're our vice president. I'm not looking to take your job," James replied.

"Just don't think anything has changed. Because nothing has."

James sighed heavily. "Is there something I can do for you, Mike?"

Mike frowned but said nothing. Then he turned, nearly bumping into Brian on his way out of the room.

"Glad to see Mike's still the same happy-go-lucky guy that we've all come to know and love," Brian sneered.

*   *   *   *

James spoke with Shannon every night, and made another date with her on Saturday night. She spent the night at his apartment—actually, she spent the rest of the weekend with him.

During the week, James had visited the gym and worked out on schedule, according to his new routine and much to Frank's astonishment. "I told you I was serious about getting in shape," James said, winking to Frank. It was the same week that James missed an entire week at the Bell Lap Tavern, much to Vincent's surprise.

James continued to check up on the Federated Wines and Liquors project. On the day of the meeting with the synagogue, James was ready. He pulled his silver Ford Taurus into the parking lot and spied the company "bucket truck"—a large vehicle with an extendable articulating arm, the end of which held a one-person plastic enclosure. He drove toward the bucket truck, parked, and got out of the car.

The bucket truck's arm was extended, angled toward a tall metal pole. Gray Mason was standing in the bucket, grasping a strand of fiber. The fiber was lashed to the side of the bucket, and the slack was dangling toward the ground. The fiber had been run from the roof of the main building, located about a hundred yards away, to the pole. Mason was reaching out over the bucket, attempting to latch the fiber onto a bracket situated at the top of the pole.

James cupped his mouth with both hands and yelled, "Mason! What are you doing up there?"

Mason looked down and waved. "Hiya, handsome! Don't you always look so nice, all dressed up in your suit and tie."

"Mason, *what* are you doing?"

"I'm running this fiber from the main building to this pole so we can extend service out to that guard shack over there." Mason pointed to a small, square, white building next to the entrance, another hundred yards away.

"Mason, I didn't sell them a fiber extension to the guard shack!" James yelled.

Mason waved him off. "Two-Boy did an additional work order. He ran it by the office."

"Who'd he run it by? He didn't run it by me. This is my project. I should be aware of any work orders."

"He tried you on your cell phone, but you didn't pick up. I think you were on an appointment. I think Two-Boy spoke to Mike."

James shook his head. Figures. Leave it to Mike to keep him out of the loop on his own job.

Mason yelled down at James. "I love my job, handsome! I love my job! The view from up here is fantastic. It reminds me of being back in the jungle. When I was on recon, flying around in my helicopter, I could see everything from up there. I sat at the door in charge of the machine gun. I would shoot everything that moved. Gooks, water buffalo, you name it, I killed it." Mason pantomimed holding large-caliber machine gun with both hands. He "shot" the ground with his invisible machine gun and made machine-gun noises.

"That sounds great, Mason." James turned to walk toward the main entrance and noticed a brand-new BMW parked behind the bucket truck, directly under the bucket. He yelled up at Mason, "Don't you think that car should be moved? You're working right over it."

Mason was securing the fiber attachment with a heavy wrench. He leaned over the side of the bucket and yelled, "What did you say, handsome?" And as he leaned over, the wrench slipped out of his hands. It tumbled through the air and crashed through the front windshield of the BMW, shattering it and sending glass flying in every direction. The car's alarm sounded, as Mason, from his perch in the bucket, stared dumbfounded at the wrench on the BMW's front seat and the huge hole in the middle of the windshield.

✳   ✳   ✳   ✳

James met Russell back at the office later in the day. Russell was dressed in a three-piece suit and bright-red tie. His hair was freshly cut; his moustache and beard were neatly trimmed.

"Very nice, Russell," James said. "I don't often see this side of you."

Since Russell started working for Cameron Voice and Data, he was rarely seen in anything other than tan slacks and button-down flannel shirts. His appearance was more lumberjack than a big-money stockbroker.

This was a different Russell, a transformed Russell. James noticed that Russell seemed more energetic and vibrant. He struck an impressive figure.

"Are you ready to do a little wheeling and dealing?" James asked.

Russell smiled confidently. "I've been dealing with the Jews all my life. If we give them what they want, they'll give us what we want. They're tough but sensible."

"Okay, Russell. It's your show." James slapped Russell on his back. "Let's get it done."

James and Russell easily found the nondescript brick building. Gold block letters mounted above the entrance read "Congregation B'nai Israel." Above the name was a gold Star of David.

This particular house of worship was small, with six rows of benches on each side of a main aisle. At the east end of the sanctuary was the ark—a simple stone altar—and hanging from the ceiling above the ark was the *ner tamid*, or eternal light.

Two men, each wearing a dark suit and a yarmulke on his head, stood waiting for James and Russell. One of the men offered his hand. "I'm Rabbi Cohn. Very nice to meet you," he said. He shook hands firmly with James and Russell, and then introduced the assistant rabbi. James and Russell moved to enter the sanctuary, but Rabbi Cohn stopped them. He indicated a small pile of yarmulkes on a small stand at the end of the foyer.

"Please don a yarmulke before entering this house of God."

They placed the yarmulkes on their heads and then followed the rabbi through the sanctuary to a doorway located on the right side of the ark. They entered a small office. Rabbi Cohn took his seat behind a small wooden desk and motioned for James and Russell to take the chairs in front. The assistant rabbi stood next to a filing cabinet, leaning against the wall.

"Thank you for taking the time to meet with us and to entertain our request," Russell began.

"Well, as you gentlemen can see, this is a very small congregation," said Rabbi Cohn. "We are working hard to help it grow, and we are confident that our new location will go a long way in accomplishing that."

Russell nodded.

"We will have a sanctuary that can seat two hundred fifty, and the building will have enough space to accommodate a small nursery and school. The congregation is very excited about our plans."

Russell nodded again.

"One of the reasons that we chose that location is that it is in a quiet area. We were aware that it was across the street from A Taste of Italy, but our congregation was comfortable with a family restaurant. We've all eaten there." Rabbi Cohn looked directly at James and then at Russell, ensuring that they understood. "But I must tell you, Mr. Davis. Mr. Cameron's opening an ostentatious steakhouse that caters to the cocktail crowd is very different from a small, quiet family restaurant. That would change the dynamic of the neighborhood. If he intended to keep everything the same, we would have much less of an issue, but this idea causes us some concern.

"And I must be frank: Mr. Cameron has quite the reputation in this town for being…a man who enjoys his drink. What happens if this steakhouse degenerates into just another bar, like every other bar in this town. What happens if it starts to attract…well…starts to attract a non-family element?"

Russell cleared his throat. "Well, Rabbi Cohn, I can certainly appreciate all of your concerns. I am here to assure you that Mr. Cameron has only the best of intentions with this venture. In fact, Mr. Cameron shares your concern about…undesirable elements that have become more prevalent in this community over the last several years. He is looking to counteract that by bringing back a certain class and charm with this new restaurant."

Rabbi Cohn's eyebrows shot up. "Oh?"

"And to further support his good intentions," Russell continued, "he has hired me to operate and manage it." Russell explained that he had a good feel for the way in which a quality establishment should present itself, as well as what he needed to do to attract appropriate clientele. He demonstrated himself to be a man of sophistication.

Rabbi Cohn nodded. "I respect your position. What will be the name of the restaurant?"

James started to answer, but Russell kicked his leg. "Mr. Cameron is still undecided on the name." Russell changed gears. "I understand that renovating your new synagogue is an expensive gesture."

Rabbi Cohn smiled. "It certainly is. But oy gevalt! God willing, we will be successful."

"Mr. Cameron fully respects your position," Russell said. "You and he would be in the same position—investing time, money, and energy in an endeavor that, when finished, will reflect the efforts put into it."

Rabbi Cohn smiled gently.

"I understand that Mr. Cameron's reputation has preceded him," Russell continued. "As a civic leader, Mr. Cameron gives freely of his time and money. Did you know that Mr. Cameron has made significant donations to several charitable groups in the area?"

Rabbi Cohn shook his head. "Actually, I know very little about Mr. Cameron's charitable activities."

"Mr. Cameron would be happy to make a significant donation to your synagogue…in consideration of his variance request."

Rabbi Cohn rubbed his chin. "What kind of donation was Mr. Cameron considering?"

Russell gave him a five-figure number.

"That's not gehakteh leber, or I should say chopped liver," Rabbi Cohn said. "That kind of donation could be very useful. Very useful indeed." He leaned forward on his desk. "Mr. Davis, you seem like a man of honor and integrity. Can you assure us that this restaurant will be as you have described it? Can you assure us that down the road we will not regret having approved this variance?"

"Rabbi Cohn, I can't predict the future. But I can tell you that as long as I'm managing the restaurant, I will run it with class. You have my word on it," Russell assured him.

"We will consider your request and let you know in the next few days," Rabbi Cohn replied. "If we do agree to grant your variance, I would ask that Mr. Cameron not make a tzimmis about it. I would prefer that it remain between us—as well as the donation."

"I understand," Russell said.

Business concluded, everyone stood, but as James and Russell turned to leave, James said to Rabbi Cohn, "I noticed that your new building doesn't have a parking lot."

"No, you're right. Parking space in this area has always been at a premium," Rabbi Cohn replied.

"I could speak to my father about letting you use A Taste of Italy's parking lot for your Saturday service," James offered. "It's a fairly large lot, and your services likely won't conflict with the restaurant's business hours."

"I would appreciate that, Mr. Cameron. It would be very convenient for our congregation." He extended his hand once again. "We will speak to you shortly. Mazel tov!"

"Mazel tov!" James and Russell repeated.

"That went well," James said when they were back in the car. "You were great, Russell. I'm very impressed."

"I didn't think we had them convinced, but when you threw in the parking at the end, I think that nailed it. They really need that parking, as much as the money. That was quick thinking," Russell replied.

James beamed at the compliment. "Can I buy you a beer at the Bell Lap Tavern?"

"Sure. That sounds good. Isn't that the place with the hot peppers?"

"Yeah. That's the one. My friend Vin manages it."

"Believe it or not, my father used to hang out there."

James chuckled. "Yes, many generations of drinkers have gotten loaded at the Bell Lap Tavern. And you know, Russell," James said, becoming serious, "I think you're going to be a smashing restaurant manager. And you know what? I'm starting to really believe in this restaurant. I think it may actually turn out to be exactly what you and my father are saying it will be."

"You're father has his issues; I won't lie to you. But he's gotten this far on his intuition, and his intuition is telling him to open this restaurant."

"I feel the karma building as we speak," James joked as he drove off toward the Bell Lap Tavern.

CHAPTER 13

▼

James was sipping coffee and reading e-mails when his telephone rang.

"You really should take this call," the receptionist told him. "I mean, you *really* should."

"Why so cryptic?" James asked. "Never mind; put it through."

A gruff voice on the other end of the line spoke. "Is this one of the Camerons?"

"Yes, this is James Cameron. Can I help you?"

"No, you can't help me, but you can help your vice president. He's hanging out of his car on Main Avenue, passed out. I think someone should get him before the cops do."

James swallowed hard. "Where is he?"

"He's out in front of Midtown Bakery. I'll tell ya, you've got some cast of characters working at that place." There was a click, and the line went dead.

"Shit!" James said. He ran out of his office. "Brian, are you here?"

Brian stood up and looked out over his cubicle. "Yeah, what's up?"

"I need your help. Mike's in trouble again."

"Again?"

"I'll explain on the ride."

Brian and James ran out of the building, jumped into James' car, and sped down the road toward Midtown Bakery. James saw Mike's black Mercedes on the right side of the road, pulled partially up onto the sidewalk. The driver's side door was open, and Mike was indeed passed out, hanging out of the car, head down. The only thing keeping Mike from falling out of the car entirely was the seat belt fastened around his chest.

James and parked behind Mike's car, and he and Brian jumped out. There was a pool of vomit directly under Mike's head. The stench made the two men gag, and Brian covered his mouth and nose with his hand to block the smell. Another pile of vomit was on the passenger's seat and around that side of the car.

"What a disaster!" James muttered. He grabbed Mike's shoulder and pushed him back into the car. Mike's face was ghostly white and clammy. James smacked his face a couple of times, but Mike was unresponsive. "Get some water, Brian," James ordered. "Quickly."

Brian ran across the street to the deli.

James continued to slap Mike's face. "Mike. C'mon, Mike. Mike, wake up, man!"

Brian came back with a large bottle of water, and James poured the cold water over Mike's head. He opened Mike's mouth and poured water down his throat.

Mike choked and opened his eyes. His breath reeked of booze and vomit. "Where…where am I?" he asked groggily.

James poured more water into Mike's mouth and splashed his face.

Mike choked again. "Okay, okay. Enough. Where am I?"

"You're sitting on Main Avenue in front of the bakery," James told him. "You threw up all over yourself."

Mike attempted to sit up. He reached for the ignition. "I have…to get to the office."

James pushed him back on the seat. "You aren't going anywhere. What the hell happened to you?"

Mike shrugged. "I met this flight attendant Friday night. We went…we went down to Atlantic City."

"Oh, I see. You partied all weekend and decided to drive back about three hours ago. Smart."

Mike coughed.

"Didn't you tell me you had everything under control? You're lucky some dude who knows you called the office. What do you think the cops would have done if they'd found you like this?"

Mike didn't respond.

"How much coke do you have on you?"

Mike coughed again. "Just take me home," he said.

James undid the seatbelt clasp and pulled Mike out of the car. With Brian's help, James dragged Mike over his Taurus. Mike's polished dress shoes slid through his vomit and left a trail of red-brown goo in his wake. James pushed Mike into the back seat, where he collapsed on the cushions.

James ran back to Mike's Mercedes and drove it off the sidewalk. He parked the car in front of an expired meter, then pressed down on the motorized controls to lower the windows. *Little good that's going to do*, he thought.

Brian was waiting for James in the Taurus. Mike had passed out again and was snoring loudly.

"Aren't you going to put some change in the meter for him?" Brian asked.

"Absolutely not," James replied emphatically. "In fact, I hope the asshole gets a ticket."

At Mike's house, Brian and James struggled to get Mike out of the back seat—he seemed like dead weight—and up the steps to his front door. James had to try a few keys on Mike's key ring before finding the one that opened the door. They half-carried, half-dragged Mike through the front door, up the stairs, and into his bedroom. They threw Mike onto the unmade bed, and Brian picked up a comforter off the floor and spread it out over him. He put his ear next to Mike's mouth to make sure he was breathing; he was.

Brian pulled off Mike's vomit-caked shoes and threw them on the floor. "Well, that's some sorry son of a bitch," Brian said.

"You could not have paid me enough to touch those shoes," James replied.

James placed Mike's keys on a large mirrored dresser, and then he and Brian returned to James' car.

"Do we need to keep this a secret?" Brian asked.

James shrugged. "Is any of this really a secret anymore?"

$*$ $*$ $*$ $*$

Later that day, Russell burst into the office, smiling broadly.

"They agreed!" James guessed.

"You bet your ass they agreed!" Russell exclaimed.

"That's awesome, Russell. What did they say?"

"I told you I thought they were still on the fence, and I was right. It was the parking that did it. They really wanted that parking."

"Glad I could be of service," James said.

Russell nodded. "I'm going to let your father know that you were a big help with this. I appreciate your help, too."

"You're welcome, Russell, but you did most of the work. I would have just walked in there and said, 'Will you sign this variance for fifty grand?' without all the schmoozing."

"Now the hard part starts."

"What hard part?"

"Actually getting the restaurant off the ground."

James laughed out loud and waved Russell out of his office. "One thing at a time, Russell. One thing at a time. Go play some video poker or something. I've got work to do."

*   *   *   *

The Bell Lap Tavern was almost empty when James walked in; only Vincent and another gentleman were in the back of the bar. They were leaning over a set of blueprints.

"Vin, what's going on?" James asked. "You look like a general studying his battle plans."

Vincent waved hello and pointed to the plans. "James, I told you my ideas would work. We're going to open up the back and relocate the staircase, and blow out the upstairs, making it one big room. And my architect here thinks this may cost me less than I first thought."

James acknowledged the architect and then said, "That's great, Vin. That's really super. When are you going to start the construction?"

"Well, it will take me a couple of weeks to draw up the actual prints," the architect said. "Then Mr. Ferrara will have to bid it out to two or three contractors. After he selects a contractor, figure a few weeks for the permits. I would say on the outside he will be able to start construction in six to eight weeks."

Vincent nodded in agreement. "It's going to be exactly as I envisioned. Come and belly up to the bar, and have a pint on the house."

The architect and James moved over to the bar and pulled up a chair. Vincent poured them each a pint and placed the frosted glasses on the counter.

"I'm just staying for one, Vin. I need to work out tonight," James said.

"You're such a sissy," Vincent teased. "How's it going with your new girlfriend?"

"It's going well. We really seem to be hitting it off."

"Just don't forget your roots, pal. Between this woman and your Adonis routine, I'm starting to feel neglected."

"Don't worry, Vin," James assured him. "I'm not going anywhere."

Vincent poured himself a beer, and the three of them raised their glasses in salute to the new-and-improved Bell Lap Tavern.

*   *   *   *

James and Russell were seated on one of the benches in the Town Hall council chamber. They were waiting for the weekly town meeting to begin so they could make sure the council approved the variance for the Mad Cow. A wooden banister separated the benches from the raised half-moon-shaped dais where the mayor and council sat.

A few other people were scattered around the room, occupying other benches. A few elderly people entered the chamber and sat toward the front of the room. James thought that these people were the standard hecklers who made life miserable for any town trying to conduct business in an open forum.

The council members came in and took their respective seats. Eventually, the mayor seated himself at the center of the dais. He turned on his microphone and tapped it. The speakers in the room made a popping sound.

The mayor asked everyone in the room to rise, and he directed them in the Pledge of Allegiance. Everyone sat down, and the mayor then asked the town clerk to begin the minutes. He reviewed the minutes from the previous week and read over a list of open items. He asked if the council wished to open up any of the items for discussion. To James' delight, no one did.

Time seemed to crawl. The mayor spent the next ninety minutes progressing through the order of business. He droned on about topics that James completely ignored, and occasionally, a councilperson would add a comment or ask a question. A few times one of the elderly people would try to address the council, and each time the mayor gave a reminder that the public could only address the council at designated times or by invitation from the mayor. The meeting inched along, and James fidgeted in his seat. He looked at his watch a dozen times and made a mental note to never, ever get involved in local politics.

Russell sat stoically through the meeting, waiting for his turn.

Finally, the mayor got to the special construction and zoning variance part of the agenda. The first item on the table was the variance for James Cameron, Sr. The mayor asked Mr. Cameron to approach the council.

Russell stood up and said, "I'm Russell Davis, Mr. Cameron's appointed representative to discuss this matter." He walked through a small gate in the banister and was directed to stand at a podium in front the council. Russell tapped his microphone lightly to make sure it was on. Most of the council and the mayor all knew Russell, and he waved and smiled at them.

"Mr. Davis," the mayor began, "I take it all the necessary paperwork has been filed with the town?" He fumbled through some papers.

"Yes, Mr. Mayor, all the necessary paperwork has been submitted for approval."

"And you've gotten permission from—" He again fumbled through some papers. "From the Congregation B'nai Israel for us to grant you approval of this variance?"

Russell responded quickly, "Yes, Mr. Mayor, they have agreed in writing to the variance request, and we have submitted that agreement."

The mayor frowned. "I'll tell you, Mr. Davis, and this is for the record. I very much enjoyed A Taste of Italy, and I'm sad to see it go. This town needs more places like that. I'm not very happy to see a bar take its place. I believe this community already has more bars than it needs."

Russell smiled. "Mr. Mayor, Mr. Cameron intends to open a steakhouse, not a bar."

The mayor smiled thinly. "Right. A steakhouse. Would anyone on the council like to add to this discussion, or does anyone have a reason why we should not grant this variance?"

A crusty old man sitting on the front bench stood up and yelled, "James Cameron is a damn dirty drunk! I knew his father, and he was a damned dirty drunk, too! And all of his technicians drive around town like maniacs in those company vans of his! I'm surprised no one's been killed. Giving him a bar is like giving an inmate the keys to the asylum!"

The mayor scolded the old man and again explained that the council was not taking comments from the public at this time.

The rest of the council sat quietly without objection.

The mayor looked at Russell. "All right, then. The town hereby approves the transfer of liquor license title to Mr. James Cameron and further grants the variance to operate the license as approved by the Congregation B'nai Israel. Congratulations, Mr. Davis. Mr. Cameron is now in business."

CHAPTER 14

▼

Spring found construction beginning in earnest on the renovations for the Bell Lap Tavern. Vincent had a hell of a time running the bar during construction, but he made the best of it. The regular crowd tolerated the dust and tarps, knowing that their favorite watering hole was getting a much-needed makeover. Everyone cheered on the day that the new smoke-eater was installed, and Vincent gave everyone a round on the house.

Even the scrawny transient who had taken to hanging around the place had gotten excited. The regulars started to call the man "Joe Vagrant"—he had not volunteered his real name, and no one had bothered to ask—but Vincent said that moniker was a little too cruel, so they just shortened the name to "Joe."

James and Shannon saw each other most weekends, and their budding relationship began to grow and blossom as well. James lost weight. He worked out three times a week like clockwork, and now that the weather was warmer, he began to take long walks. He stayed out of the bars, for the most part, but still frequented the Bell Lap Tavern a few nights a week, if only to appease Vincent.

Booby returned from vacation and continued arguing with his wife. The stitches in his forehead had been removed in Belize by a local doctor, who also suggested a prescription for malaria pills, which Booby had declined. When he returned to the office, his wound was healed, but an angry red scar ran down the top of his bald head. Booby seemed to not pay it any attention.

The same architect who Vincent hired to draw up the renovations to the Bell Lap Tavern was hired to draw up the plans for the Mad Cow.

James frequently checked on the Federated Wines and Liquors project, which continued to make good progress under the watchful eye of Two-Boy—he also lost a little weight, but not enough to even come close to putting his nickname in jeopardy.

Mike reported to the office the day after the "Main Avenue Incident," as Brian dubbed it, but never said a word about it. When Booby returned from vacation, James explained to him what had happened, and he asked Booby to speak to Mike.

Booby was only able to elicit weak promises from Mike: "I promise I won't let something like that happen again" and "I'll try to not do cocaine anymore." James knew it was pure bullshit, but he was helpless to control it. Booby seemed to believe Mike, to no one's surprise.

But it was a surprise when Mike actually started to behave himself. He still was his usual grumpy, moody, pain-in-the-ass self, but that was what people expected, so everything was status quo.

At the end of March, a sheet was posted just inside the main entrance to Cameron Voice and Data's office for people to sign up for a company fishing trip. Meridian got it into his head that the office and field employees needed to spend some time "bonding," so he figured the best way to do that was to get everyone on a bus at five in the morning and drive down to the shore to go fluke fishing on a big party boat. It didn't take long for the sign-up sheet to get completely filled in; another sheet had to be added to accommodate all the additional names.

*   *   *   *

On the last Friday in March, James got on the train and headed into Manhattan to meet Shannon. Their Friday date night had become something of a routine. The night was unusually warm for late March, reaching almost sixty degrees. The sky was clear, and a light breeze blew in out of the south.

James, in his light gray dress pants and tan turtleneck, was dressed perfectly for a jaunt around Manhattan.

There weren't many passengers on the inbound train to Manhattan; most of the passenger traffic was heading the other way, taking people back to their lives in the suburbs. James idly watched the towns go by. He picked up a copy of *The New York Post* off the floor of the car and scanned the headlines. The train disappeared into a tunnel, displacing the warm moonlight with cold artificial light. James threw the paper back onto the floor and waited for the train to emerge from the tunnel.

The train traveled under the Hudson River and exited into the newly reopened World Trade Center station. James stared out the window into the neatly excavated pit that once housed the World Trade Center complex. He marveled at the enormity of it, and wondered how so much rubble and ruin could be made to look so scrubbed and sanitized.

The train stopped at the platform, which was the restored original platform, now located about half way up the hole. James had taken this train dozens, if not hundreds, of times and always saw—and smelled—Famous Original Ray's Pizza as soon as he got off the train; it was the first shop in the cavernous underground mall that formerly existed on this level.

The mall was gone, as was Famous Ray's, and James keenly missed it. He sighed, walked out of the train onto the platform, and headed up the long flight of stairs toward the street.

From the station exit it was a short walk south to Battery Park City; the walk took less than ten minutes.

James entered the esplanade of the massive structure, a collection of interconnected buildings, but he knew exactly how to find Shannon's apartment building. He'd barely knocked on her door when it flew open, and Shannon launched herself into his arms, giving him a big kiss.

"James, it is so beautiful out tonight. I am so happy spring is finally here. I could not wait for the winter to end."

"Good to see you, too, my dear!" James replied enthusiastically.

"Let's make sure we have a good time tonight," she said.

Shannon's apartment was modern but small—typical for Manhattan. The living area was well appointed, and three huge windows overlooked the Hudson River. Venetian blinds covered the windows, but they had been pulled up to let in the moonlight, and the view was spectacular.

Next to the living area was a small eat-in kitchen, which opened to a small dining nook. Under a row of cabinets was a granite counter that opened onto the living area. An empty fruit bowl sat on the counter. A round modern-looking dining table occupied the dining nook. Four chairs were pushed in under the table.

Past the living area was a short hallway that led to the master bedroom, and off to the left was a small study, which Shannon used for storage. She also had a bookcase that contained her small library.

Shannon ran back into her bedroom. "I'm just about ready," she called over her shoulder. "Just give me another couple of seconds."

Shannon was dressed in black pants and a red wool pullover. She wore red high-heeled shoes. She considered herself in the mirror, nodded to her reflection, and then returned to the living room. "Okay, I'm ready to go."

They talked about what they should eat for dinner and decided they were in the mood for Italian, so they left the building and headed north toward Little Italy.

"Should we walk or take a cab?" James asked.

"Let's walk," Shannon replied.

They held hands as they strolled down the sidewalk, taking their time and enjoying the springtime sounds and smells of Lower Manhattan. Finally, they reached Mulberry Street in Little Italy. Over the last thirty years, Little Italy gradually had been encroached upon by Chinatown, which now had it surrounded. Mulberry Street was the heart of what was left of Little Italy, and it extended for about four blocks. On each side of those four blocks, however, resided an impressive array of restaurants that catered as much to the natives as it did to the tourists.

James and Shannon walked the length of Mulberry Street, scanned the menus, and looked in the front windows. They finally decided on Angelo's, an old eatery that had been a Little Italy fixture for almost one hundred years.

They were greeted by the host, an old, thin Italian man, dressed completely in black. "Buona sera!" he said with a smile.

The restaurant was narrow but long, and it occupied two levels. The host led them to a small table in the back of the restaurant. He ceremoniously lit a candle in the middle of the table.

"Buon appetito; enjoy," he said graciously.

A server appeared and took drink orders. James asked for a recommendation on a nice Chianti. The bottle of wine was brought over, opened, tasted, and poured.

James and Shannon toasted each other and sipped their wine.

Menus were delivered, and the two sat for a few minutes, contemplating their dinner selections. They decided to share two appetizers, and they each chose pasta for their entrées: James, a vodka pink sauce, and Shannon, a primavera.

"So, how was your week at work?" James asked.

Shannon took a sip of wine. "It was fine. We just booked this new customer, and it's going to be a major software deployment. They are already being difficult. We're still in the transitional phase from sales to implementation, so I'm getting caught in the middle. You know what they say—"

"No good sale goes unpunished!" James laughed.

"We have not been dating long enough to finish each others sentences," Shannon teased.

"I know. It's just that we have that 'connection thing' that you keep telling me about."

"We really are very similar. Aren't we supposed to be dating people not like us? I thought opposites attract."

"We are opposites," James said.

"How do you mean?"

"I have a penis, and you have a vagina."

Shannon choked on her wine, blushed, and giggled. "Stop. Don't be rude."

"Seriously, I don't know why, Shannon. Maybe we're enough the same to understand each other, but different enough to keep each other interested."

"See, that's one reason why I like you. You are very good with words."

"Does that mean I get to say penis and vagina again?"

"And I have been trying so hard to elevate your mind out of the gutter."

Their repartee continued until their appetizers arrived. James had ordered fresh mozzarella and roasted peppers, and a heaping plate was placed in the center of the table. Shannon had ordered stuffed mushrooms, and that plate was arranged next to the first appetizer. The aroma of both dishes made their mouths water.

After they finished eating, James reached his hand across the table, and Shannon held it and kissed it.

"I do really like you, James," she whispered, gazing into his eyes.

James reached into his coat. "I almost forgot," he said nonchalantly. He pulled out a small, rectangular black-felt box and handed it to her.

"Now, James, what is this?"

"Open it."

Inside was a gold necklace. Looped to the necklace was a large emerald pendant set in gold. Also in the box was a gold bracelet, and hanging from the bracelet were small emerald charms.

"James, these are beautiful! I don't know what to say."

"You can say 'Thank you,'" James teased. He clasped the necklace around Shannon's neck and gave her a peck on the cheek.

The wait staff, witnessing the scene, clapped softly. A few patrons held their glasses up in toast. The head server came over with two apéritif glasses filled with Sambuca. "It's nice to see two young people in love," he said. "This is on the house."

James and Shannon raised their glasses and toasted.

"Salud!" James said.

"Salud!" Shannon repeated.

Shannon put on the bracelet, admiring the emerald charms. "These must have been expensive, James. Thank you."

"It was a mere pittance," he assured her.

They took another sip of wine and gazed into each other's eyes.

"So, was the waiter right, Shannon?"

"About what?"

"Are we two young people in love? Are we falling in love?"

Shannon sighed and blinked a few times. She considered her words carefully. "James, I think you're great. I really do. I like you very much. And I think I absolutely could love you. I do love you. But…."

"But?"

"James, I had a long relationship with someone who just didn't know who he wanted to be. And it made him miserable. And it made me miserable, too." She gently caressed his hand. "James, you remind me a lot of him. And that scares me." She sighed. "Look, I'm a tough cookie. I make my own way in this world. I don't need anybody to take care of me."

"I'm not here because I'm looking to take care of you," James said defensively.

Shannon shook her head. "That's not what I meant. Look, I don't fall in love easily. I'm careful not to let myself. I thought I was in love once before, and I invested a lot of time, energy, and emotion into that relationship, and it didn't work out."

"Shannon, I don't understand. What do you want me to be?"

"See, James, that's the point. Your life is not about what everyone else wants you to be. It's about what *you* want to be; it's about finding out what makes you happy."

James stared down into his wine glass.

"James, I don't care what you do," Shannon said urgently. "Sell voice and data networks, if that's what you want. Become a teacher or a pilot or a circus clown—I don't care. What I do care about is that you care about what you do."

"Now who's being clever with words?" he joked. He took her hands in his, carefully considering what he wanted to say. "Shannon, these things are not that simple. I can't just decide tomorrow to change my whole life."

Shannon kissed his hands. "Oh, James. Don't be silly. Of course you can." She softly touched his cheek, whispering, "James, I would love to some day get married and have babies and have my little white house with my white picket fence. I really would. And I could see myself being there with you."

James smiled weakly, waiting for her to continue.

"But please don't ask me to commit my life to you until you figure out your own life first. If you really love me, or want to love me, then you have to do that before we can even talk about us."

He stared into her bright, green eyes. "Okay, Shannon. Okay. We probably shouldn't have even had this conversation tonight. We've only been dating a little while. All of this was purely hypothetical anyway, right?"

"James, I meant every word I said."

James downed the rest of his wine and poured himself another glass; he drank that in two gulps. He reached for the bottle and began to pour another. Shannon grabbed his arm. She had tears in her eyes.

"Don't do this to yourself, James. Please. If you're going to do this, then we should call it a night."

James finished filling his glass and put the bottle down. "I'm sorry, Shannon. You really are the only good thing going in my life right now, and it just hurts when you say these things to me."

"I'm sorry, James. Sometimes the truth hurts."

"But I am going to think about what you said. I promise." He took another small sip of the Chianti. "Believe me, Shannon, I really do want to be happy. I'm desperate to be happy," he said in a husky voice.

She looked into his eyes. "I know, James."

Their dinners arrived, and they spent a few minutes picking at their pasta. The food was delicious, and eating it improved their moods. When they finished, they ordered a cannoli pastry to share and two small cappuccino coffees.

Shannon paid the tab for the meal. James started to protest, but Shannon interrupted him. "These presents probably cost you ten times what this dinner cost. I'm picking up the pasta."

They decided to complete the night with dancing—it would help work off some of that rich Italian food. They walked arm in arm up to corner, with the intention of hailing a taxi.

Shannon gave James a light kiss on the cheek. "I know you're going to be fine, James. I know you're going to find what you're looking for. There's no rush; I'm going to give our relationship a good chance."

James patted her hand.

They went dancing for several hours and had a great time. Neither drank very much, and they left the club, tired and sweaty. They walked south, cooling off in the night air and holding hands. They went back to Shannon's apartment and made love.

Afterward, Shannon lay sleeping next to James, breathing softly. James, exhausted, would not be rescued by sleep. He stared at the ceiling in the blackness of the room, lost in his thoughts.

CHAPTER 15

▼

Booby and James wore hard hats as they stood in the middle of the former A Taste of Italy. The entire restaurant had been gutted, including the sheetrock walls and carpeted floor, and was bare down to the studs. Piles of debris were everywhere. Construction workers hauled the remaining pieces of floor and wall out the front door, which had been removed from its hinges and was leaning against the side of the entrance. Dust floated in the air. James coughed.

Booby smiled and put his arm around his son's shoulders. "This is going to be top-notch. Really top-notch."

"Did you have to rip out the walls, too? They didn't look to be in bad shape," James commented.

"I wanted to start from scratch, booby. I wanted to make sure everything was perfect from the ground up."

"Well, you certainly left no stone unturned."

They stepped carefully through the main dining room and into the kitchen, which had also been gutted and was in the process of being rebuilt. Copper plumbing pipes jutted out from the roughed-in walls. A new tile floor had been laid down, over which a thin layer of sand had been spread to protect the surface from the workers. The rear entrance was open, and a large delivery truck was parked just beyond.

Three men maneuvered a dolly carrying a huge stainless-steel broiler into the kitchen.

"What's that?" James asked.

"That, booby, is going to be the heart of the Mad Cow. That's our new state-of-the-art commercial stainless-steel steak charbroiler. That unit heats up to nine hundred degrees. That's how you cook fine steaks, son. That oven is so hot it sears the meat in seconds and locks in the juices; that's what defines the flavor. That broiler is what all the good steakhouses use."

"Where'd you find that?"

"Russell and I went over to the New York Restaurant Exposition show at the Javitz Center last month. We talked to a bunch of restaurant consultants, and they said this was the way to go. Russell and I have been doing our homework."

"Sure looks like it. Did you hire any of the restaurant consultants you spoke to?"

"Of course not, booby. They wanted a lot of money!"

The men positioned the broiler against a wall in the kitchen.

James admired it. "It looks expensive."

Booby winked. "It was."

"Well, don't tell Mike. He'll just flip out on you again."

The two men laughed.

Booby evaluated his son. "You seem in a better mood lately, James. You look good, too. I see you've lost weight. Anything you want to share?"

"I don't know if there's much to tell. I'm still dating Shannon—"

"Whom I still haven't met, booby."

"Well, you'll meet her soon. I'm thinking of asking her to come on that fishing trip next month, so I guess you'll meet her then."

"Your mother's not going to be happy about that," Booby chided.

"Tell Mom I'm not ready yet to bring Shannon home to play Meet the Parents, okay?"

✳   ✳   ✳   ✳

The end of April brought the opening-day golf tournament at Forest Hills Country Club. It was a beautiful spring day, warm and sunny. The trees and bushes had greened up nicely, and birds chirped all around. An arrangement of bright-red and white flowers had been planted around the edge of the patio. A light breeze blew, fresh and fragrant.

Booby, James, Meridian, and Mike sat at a lawn table on the brick patio overlooking the first tee. They were enjoying their beers and hot dogs and hamburgers. The club started the tournament with a grilled lunch on the first tee-side brick patio at noon and ended the tournament with a lavish buffet dinner.

A massive outdoor grill released a cloud of charcoal smoke. The pleasant smell of cooked meat mingled with the other spring scents the air. On a table next to the grill was a spread of burger and hot dog fixings, pasta salads, and potato salads. A round plastic tub was filled with beer, soda, and ice.

"Can't beat a grilled burger on a day like today," Meridian said. "I think I might go get another one."

"Don't eat too much, Meridian. You won't be able to swing your driver," James said.

Meridian shrugged, burped, and got another burger with the works and a fresh beer.

"Could you try to exercise a little more tact, Meridian?" Mike scolded. "This is a country club."

Meridian took a long swig of his beer; he burped. "Sorry, Mike. I'll try not to embarrass you. By the way, I didn't ask to come to your exclusive little social club. James invited me."

Mike frowned at Meridian.

"Let him be, booby. We're all here to have a good time today."

James looked at his watch. "We should be teeing off pretty soon. I'm going to go do a little putting." James joined half a dozen other golfers on the putting green.

Meridian enjoyed his second burger and drank his beer. "You'd think all this practicing would help these yo-yos. Most golfers on these courses stink."

"A private course isn't like a public course," Mike said. "You get a better class of golfer here. People who can afford to belong to a country club tend to take their game more seriously."

"Now don't be an elitist, booby," Booby said. "It's not nice to make people feel inferior."

Meridian laughed. "Don't worry, Booby. Mike doesn't intimidate me. I'll tell you what I think of these country club types at the end of the round."

The starter appeared and called for the Cameron group to tee off.

The men grabbed a few additional beers and got into their respective golf carts. They pulled up to the first tee. The remaining golfers on the patio watched the men hit their first drive. James felt that making golfers hit their first shot of the day in front of a gallery must have been some kind of insidious joke perpetrated by the membership, the sole purpose of which was to psyche out the guests and high handicappers.

Meridian volunteered to go first. He pulled his driver, an old beat-up knock-off, out of his golf bag. "This is my K-Mart special." He whipped the club around his body a few times to loosen up. "I call it Big Blue Light." He poked his tee into the ground, positioned his ball on it, and stood at address. After concentrating for a few seconds, he took a mighty swing. The ball exploded off the center of his club and flew straight and long down the middle of the fairway. A few golfers sitting on the patio cheered.

"Nothing to this game," he declared.

Mike was next. He lined up his shot and worked through a lengthy pre-swing ritual. He finally moved to address the ball.

James popped open a fresh beer and said, "Let's go, long and wrong. Enough with the ballet. Just hit the ball."

Mike shot James a dirty look, then turned to concentrate on his shot. He smacked the ball. It went straight down the fairway a good distance before slicing and disappearing into the trees. "Shit," Mike said.

"Watch that language, Munro. This is a country club, remember?" Meridian teased.

James went next. He had a good set of clubs and, after taking lessons and practicing, had turned himself into a passable golfer. He set up his shot and swung smoothly through the ball. The ball launched off the club and traveled down the middle of the fairway, coming to rest about fifty yards short of Meridian's shot.

"Not bad," he commented to himself. The other three men nodded.

Booby was a boater and not much of a golfer. He justified the country-club membership as a good way to entertain consultants and customers, but he didn't actually come to play golf very often. He had a full set of clubs, but typically, he played with only one: the eight iron. He seemed to have a problem hitting the rest of his bag, but he got along well with the eight iron. Ironically, he didn't play much worse than most of the other golfers who strategically attempted to use every club they owned.

Booby stamped out his cigarette in the grass and placed the ball on the tee. Without much setup, he hit the ball. The ball traveled in the air a short distance and bounced down the fairway, coming to rest about fifty yards short of James' shot.

"All right! The game is on!" he exclaimed.

The men headed for the carts to chase after their balls.

The round was good fun. The men had a fine time and posted scores better than expected, although far from what was needed to win. The afternoon was gorgeous, one of those rare days that is bright, warm, and sunny without the associated humidity, which rises quickly and plagues every summer on the Atlantic coast.

After the golf tournament, the men showered in the clubhouse and donned dress pants and sport coats and headed upstairs to the main dining room. They bellied up to the oak bar and each ordered a "Transfusion," the traditional post-golf-round drink. The drink, comprised of vodka, grape juice, orange juice, and Seven-Up, was served in a large round glass. It was a tasty and refreshing drink.

The men lingered at the bar, making small talk with the other golfers who slowly made their way up to the reception. The resident golf pro indicated that the awards would be given out soon, and he asked everyone to help himself to food and then find his seat.

A lavish buffet had been set along the far wall. In the center of the table was an ice sculpture of a golfer. Sitting among the carved ice were bottles of vodka, traditional and flavored. Also carved into the sculpture was an ice platform. Resting on the platform were three large tins of caviar. In front of the caviar was a series of bowls containing chopped egg whites, onion, and capers.

A seafood buffet and raw bar were to one side of the ice sculpture; to the other side was a collection of salads, breads, and a tray of Italian deli meats and cheeses. Across the room, a server staffed a pasta station boasting five types of macaroni and five types of sauces. Adjacent to the pasta station, another station offered prime rib, turkey, and ham.

The men each grabbed a plate and piled on an assortment of food until the plates could not support another morsel. They carried their meals back to the table.

Meridian placed his plate on the table and then stood in front of the ice sculpture, eyeing the caviar and vodkas.

His lower lip trembled. An older gentleman tried to walk in front of Meridian, but Meridian reached out and grabbed the man's shoulders. "I have died and gone to country-club heaven!" he exclaimed.

The older gentleman backed away from Meridian, glancing over his shoulder as he moved off.

Meridian picked up a highball glass off the table and tossed in a few ice cubes. He randomly chose various vodka bottles and filled his glass with a little of each. He filled another plate with an assortment of crackers, caviar, and caviar accoutrements and then sat down at the table.

Mike looked at both of Meridian's plates. "Have some manners. The food's not going anywhere," he said flatly.

Meridian threw Mike a dirty look. "Give it a rest, Mike. Just remember who kicked your ass in golf today."

"By one stroke," Mike replied.

"One is all I needed."

The four men ate heartily, as the food was delicious, of good quality, and plentiful. Sated, they sat back and sipped their respective drinks.

The awards were presented. The Cameron group didn't win anything, until the raffle was drawn. Like most tournaments, every golfer in the room received a prize of some sort.

Booby was the big raffle winner, receiving an expensive blue designer wind breaker.

"All I got was this lousy umbrella," Meridian complained.

"I got an umbrella, too," James said.

After the awards, the men headed up to the bar, sipped cocktails, and talked golf with the other people who were inclined to stay and finish out the evening. James noticed that Mike was running to the bathroom a little too frequently, considering the amount he was drinking. At the end of the night, all four were a little drunk, with Booby and Meridian in the lead. They decided to call it a night. Meridian was Booby's ride home; Mike was James'.

"Want to stop at the Bell?" Meridian asked James.

"Sure, I'll meet you down there," James replied.

*   *   *   *

Once in the car, Mike told James he was going to take a detour and make a quick stop. "I just need to run in and drop something off. I'll be in and out in two minutes."

"No problem. You're driving," James replied.

Mike drove to a neighborhood that looked a little run-down. Mike pulled up in front of an older Dutch colonial with dirty white siding. He put the car in park and got out. "I'll be back in a minute," he promised.

James sat in the idling car and fiddled with the radio.

Mike walked up to the front door and knocked. The door opened, and he was let in. The door shut behind him.

James found a song he liked and started to sing along to it.

Several minutes went by.

James stared at the house, hoping to see in through the front window, but the window was darkened. Several more minutes went by. James was starting to wonder what was going on. He changed the radio station again and found an old Doors song; he sang along to that. James looked toward the front door. Still no Mike. He glanced at his watch and realized that he had been waiting for nearly half an hour. *What the hell are you doing in there?* he thought.

James turned off the ignition. He took out the keys and put them in his pocket. Then he got out of the car and walked toward the front door.

A bright light shone directly in James' eyes, blinding him.

"Freeze!" a voice commanded. "Put your hands in the air where we can see them and place them slowly on your head!"

James did as he was told. His eyes adjusted to the light, and he saw the police officers. These officers, however, wore black Kevlar vests with "Police" written in bold white letters across the front and back, and they wore black military style helmets.

Two of them were pointing automatic rifles at him. These were no ordinary police officers.

"I don't understand, officers, what seems to be the—"

"Shut up! Don't say a fucking word! We knew you were going to be making your drop tonight, and now we've got you cold."

"Drop? What drop? I don't—"

"I said shut up!"

The officer approached James and hit him in the stomach with the butt of his rifle. James doubled over and fell to the ground. Another officer grabbed James' arms, pulled them behind his back, and handcuffed his wrists together, as James lay coughing on the ground.

Two more officers approached the front door. They nodded to each other. One steadied his rifle, and the other kicked, his heavy boot slamming into door. The door flew open in a burst of wooden splinters.

Both men ran into the house, followed by two more.

James looked up and saw a line of police cars coming up the block, lights flashing and sirens blaring. A black van pulled up in front of Mike's Mercedes, blocking any attempt at escape.

James heard shouting in the house, a few screams, and noises that sounded like people struggling.

The back door opened suddenly, and a man burst through the screen door. The door fell into the yard. The man ran around the side of the house to the street. One of the officers moved in the man's direction and raised his rifle.

"Stop!" he shouted. "Stop, or I will fire!"

The man continued running down the street.

The rifled cracked.

The man fell to the ground, clutching his leg.

The line of police cars had arrived, and an officer jumped out of the still-moving lead vehicle and ran over to the downed man, handgun drawn. He grabbed the man's arms and cuffed his wrists behind his back.

James watched incredulously as the scene unfolded.

Half a dozen police officers ran into the house, guns drawn.

A few minutes later, the officers came out with a line of handcuffed people. One of those handcuffed was Mike Munro.

James was pulled up off the ground and spun around. Before him stood a man who was wearing a suit and smoking a cigarette. The man threw the cigarette down and ground it out with his heel.

"I'm Detective Gillespie. And you're under arrest." He read James his Miranda rights.

When Gillespie finished, James blurted out, "Detective, I don't know what the hell is going on tonight, but you've got the wrong guy. My name is James Cameron. I work for Cameron Voice and Data on Rutherford Turnpike. My father is James Cameron, Sr." James looked into the detective's eyes for any hint of recognition. "You know...Booby?" Gillespie studied James coldly. "For Christ's sake, I just came from a golf tournament!"

Gillespie reached into James' back pocket and pulled out his wallet. He looked at his license and studied James' face. He pulled out James' credit cards and flipped through the miscellaneous assortment of business cards and pictures the wallet contained. The detective's face softened. "James Cameron. Yeah, I know your father. I heard he bought the old A Taste of Italy. He's opening up a new place?"

"Yeah. He's going to open a steakhouse."

"What's he going to call it?"

"The Mad Cow."

"What? Like the disease?"

"Something like that."

The detective looked dejected. "Kid, I don't know what you're doing here, but if your story checks out, you just ruined two months of investigative work for a whole lot of people."

"What are you talking about?"

"Cameron, we've been staking out this house for months. The asshole who lives here is the biggest distributor of coke and crack cocaine in the area. Our sources told us he was supposed to get his monthly delivery from his supplier tonight. A big one. We were told the drop would be made in a late-model black Mercedes.

"We weren't just going to get that asshole but also conclusively pin down his supply. This was supposed to be our big chance to break open the local network." Gillespie pointed to Mike's car on the street. "The SWAT boys thought they'd nailed it, and I wanted them to wait until you made the drop, but they jumped the gun." Detective Gillespie lit another cigarette. "Is that your car?"

"No, it belongs to Mike Munro. He works for my father, too. He was also at the tournament today."

Gillespie nodded his head and frowned. "I know Mike Munro. I remember him when he was a kid running around the old neighborhood. Was he in the house?"

"Yeah. I saw them take him out while I was lying here on the ground."

"He's in the back of the van. They're taking the bunch of them in for questioning." He looked at James. "You know, you're still under arrest until we can straighten this whole thing out. You're going to have to answer a lot of questions. At this point, the department needs to start playing cover your ass." He studied James. "You were here to buy coke?"

"No! Not me. I don't play with that shit. Evidently, that's what my executive vice president was here to do."

"You didn't know where he was going?"

"No. He said he had to drop something off somewhere. I really wasn't paying attention."

"So you were just along for the ride?"

"We'd gone to the opening-day golf tournament at Forest Hills Country Club. We're both members there. Mike picked me up this morning. He was driving me home. Actually, he was dropping me off at the Bell Lap Tavern."

"The party's over for you tonight, kid."

"I know that."

Detective Gillespie inclined his head toward the sky and breathed in the night air. "Mr. Munro chose the wrong night to come here to cop drugs," he stated. "They're going to give him a hell of a time down at the station." Gillespie grabbed James by the arm and led him to his brown unmarked sedan.

"Detective Gillespie," said a uniformed officer. "What do you want us to do with the Mercedes?"

"I want you impound it and strip it. Take it apart. If there are drugs in there, I want them found," he replied.

The officer nodded.

"Detective, Mike may be a user, but he's no dealer. You're not going to find anything," James said.

"You're right; I'm probably not. But after the trouble you two just caused me, I'm not taking any chances. And your friend there deserves it." Gillespie pushed down James' head as he guided him into the back seat.

"Can I give you some advice?" Detective Gillespie asked on the way to the police station.

"Please do," James responded.

"You seem like a good kid. But you're getting too old to be getting mixed up in this kind of shit, accident or no." He eyed James through the rear-view mirror. "If I were you, I would give some serious thought as to where you think your life is heading. I would also give some thought as to the type of people you choose to associate with, and whether or not those people are going to help you get to where you want to go."

James rolled his eyes. "Who are you? Doctor Phil?"

"Don't be smart, Cameron. Until I say so, you're ass is mine."

"Sorry," he said sullenly, slouching down in the seat.

They drove the rest of the way to the police station in silence.

CHAPTER 16

▼

"It's really not that funny, Vin," James said.

Vincent leaned over the counter, laughing hysterically. "No...." he insisted, tears streaming down his cheeks. "That...that is the funniest thing I've ever heard!" Vincent wiped the tears from his eyes with the back of his hand.

James sighed. He sipped his beer. "It wasn't that funny, if you were there."

"So?" Vincent prompted James. "What happened next?"

"They took us down to the station. They threw me in the drunk tank and left me in there for three hours. Then they took me into a room, where I had to take off all of my clothes. This really fat dude came in, and he did a cavity search."

Vincent pressed his lips together, trying to keep from laughing, but he couldn't control himself; laughter exploded from his mouth. Finally, he asked, "Did they find anything of interest?"

James took a gulp of beer. "Funny, Vin. Really funny."

"They were messing with you, man."

"I don't blame them, really. We ruined their big sting operation. I'm surprised they didn't beat the shit out of me, like they did Mike."

"Yeah, so what happened to Mike?"

"I'm not sure. The separated us. After they had their fun, they put me in a cell for another couple of hours, and then they brought me to an interrogation room and asked me stupid questions for an hour. I must have repeated the same story fifty times."

Vincent nodded. "That's what they do. They ask you the same thing over and over to see if you'll slip up and say something different."

"And you learned this...where? In detective school?"

"Don't be a dick. I'm not the one who spent the night in jail. So then what happened?"

"They let me go. I finally got to bed about six in the morning. I don't know if Mike was still in there, but I assume he was. As soon as I got home I called my father; my call woke him up."

"He must have been happy about that."

"Actually, when he heard my story he became very upset. He was concerned that something really bad could have happened to me. For God's sake, I saw a guy get shot! And he was not happy with Mike." James clenched his hand tightly around his beer glass. He finished his beer in one gulp. Vincent got a fresh, frosted glass out of the freezer and poured James another.

"What did your father say to Mike?" Vincent asked.

"We both went over to his house—it was a come-to-Jesus meeting. My father told him that he either had to go to rehab and get clean or he was fired."

"Wow. That must have been hard for Booby to tell Mike."

"He was livid. I don't think he was thinking about Mike's feelings at that point."

"What did Mike say?"

"What could he say? He apologized. To me and my father. He also agreed to go to rehab."

"Booby actually got him to go to rehab?"

"It's not like he had much choice. My father checked him in at Fair Oaks in South Jersey on Monday. Thirty-day program. I'm sure he's knee-deep in mineral water and miniature golf as we speak."

"Do you think he's going to take rehab seriously?"

"He hasn't been sober for thirty days straight in years, so who knows what effect the program will have on him? I hope it's a positive one."

Vincent chuckled. "Rehab is for quitters." He poured himself a beer and contemplated his new, powerful, quiet-running smoke-eater. He turned back to James. "Did you ever find out why he was in that house for so long?"

James smiled. "Yeah. He was getting a blow job by one of the crack whores who was hanging out in there."

Vincent cringed. "Dude, that is scraping the bottom of the barrel. So what happened to him in jail?"

"Mike said they interrogated him all night. The cops smacked him around. They finally charged him with possession of an illegal substance, but he didn't have that much coke on him, so they couldn't get him with intent to distribute. Eventually, the cops had to let him go."

"He's lucky. He got off easy."

"Not that easy—you should see his Mercedes. The cops totally ripped it apart. It's sitting in pieces down at Afton Auto Body right now. Rebuilding that car is going to be like trying to put Humpty-Dumpty back together again."

"That's a shame, because it was a beautiful Mercedes." Vincent shook his head. "Say, did you tell Shannon?"

"Of course I told her. I didn't do anything wrong. Still, she wasn't very happy."

"What did she say?"

"She asked me if I enjoyed the cavity search." James changed the subject. "Don't forget about the fishing trip. It's in three weeks."

"I'm in. And don't forget the following weekend is the big relaunch party for the new-and-improved Bell Lap Tavern."

"I wouldn't miss it for the world," James assured him.

A lot of work had been done in the bar in a short amount of time. A brand-new hardwood floor had been installed, and the walls had been repaired and painted a dark green. A new plaster ceiling was in place, painted a soft white.

The bar counter had been sanded and refinished, and its waxed surface gleamed. Vincent had also added a rounded mahogany cornice to the counter edge to give it a richer look. The brick wall behind the bar had been scrubbed of the decades-old buildup of grease and grime, and the red bricks looked practically new.

"Vincent, the Bell Lap is looking great," James commented.

"I'm getting all new bar stools. They should be coming in a few weeks."

James finished his beer. "Okay, I have to go. Shannon's coming in this weekend, so we'll stop by on Saturday night."

Vincent held up his hand. "Wait," he said, coming out from behind the counter and putting his arm around James. "Before you go, I have to show you this." He led James over to the brand-new jukebox. The new unit was bigger than the old one and was completely computerized. Instead of containing rows of CD disks that rotated out on arms, a large color touch-screen occupied the middle of the machine, displaying neatly arranged boxes of artists and song titles.

"I got this baby hooked up with high-speed Internet access, so if the song you want to play isn't listed, you can request it, and it will download and play in a couple of seconds. My customers will have access to literally millions of songs." Vincent winked. "All for an extra charge, of course."

James smiled. "Vin, you are turning into a regular entrepreneur," he said, clapping Vincent on the back. "See you later."

Vincent pressed some icons on the jukebox display and a song started to play—the theme for the television show "Cops." James laughed and waved good-bye as he went out the door. Vincent sang loudly after him: "Bad boys, bad boys, watcha gonna do, watcha gonna do when they come for you...."

*   *   *   *

On the last Friday in May, James drove to Federated Wines and Liquors to meet with Two-Boy. It was the last day of the cabling portion of the project, albeit the most time-consuming and demanding one.

James noticed a new fiber stretching out to the guard shack on his left as he pulled into the parking lot. *Good boy, Mason*, he thought. James expected to be one of the first people to arrive this morning. To his surprise, parked outside of the main entrance was a line of Cameron Voice and Data vehicles. At the end of the line sat Two-Boy's monstrous yellow Hummer.

James parked next to the Hummer and got out.

Standing in a group next to the last van were the McGirk brothers, Gray Mason, and Two-Boy. They started to applaud as James approached them. Two-Boy offered James a cup of coffee and grinned at him through the cigar in his mouth. "I told you, Cameron, when you hire me, you hire the best. We're all finished here, and I built you a showcase. Are you ready for your walk-through?"

James nodded. "Let's do it."

Two-Boy held the glass door open for James as he entered an air-conditioned room permanently set to sixty degrees. Along one long wall stood an array of communication racks and panels—four long rows of them, all neatly assembled and labeled.

"Four thousand terminations," Two-Boy said proudly. "As per contract and per spec."

"Wow," James said. "That is a thing of beauty."

"My work here is finished," Two-Boy stated dramatically.

James shook his hand. "You cost my old man a fortune, but you were worth it!"

Two-Boy eyed James seriously. "Don't forget about my dinner."

James laughed. "I won't."

The other men entered the room and all stood admiring their handiwork.

"We did good, handsome. Real good. I hope we made you proud," Mason said.

James slapped Mason on the back. "Yes, you did," he agreed.

"Who started the freakin' party without me!" a voice shouted from out in the hallway. Meridian and two other men pushed a large industrial dolly into the room. Sitting on the dolly was a bubble-wrapped, square, plastic-encased monstrosity. The next phase of the project was the actual communications system, and the system had arrived.

Meridian eyed the men. "Holy shit, Two-Boy, you're even fatter than the last time I saw you." He pointed at Mason and the McGirk brothers. "I hope you children are finished playing with your little wires, because it's time for the real men to take over."

"You weren't supposed to start until Monday, Meridian," Two-Boy retorted. "What happened? You needed to run over here and get pointers on how to do professional work?"

"At least I don't go home every night and jerk off to a ham sandwich," Meridian said, grinning at him.

Two-Boy laughed good-naturedly. "You're just jealous because I made more money on this one project than you'll make all year."

Meridian gave him a look of mock confusion. "Oh, I'm sorry...was that your Hummer that I pissed all over in the parking lot?"

"Okay, guys," James said, holding up his hand to interrupt the banter. "The match is over, and I call it an even draw." James turned to the crew, ready to get down to business. "Mason, you and your men can have the afternoon off. Two-boy, before you go, we need to do the dog-and-pony show for the customer and have one final project meeting."

"No problem."

"Will we be seeing you tomorrow for the fishing trip?" Meridian asked.

"Wouldn't miss it," Two-boy replied.

"Then you'd better go home and eat some salad," Meridian teased. "I want to make sure you can fit in that bus seat tomorrow."

James rolled his eyes at Meridian and led Two-Boy down the hallway. "This shouldn't take too long. And then you and I will spend the rest of the afternoon digging into a few nice steaks and drinking some fine wine."

Two-Boy rubbed his belly. "That sounds great. I could go for a porterhouse. Or three."

CHAPTER 17

▼

A silver charter bus with black tinted windows sat in the parking lot of Cameron Voice and Data. It was five-thirty in the morning.

James and Shannon got out of his car with coffee in hand, and yawned.

James yawned and stretched. "This is my favorite part of the trip," he said dryly.

The early-morning dampness clung to their skin. The air was cool, which indicated it would be a warm day. Pale light started to creep over the horizon in the eastern sky.

James popped open his trunk and took out a duffle bag and a small cooler. The duffle bag contained an extra T-shirt and a pair of shorts for each of them; the cooler held sandwiches, water, and soda.

Shannon twisted her hair into a bun on top of her head. "I can't remember the last time I went fishing on a party boat," she commented.

"Today is going to be a white-trash fandango," James joked. "At the very least, it will be entertaining."

They joined the growing crowd milling around the bus, and James introduced Shannon to everyone. A lime-green vintage Volkswagen Beetle arrived next. Out stepped Vincent, also with coffee in hand. He walked over to James and Shannon. "Damn, it's early," he complained.

A white Cameron van screeched into the lot, honked at the assembled group, and pulled up next to the bus. Booby and Meridian jumped out and went immediately to the back of the van. Meridian threw open the doors to reveal the floor-to-roof stacks of cases of beer.

"Let's get this party started!" Meridian yelled.

"That's a lot of beer," Shannon observed as Meridian and Booby loaded the beer into the storage compartment of the bus.

James nodded. "I told you. This crowd doesn't screw around."

Booby was as excited as a kid on Christmas morning. He was dressed all in white and wore a white admiral's hat, complete with gold-leaf braiding. A cigarette dangled from his mouth as he bopped around, cracking jokes and laughing. "I'm real happy we got so many people to go on the trip," he called out to the crowd, "and I want to thank Meridian for setting up the whole thing. I just want to let everyone know that I'm paying for all the beer for today's trip. So drink up and enjoy!'

The crowd applauded.

Meridian walked through the crowd, giving out cans of beer, making sure everyone got at least one. James and Shannon dumped their remaining coffee onto the ground and popped open their beer cans.

"Breakfast of champions!" James said.

Another series of white vans arrived, and the McGirk brothers emerged amid a cloud of smoke. The oldest McGirk brother wore a black pirate's hat and eye patch. A plastic parrot was fastened to one shoulder of his black pirate's vest. "Aye, matey!" he yelled, waving a plastic cutlass in the air. "Who cares about catching fish, as long as we all catch a buzz!"

Gray Mason got out of his van, wearing camouflage khaki army pants and a Bruce Springsteen concert T-shirt. His hair was scattered more wildly than usual.

"It's fucking early, handsome," he said to no one in particular as he joined the group. "Back in 'Nam, this is about the time of the morning that we went out on our seek-and-destroy missions. The early morning is always the best time to kill gooks. Get 'em right as they're about to eat their fucking gook rice breakfast."

Two-Boy was the last to arrive, his yellow Hummer dwarfing the other vehicles in the lot. He climbed down from the Hummer, inserted a cigar into his mouth, and made his way over to the group, where he was handed a cold beer. "What time is breakfast?" he asked.

Booby signaled that everyone should get on the bus; when everyone was aboard, there was not an empty seat to be had.

The bus driver put the bus in gear and drove off toward the highway. The crowd cheered.

During the trip, Meridian walked up and down the aisles, handing out beers, making sure no one went thirsty. Booby sat in the front, chatting up the bus driver.

The McGirk brothers positioned themselves in the back of the bus, lit a series of joints, and passed them around. Soon, the cabin started to fill with the pungent aroma of marijuana smoke.

A joint was passed to James, and he looked at Shannon for permission. She shrugged, and he took a long drag and coughed. He handed it to her. She started to pass it along but then reconsidered it. She took a big pull on the joint.

"When in Rome…" she explained through hacking coughs.

She passed the joint across the aisle to Vincent, who passed it on.

The bus driver sniffed the air and said to Booby, "I can't have your employees smoking pot in this bus. You need to tell them to put out that shit."

Booby stood up, holding a beer in one hand and a cigarette in the other. "All right, everybody. I need your attention. You need to smoke that stuff on your own time. The bus driver just told me that you're going to have to put that out."

A loud chorus of boos erupted from the crowd. Half a dozen empty beer cans were launched at Booby and the bus driver.

Booby protested, "Now, booby—" He was interrupted by another loud chorus of boos and several more beer cans.

"Hang the son of a bitch!" a voice yelled.

Booby handed the bus driver a hundred-dollar bill. The man sighed, but accepted it.

"Just keep these people under control," he pleaded, as Booby smiled expansively. "They don't pay me enough for this," the bus driver muttered under his breath.

As the ride continued, the passengers became more and more boisterous. The beer flowed freely. Meridian started a sing-a-long in his best Scottish brogue. "You cannot throw your granny from the bus! No, you cannot throw your granny from the bus! You cannot throw your granny, 'cause she's your mammy's mammy. You cannot throw your granny from the bus!"

Stoned, James and Shannon started making out and were soon bombarded with empty beer cans. "Get a room!" someone yelled. They hugged each other and giggled.

The bus finally arrived at the Point Pleasant Charter Marina on the Jersey shore. Half a dozen large charter boats were lined up in a row, birthed in slips connected via a wooden dock. The last boat in the line, the *Sea Hag*, was the charter that Meridian had arranged.

The *Sea Hag* was a modern commercial fishing vessel. The deck and cabin were white fiberglass, and the hull was painted midnight blue. A steel railing ran the perimeter of the deck, punctuated every few feet by a steel fishing-rod holder.

On top of the main cabin sat a smaller observation cabin, and forward of that was the command bridge. An array of electronics were mounted to the top of the command bridge.

A tanned, swarthy, stubble-bearded captain stood in front of the *Sea Hag*, sipping coffee. A group of young mates were busy on the boat itself, arranging fishing poles and prepping the boat for departure.

The bus parked in a sandy lot in front of the *Sea Hag*. The McGirk brother who was dressed in the pirate outfit swung out the door, hanging from the hinge and yelling, "Arrgg, matey! Cameron Voice and Data is here! And if we don't catch any fish, you will all walk the plank!" He jumped out of the bus, followed by the rest of stoned, drunken passengers.

The captain rolled his eyes.

Meridian gathered a few people to help carry the beer from the storage compartments to the boat. It was a beautiful late-spring morning, with not a cloud in the sky. Booby approached the captain, introduced himself, and shook his hand. The captain looked at the sky. "Might rain," he said.

Booby laughed politely and handed the captain a few crisp, hundred-dollar bills. "I'll take care of my people. Just make sure we catch some fish."

The captain studied the group. "Look, I'm not here to baby-sit a bunch of drunks, okay? I'm running a fishing charter. These people look whacked already. I'll take you out, but if they get out of hand, we're turning around."

"Don't worry, booby," Booby said. "Everything's going to be great."

A group of people, including Two-Boy, headed over to the convenience store on the marina property for more food. Two-Boy came back carrying two large submarine sandwiches wrapped in wax paper; he was finishing a breakfast sandwich of bacon, egg, and cheese.

"Hey, Two-Boy!" Meridian yelled, "I hear we're going to have rough seas today. You better eat up; we need the extra ballast."

A few people laughed. Two-Boy gave Meridian the finger.

About half an hour later, everyone was on the boat and had donned their life vests and popped fresh beers.

The captain blew the horn a few times; the sound was loud and sharp. The boat had been idling, warming up, and the captain now put the engine into gear. The mates ran along the side of the boat, freeing the coarse rope lines and throwing them back onto the dock. The *Sea Hag* pulled out of the slip and glided slowly through a no-wake zone. It entered a channel, getting in line after a group of other boats.

A stone jetty protruded out from each side of the channel into the ocean, and standing on the jetties on both banks were people who waved at the boats as they passed by. James, Meridian, Shannon, and Vincent stood at the railing in the middle of the boat, holding beers and waving back. The captain blew the whistle a few times in acknowledgement.

The *Sea Hag* passed through the channel into the open water of the Atlantic Ocean. As soon as it did, the waves grew in intensity. The *Sea Hag* headed east and picked up speed, her engines droning loudly and the noise breaking over the waves.

The group held on to the railing with one hand and sipped beer with the other. The smell of the sea was in the air: clean, fresh, and invigorating. Salt water splashed up and sprayed the boat each time the *Sea Hag* rolled down a wave.

The *Sea Hag* headed east for a while and then turned due south. It traveled on for several miles and then came to a halt.

The captain announced over the loudspeakers: "We just got a big hit on the sonar, so we'll stop and fish here first. Good luck…and please remember to drink responsibly."

With that, the boat cheered, and people turned and saluted those around them by clinking their beer cans together.

The mates came out, carrying baited poles, and moved up the deck, handing them out. They offered assistance to anyone who didn't know how to use the fishing poles, but most people declined, as they were experienced.

The captain blew the whistle, and all along the railing of the *Sea Hag*, fishing lines dropped into the water.

James watched his line spool out down into the water, and he felt the sinker hit bottom. He cranked the wheel of the reel and held out the pole. He then helped Shannon get herself situated.

"Now we just wait, right?" Shannon asked.

"Right."

They didn't wait long.

Shannon felt a tug on her line. "Is that a fish?"

James reached over and put her line between two fingers. He felt the line vibrate. "That's a fish! That's a fish! Pull the tip of your pole up!" he instructed excitedly.

Shannon jerked up her pole.

"Now start reeling it in!" he told her.

Shannon reeled in her line, steadily and deliberately, so she wouldn't rip the hook out of the fish's mouth. A long flat fluke broke the water and flapped around the surface.

"Don't lift it out! You might lose it," James warned. "Fish on!" he yelled to the mates.

One of the mates ran over with a long netted pole. He reached over the boat and scooped up the fish. He brought it up onto the deck, took it out of the net, and held it up. The fluke's puckered mouth opened and closed reflexively. "That's a nice one," he said. He measured the fish and made note of the length. The mate took the fish and tossed it into an ice filled chest.

"I caught a big fish!" Shannon exclaimed. "This is fun; I want to catch another one."

Shannon was the first, but then people all over the boat started pulling in fish. James, Meridian, and Vincent got in on the action, too. The mates moved quickly up and down the deck, netting fish, removing hooks, and then hooking and baiting lines so people could fish again. Soon, the mates were sweating profusely.

The group fished for almost two hours, and everyone caught at least two fish. The sun was now high in the clear midday sky.

"It's getting hot," Vincent stated. He looked at James' and Shannon's faces, which were turning bright red. "Did you two forget to put on sunscreen?"

James and Shannon looked at each other, hooked their poles, and ran into the cabin. James found his bag and rummaged around for the sunscreen. He helped Shannon liberally apply it on her face, neck, and arms; she returned the favor.

"I'm so sorry, Shannon. I forgot. I meant to put it on before we left, but I was too stoned to remember."

"Don't worry, loverboy. I didn't remember, either."

They changed out of their jeans and into shorts and applied sunscreen to their legs. James pulled out a couple of baseball caps. He handed one to Shannon and put the other on his own head.

They gazed into each other's eyes, clearer now than they had been a few hours earlier. James' light-blue eyes blazed out of his sunburned and wind-blasted face.

"You're going to have one hell of a sunburn," he commented.

Shannon nodded, unconcerned. "Have you ever had sex on a boat?" she asked.

"What? I don't—"

"Come with me."

Shannon led James upstairs to the empty observation deck. They could see the other people, talking and laughing. Here and there, a cheer would rise up, indicating a hooked fish. The boat swayed and rocked on the ocean. They found a bathroom at the far end of the room and went in, locking the door behind them.

They emerged a little while later.

When they came out, they heard the whistle.

"Shit! The boat's about to move!" James said. "We'd better get back downstairs."

The Captain already had started the engines, and water was churning up at the rear of the boat. James and Shannon returned to their fishing poles, only to find that one of the mates had already secured them.

Meridian came up to them, carrying three fresh beers. "Where the hell did you go? Vincent and I thought you fell overboard." He handed them each a beer.

"We had to apply some sunscreen," James said.

"Yeah, and we changed into shorts," Shannon added.

Meridian took a big gulp of beer, eyed them suspiciously, and burped. "You two were off screwing somewhere." Meridian pointed straight up. "You know, the Mile High Club is exactly one mile higher than where we are right now. What are you starting? The Sea Level Club?"

James and Shannon blushed, but their sunburned faces hid the redness. They joined Vincent next to the railing as the boat moved south.

The *Sea Hag* stopped at another two fishing spots, which netted some fish, but the catch was not as good as the first stop. After six hours on the water, the boat turned around. The captain throttled her up, and the *Sea Hag* traveled back to the marina.

The four friends stood at the railing. They were all a little dehydrated. *Man, I'm a little drunk*, James thought. *Well, maybe more than a little drunk.* He and Shannon stood close together, facing into the wind. The boat was traveling fast, and waves splashed up and wet their faces. The cold ocean water was refreshing, but the salt spray stung their sunburned skin. The sun had started to dip lower in the sky, and the rays didn't feel quite as warm. The ocean shone blue-gray, and the sun's rays glinted off the surface. Out in the distance, a line of dolphins moved gracefully in and out of the water. One of the dolphins broke the surface and sprayed a fine mist into the air.

Shannon put her hand gently on James' face. "I love you, James," she whispered.

"I love you, too," he answered.

The *Sea Hag* motored back to the marina.

To the captain's—and to a large extent, Booby's—surprise, the Cameron Voice and Data fishing expedition failed to turn into a riot. The group was loud and drunk, but for the most part, they were well behaved. Several employees became sick during the excursion and vomited over the side of the boat, but it was unclear whether that was caused from drinking or seasickness. Either way, the vomit made good chum and didn't adversely affect the proceedings.

When they got back to the dock, the mates began cleaning and skinning the fluke into filets at a station at the rear of the boat. The passengers disembarked, most wobbly on their feet, and loaded their belongings back onto the bus.

Booby and Meridian organized a group to clean out all the empty beer cans scattered around the *Sea Hag*. The effort took several trips.

Two-Boy won the pool for "Biggest Fish"; of course, he was heckled mercilessly.

James and Shannon stood with a group of people waiting to board the bus. They were joined by Vincent. "You two look like the poster children for aloe vera," he said.

The mates placed a Styrofoam cooler containing a few hundred pounds of fish packed in ice in the storage compartment of the bus. The captain shook hands with Booby and then with Meridian. "You had a wild group," he said, "but they took the fishing seriously. I liked that. If you ever want to do another trip, I'd be happy to offer you a repeat-customer discount."

"Thanks, Captain," Booby said.

The captain grinned. "And as you can tell by the catch, I know where the fish arc."

CHAPTER 18

▼

The beer flowed freely once again as the bus traveled north up the highway. Since early morning, the relative level of drunkenness in the group had ebbed and flowed several times, and now, like the tide, it was high again.

Meridian started up a sing-along. Someone passed around a bottle of scotch whiskey. About halfway home, Booby stood up and addressed the bus. "Who's up for a fish fry back at my house?"

Everyone cheered.

"I just opened my pool, and the water's crystal clear!" he yelled.

Everyone cheered again.

James looked wide-eyed at Shannon. "This is going to get interesting. Say, how would you like to meet my mother?"

Booby sipped scotch and called out directions to the bus driver. As they came to Booby's street, the bus driver asked incredulously, "You want me to go up that street?"

"That's the street where I live," Booby answered.

"Isn't it a little narrow for a bus?"

"Don't worry, booby, you can make it!"

The bus driver had to turn, back up, and turn again as he maneuvered the bus up the narrow street. He narrowly missed clipping a parked car more than once, and each time, the crowd yelled wildly and threw beer cans at the bus driver.

Finally, the bus pulled in front of Booby's home. The oldest McGirk brother, still dressed like a pirate, ran to the front of the bus and waited for the door to open. When the driver opened the door, McGirk hung out and yelled, "Arrgg!

Surrender your rum and your women, and we may let you live!" McGirk howled loudly at himself.

Meridian and the others pushed past him, and the bus began to empty. They unloaded the fish and what remained of the beer. Booby led the group to a gate that opened up to his backyard, patio, and pool.

At front door, Jane Cameron surveyed the scene. Her face was crimson with anger. "James! James Cameron!" she shouted. "What are you doing?"

Booby waved to her and skipped into his backyard, with everyone following behind.

"James!" she screamed at him. "I absolutely forbid all of these people to come into my house. James!"

Booby ignored her.

As James helped Shannon off the bus, he could see that his mother was growing more hysterical by the minute. James grabbed Shannon's hand and hurried up the steps to the front porch. "Hi, Mom!" he said abruptly. "How are you doing? This is my girlfriend, Shannon."

Mrs. Cameron stopped shouting in mid-sentence and turned to consider her son. "James, what is your father doing? I thought you were going fishing today?"

James sloppily kissed his mother; he was more than a little drunk. "We did. The fishing trip is over. Dad invited people back for a fish fry."

"The whole bus?" she asked, exasperated.

"Don't worry, Mom. I'll make sure they stay outside. I won't let anyone roam around the house."

Mrs. Cameron turned to Shannon. "I'm sorry. This whole thing just took me by surprise." She extended her hand. "I'm Jane Cameron, James' mother. I am so happy to finally meet you." She gave her son a reprimanding look as she sniffed the air. "You two smell like fish and beer."

"Mom, I better get back there and help Dad. Why don't you come outside and hang out with us?"

Mrs. Cameron frowned. "I'm not really in the mood to socialize with a bunch of drunk people."

James shrugged. "Okay, Mom. We'll be around back if you need us."

Shannon attempted to defuse the situation. "Mrs. Cameron, why don't you and your husband join James and me for dinner next weekend in Manhattan? I know this great little French bistro. My treat."

Mrs. Cameron smiled thinly. "Thank you, Shannon. We'd be delighted."

"I'll make arrangements with you during the week, Mom," James said, as he pulled Shannon down the front steps. "We'll be around back if you change your mind."

"Stop drinking!" Mrs. Cameron yelled after them.

James and Shannon walked around to the backyard and the pool area. James' father had a sweet setup: A large pool was in the middle of the yard, surrounded by a stamped concrete walkway. On either side of the pool was a rectangular yard. The yard was arranged with an assortment of plastic chairs and reclining loungers. A sizable patio occupied the front third of the yard, also of stamped concrete. An ornate metal patio set sat off to the left, and to the right a customized brick gas grill was already smoking. The patio exited down to a door that connected a large, tiled basement, complete with kitchen, to the pool area.

People jumped in and out of the pool in various stages of undress. Meridian and Two-Boy had taken to wresting in the grass and had attracted a small crowd. Booby came out of the basement, carrying a broad-rimmed martini glass filled to the brim. Sitting in the liquid at the bottom of the glass was a three-olive toothpick.

Music echoed through speakers strategically located around the patio.

"Mom's a little stressed out," James told his father.

"She takes things too seriously," Booby said, waving his hand dismissively.

"Would you like me to start cooking the fish?"

"That would be great, booby. I'll entertain the guests."

"Would you please get us a drink, Shannon?" James asked.

"Beer?"

"I'll have a vodka and tonic on ice, with a lime. I don't think I can stand any more beer."

Shannon laughed. "You are such a lightweight. Easy on the vodka?"

"Please."

Shannon disappeared into the basement.

Vincent joined James, obviously drunk. "Where's your beer?"

"Shannon's making us a couple of mixed drinks."

"You are such a lightweight. When are we eating?"

"We'll eat after I cook the fish. That's what I'm about to do."

Vincent staggered away.

Shannon came out of the basement carrying a cocktail glass and a beer. She handed him the glass. He pointed to the beer.

"It has been way too long a road for me today to switch now."

James reached into the Styrofoam cooler that had been placed next to the grill and pulled out several freezer bags stuffed with fish. He spread the filets out neatly on the grill and then ran to the basement to rummage for some lemon and butter.

The party continued, with people becoming more and more drunk. Booby finished off his first martini and then had another. And then another after that.

The aroma of fresh-grilled fish cooked in lemon and butter permeated the patio. James asked Shannon to go bring out some paper plates and utensils from the basement. Soon, the first batch of filets was cooked, and James called out for people to come and eat. After the first stampede was served, James grilled up another batch. He served that and then cooked a third and a fourth.

Shannon put her arms around James' waist and whispered huskily, "I like the way you work that grill. It's very manly. You turn me on." She gave James a beer-soaked kiss.

As they kissed, James noticed something out of the corner of his eye. "Would you look at that? I am now permanently psychologically damaged."

Shannon turned. "Oh…my…God," she said.

Two-Boy stood on the diving board. Naked. Slowly, people in the yard started to notice, and laughter broke out around the party.

Two-Boy spread his arms. His belly, all four, thick folds of it, hung down over his waist, practically covering his genitals. Two folds of fat hung over his hips, like saddlebags.

Booby stood in the middle of the pool, smoking a cigarette and holding a martini, with his back to Two-Boy. He was engaged in a conversation with three people.

Two-Boy began jumping up and down on the diving board, the folds of his belly shimmying. He jumped higher and higher. His penis flopped up and down as well, a mere sideshow to the spectacle of his undulating girth.

People were now rolling around in the grass, laughing hysterically.

James and Shannon started to laugh and soon were laughing so hard, tears were rolling down their cheeks.

Two-Boy jumped high in the air and grabbed his legs. He descended like a cannonball. Right toward Booby.

Too late, James reacted. "Dad! Watch out!"

Booby looked up, and Two-boy slammed into his back, knocking him face-first into the water. They both went down hard, with Booby hitting the bottom of the pool.

Two-Boy easily stood up. He reached down and grabbed Booby, pulling him up out of the water.

As soon as Booby's head cleared the water, he let out an agonized yell. "My knee! My knee! I think my knee is broken! Call an ambulance!"

Two-Boy, now completely mortified, helped Booby to the side of the pool. A few people reached down and pulled him out of the pool.

Booby, too drunk to stand, collapsed in agony, "My goddamn knee! Somebody call an ambulance!"

The commotion had brought Mrs. Cameron out to the elevated back porch, where she stood looking down on the patio. "What happened?" she demanded as James raced over to her.

"Somebody jumped on Dad. I think he's hurt. We need an ambulance."

Mrs. Cameron turned beet red. "That's it!" she yelled, "Everybody out! This minute! I want everybody to leave. Now! Don't make me call the cops!" She rushed back inside to call 9-1-1.

"Mom's calling an ambulance," James told his father. "It'll be here soon."

Booby's face was ghostly white; he looked terrified. He could barely speak from the pain, and he gripped his son's hand tightly.

The party suddenly became very quiet. Vincent shut off the music, and people started to leave, heads down. Two-Boy, dressed now, looked concerned.

"James, I am so sorry," he said. "It was an accident. I didn't mean it. I am so sorry."

James looked up. "I know it was an accident, Two-Boy. Let me just get my father taken care of."

Two-Boy nodded, apologized repeatedly, and then quietly left the yard.

Shannon appeared with some aspirin and a glass of water for Booby. Mrs. Cameron joined them and placed her hand on her son's back. Soon, they heard the ambulance's siren, and three paramedics entered the backyard. One bent down and examined Booby's leg and knee; he frowned. He barked some directions to the other paramedics, who ran back to the ambulance.

They placed Booby's knee in a brace, the process causing him to let out a series of screams. He lay on the ground, soaking wet and in shock. They placed him on a stretcher, loaded him into the ambulance, and sped off to Hudson General.

Mrs. Cameron gave James a quick kiss. "I'd better follow them."

James nodded mutely. He and Shannon stood motionless in the back yard, the smell of cooked fish still lingering in the air.

"Wow, that's a bummer," Vincent said. "I hope your father is all right." He swayed back and forth on unsteady legs. "Do you want to—" He hiccupped. "Want to go to the Bell Lap?"

James grabbed his arm. "I think the party's over, Vin. I'm exhausted, anyway. We should just call it a night."

"James is right," Shannon agreed.

"Well, I'm going to the Bell," Vincent said firmly.

"Shannon and I will walk with you. Then we're heading home."

James locked his parents' house, and then the three walked down the hill to Main Avenue. Vincent put his arm around James' shoulder as they walked— partly in friendship but mostly for support. "I love you guys," he hiccupped. When they reached the doorway of the Bell Lap, Vincent asked again, "Are you sure you don't want to come in?"

"No thanks, Vin. I'm wiped out." James grabbed his friend and kissed his forehead. "I'm going to be drinking with you at this stupid bar for the next fifty years. I think you can let me go for one night."

Vincent gave Shannon a big hug and kissed her. "You know, for one of those snobby corporate chicks, you're pretty cool," he joked. Vincent turned and stumbled into his bar.

"Good night, Vin!" James and Shannon called out.

Back at James' apartment, they showered and then lay together in bed, staring at the television.

"I hope your father is going to be okay," she said.

"I don't know. He hurt himself pretty bad today. We'll know more tomorrow."

Shannon moaned and rubbed her temples. "I think I'm going to have a hangover for the next week."

"That's one of the things I like about you. You can practically out-drink me when you put your mind to it."

Shannon grimaced. "I don't know if I would exactly call that a positive attribute."

"You're Irish…I'm Scottish. We come from two serious two-fisted drinking cultures. It's a wonder I'm not an alcoholic."

"You're not?" she asked.

"Very amusing," James said, feigning annoyance. "And what's all this with making dinner plans with my mother? You made me look like an ass."

"There are just some things that women are better at," Shannon explained. "Like keeping mothers happy. I take it she's been waiting to meet me."

"Well, I didn't think it was time yet," James said defensively.

"You and I will have a fine time at dinner with your parents," Shannon assured him.

James nodded. He rested his head on her chest and wrapped his arms around her. Within minutes they were both fast asleep.

CHAPTER 19

▼

Vincent waved to James and Shannon as they walked through the brand-new heavy-oak front door. The Bell Lap Tavern was packed. People stood elbow to elbow at the bar, and the crowd extended a few rows back. Music blared from the jukebox and also from speakers mounted on the ceiling in the corners of the bar. People walked up and down the stairs that led to pool tables and dart boards on the second floor. The smell of cigarette smoke in the air was present but not overwhelming. The new smoke-eater was doing its job.

James and Shannon pushed their way up to the bar. They noticed that Meridian was leaning against the counter, beer in hand. Meridian held his pint up in greeting.

"Vin, this is awesome! The Bell Lap is packed!" James yelled.

Vincent grinned in agreement. A young woman ran behind Vincent, carrying three pints of beer.

"New bartender?" James asked.

"Yeah, and I got one upstairs, too. I figure I'm going to need them on the weekends."

"You have two bartenders? What's that make you now? The manager?" James joked.

"I'll pour you guys a couple of pints—"

"And a round of shots! One for you, too, Vin."

Vincent quickly poured the beers and then lined up four shot glasses on the new counter. He poured four shots of whiskey, and the brown liquid splashed over the sides.

James handed a shot to Meridian and Shannon, and Vincent lifted his own.

"To the Bell Lap Tavern!" James toasted.

"To the Bell Lap Tavern!" they repeated and clinked their glasses together.

They downed the shots in one gulp.

Vincent wiped his mouth and scanned the crowd. "I have to see to my customers," he explained. "I'll talk to you later. It's time to make some money."

"I've never seen him so energized," James said to Meridian.

"Yeah, he's really excited. He finally got what he wanted. Good for him." Meridian took a big gulp of beer.

James looked around the crowd. "Meridian, there are a lot of good-looking girls here tonight. Maybe one of them would be interested in a low-class slob like you."

Meridian frowned and took another gulp of beer. "Hey, James, can you stop playing cupid for once? I'm sick of everyone telling me what I need to do. If I want to talk to girls, I'll talk to girls. I see that there are women here. I'm not blind."

"Sorry, Meridian, I wasn't trying—"

Meridian interrupted him. "Look, I know everyone is trying help, okay? But I don't need any help. I'm fine. But I would appreciate it if everyone would just leave me alone."

The new, young bartender ran by, and James reached out over the bar and grabbed her arm. "On your way back, can you bring us three more shots of whiskey?"

This time, the three toasted each other and drank the shots in one gulp. The warm liquid burned as it went down their throats a second time, and their faces grew flushed.

"All right, Meridian. I won't bother you anymore about your love life." James crossed his fingers and put his hand over his heart. "Scout's honor. But if you ever want to talk, I'm here."

Meridian nodded and drank his beer.

"If this is any indication how Saturday nights are going to be from here on out, my man Vincent is going to be doing pretty well for himself," James commented to Shannon.

"I'm very happy for Vin. He really deserves this, considering all he's been through," Shannon said.

An older gentleman moved through the crowd, smiling. "Well, would you look at that?" James said to Shannon, as he pointed to the man.

Joe Vagrant, clean-shaven and neatly dressed, recognized James and made his way up to bar. He held out his hand. "You're James, Vin's friend, right?"

James shook the man's hand. "Good to see you...Joe?"

"I'm here to pay my respects to Vin." Joe took a ten-dollar bill out of his pocket. "And to buy my own way tonight."

"He went upstairs," Meridian said.

"You're looking better these days, Joe," James commented.

Joe nodded. "I think things are looking up."

Vincent came back downstairs and hopped behind the counter.

James yelled out, "Hey, Vin! Look who made an appearance." He pointed at Joe.

Vincent reached over and shook Joe's hand. "Good to see you tonight, Joe."

The bartender brought over a pint of beer for Joe, and the group toasted each other and clinked glasses.

Vincent gave them the thumbs up, his face beaming.

*   *   *   *

On the following Monday morning around eleven, Vincent let himself into the Bell Lap Tavern. He was tired and still a little groggy from the long weekend. The grand re-opening had been a huge success, better than he ever expected.

Vincent had been smart. He had taken out full-page ads in the weekly town newspaper for the last month, which talked up all the improvements to the bar. And he had started a grassroots campaign to spread the word. It had all turned out well for him.

Although he was never one to drink much when he was working, this weekend had been an exception. He imbibed a little more than he usually did on Friday, got absolutely pie-eyed on Saturday, and wound up drunk again on Sunday night. It seemed the whole town had come out to wish him well and buy him a drink, and he couldn't refuse them.

Vincent turned on the lights and walked behind the counter, where he put on a pot of coffee. Thank God he was off tonight. He'd scheduled one of his weekend bartenders to start working the Monday shift, and she started tonight. She seemed ambitious; she was working her way through college, was bright, and most importantly, was trustworthy. She reminded Vincent a lot of himself at that age.

If she worked out, and if the weekends were good enough, he might even let her work Wednesday nights, too. Vincent could not remember a time when he didn't work at least six nights a week.

The coffeemaker gurgled, and the pot filled. Vincent poured a cup of black coffee, took a few tentative sips, and placed the cup on the counter.

He reached under the counter and pulled out Big Al's old metal safe. The space inside was stuffed with cash. It had been a good weekend.

Vincent frowned. Because of his loan, most of the money in the safe would have to be deposited in the bank. And most of that would go to pay the loan. It was a double whammy. Debt and taxes. Big Al never had these problems. He sighed, closing the door to the safe. He was reaching for his coffee when he heard the door to the Bell Lap Tavern swing open. *I always forget to lock that damn door*, Vincent swore to himself. A gaunt man entered; Vincent recognized him immediately.

"I'm not open, Joe. Come back around two. The bar should be open by then."

The man entered the bar and shut the door. He walked over to Vincent.

"Joe, I said I'm not open, dude. You need to leave."

Joe stood in front of Vincent, his eyes cold and calculating. He raised a pistol, and pointed it at Vincent. "First give me all the money in that safe, and then I'll leave."

Vincent backed up, eyes wide, and stared incredulously at the man. "Joe, you have got to be kidding me. Is this some kind of a joke?"

"I'm not joking."

Vincent took a deep breath. "Joe, you've been coming in here for months. Do you know how much free beer I've given you? And when it was cold, didn't I let you come in and sit at the bar, just to keep warm?"

"Just give me the money."

"Joe, everyone in this bar knows who you are. You can't just rob me. They're going to catch you."

"Give me the money!" Joe demanded.

Vincent's heart was pounding. "Joe, this is bullshit! Look, there isn't even all that much in the safe. This is a neighborhood bar."

"I saw the crowd in here this weekend. I'm sure there's a lot more in that safe than you're letting on."

"Joe, just put the gun down and leave. I promise I won't even call the cops. We'll just pretend like this never happened."

Joe's grip on the gun grew tighter. "Give me the money now."

"Or what? You're going to shoot me? You're not going to shoot me."

"I'm not going to ask you again," he said icily.

"Fuck you, Joe. I'm not giving you the money."

The gun fired.

Vincent felt a burning sensation in his stomach. He touched his stomach and felt blood. The acrid smell of gunpowder stung his nostrils. He looked up, surprise clearly written in his eyes as he stared at the man. "Joe...?"

The gun fired again. The bullet ripped through Vincent's throat, and he fell back against the wall, knocking over a shelf. Bottles spilled onto the floor, and there was the sound of shattered glass.

Vincent clutched his throat and made a gurgling sound. Blood spilled out between his fingers, flowing red down his white sweatshirt. He collapsed onto the floor. Shards of glass dug into his arms and back.

The man looked over the counter at Vincent. "The name's not Joe." He picked the safe up off the counter, then turned and walked calmly away from the bar. The new door of the Bell Lap Tavern closed quietly behind him.

Vincent knew he didn't have much time—darkness was creeping in around the edges. He focused on the telephone sitting on the shelf against the wall. He reached out, grabbed the line cord, and pulled the phone off the shelf. The phone crashed onto the floor, the receiver bouncing away from Vincent. He pulled the phone closer.

Vincent held the switch hook down for a few seconds and then let it rise. He dialed 9-1-1. He grabbed a bar towel and put pressure on his throat. Blood continued to pour out between his fingers and dripped onto the floor. The darkness around the corners of his eyes closed in.

A voice coming came from the telephone's receiver, just out of Vincent's reach. "Emergency assistance. What is the nature of your emergency? Hello? Are you there? Can you hear me? This is emergency assistance...."

The voice trailed off as Vincent slipped into unconsciousness.

*   *   *   *

James was finishing the last of his turkey sandwich when his phone rang. He quickly chewed the food in his mouth, washed it down with a swig of soda, and answered the telephone.

"James, it's Meridian." His voice was shaky. "You have to get to the hospital right away. Vincent's been shot."

"Shot?" James responded stupidly. Had he heard Meridian correctly?

"They're operating on him right now. They said he was shot in the stomach and the throat. You have to get down here. It's bad."

"What...what happened?" James stammered.

"It was a robbery."

"Who called you? How—?"

"One of the paramedics. He knows I'm Vincent's friend, so he called me. Look, none of that matters! Just get down here!"

"On my way."

Mike stood in the doorway, blocking James' exit. "James, this is my first day back, and I wanted to talk to you for a couple of minutes—"

"Mike, not right now." James pushed past him. "Vincent has been shot. Out of my way." James rushed out of the office, ran to his car, and sped off toward Hudson General.

✳   ✳   ✳   ✳

James and Meridian waited on a small bench in the middle of a hallway in the trauma center wing of Hudson General. Neither spoke. Hospital personnel rushed quickly back and forth, and doctors, nurses, and orderlies moved with purpose.

Every so often, there would be a rush of activity when a new patient arrived and was whisked down the hallway to the operating room. *Too much activity*, James thought absently, his mind seeming numb. *Too much.*

After two hours of sitting on the bench, a doctor approached the men. "Are you here for Vincent Ferrara?"

"Yes," they answered in unison.

The doctor's mouth was a thin line. "I'm Doctor Zimmerman. I operated on Mr. Ferrara."

James and Meridian nodded, waiting.

"When Mr. Ferrara was brought in," the doctor began, "he had already lost a significant amount of blood. He suffered a serious stomach wound. We removed the bullet from his stomach and repaired the damage as best we could. The bullet that passed through his neck lacerated the carotid artery, which caused most of the bleeding. It's a miracle he made it here alive. He's in recovery now, but his condition is critical. The neck wound bled into his lungs, causing extensive damage. We've done what we can."

Meridian grabbed the doctor's arm. "Is he going to make it?" he cried. "Is Vincent going to live?"

Doctor Zimmerman placed his hand on Meridian's shoulder. "I don't know. I wish I could say yes, but I honestly don't know. As I said, we've done all we can."

"We'd like to see him," James announced.

"Well, you're not blood relatives. I'm really not supposed to—" He sighed, taking in their plaintive stares. "All right. Follow me." Doctor Zimmerman led them to another wing of the hospital. "He may or may not be responsive," the doctor cautioned them as they stood outside Vincent's room. "And you shouldn't stay long."

James nodded in understanding as he slowly pushed the door open. He and Meridian entered the room.

Vincent lay on a bed in the middle of the room. He was hooked up to a heart monitor, which beeped softly. His face was pale, and his neck was bandaged.

James and Meridian looked down at their friend. His shallow breathing barely raised the sheet pulled up over his chest.

Without a word, the two men pulled up chairs next to the bed and took up their vigil. They sat without speaking for almost an hour, barely acknowledging the frequent nurse visits.

Finally, Meridian stood. "James," he said quietly, "I'm going to get a soda. Do you want one?"

James shook his head. He slouched forward in his chair, elbows on his knees, and put his face in his hands. James began to cry.

Suddenly, Vincent's hand twitched. His eyes fluttered. James sat up, wiping his eyes and reaching for Vincent's hand. "Vin. Hey, Vin. It's James," he whispered. "How are you doing?"

Vincent coughed weakly. "Not...not too good."

James moved to get up. "Let me go get a doctor."

Vincent gripped his arm. "Wait."

James focused back on Vincent. "Who did this to you, Vin?"

Vincent coughed. "That guy, Joe...Joe Vagrant...know who I mean?"

James' face reddened. "That son of a bitch. I told you that guy was no good, Vin. You should have listened to me."

"A little late for that now...don't you think?"

"Don't you worry, Vin. We're going to get that son of a bitch."

Vincent nodded.

"Don't you worry, Vin," James said again. "The doctors said they got you all patched up. Just hang in there. You're going to be fine."

Vincent smiled weakly and closed his eyes. "James?"

"I'm right here, Vin."

"James...do me a favor."

"Anything, Vin," James answered, squeezing Vincent's hand.

"Don't...don't...let your life...turn out like mine."

"What are you talking about? What do you mean?"

Vincent's breathing was labored, but he struggled to continue. "Follow your heart." Vincent wheezed and grimaced. "You have...potential."

"What do you mean, Vin? What do you want me to do?" James cried. Tears ran down his cheeks.

Vincent opened his eyes slightly, and James could see that they were yellowish and sunken. Vincent gripped James' hand as tightly as he could. "Make yourself happy, James," he whispered with obvious effort, "and live a long life." Vincent closed his eyes again, and James listened only to the sound of Vincent's shallow breathing. Then Vincent's lips moved, almost imperceptibly.

"What is it, Vincent? Do you want to tell me something?"

The corners of Vincent's mouth turned up slightly, almost in a smile. "Turned that bar into something special, didn't I?"

"You did a great job with the Bell Lap Tavern," James agreed. "It turned out perfectly."

Vincent nodded. "Tell Meridian something for me."

"He's here, Vin. He just went to get a soda. What do you want me to tell him?"

"Tell...tell him...I said good-bye." Vincent slipped into sleep.

Meridian came back into the room and noticed James' teary eyes. "What happened?"

James looked up at him, his great sadness written on his face. "He said...he said good-bye."

The two men hugged tightly. James sobbed onto Meridian's shoulder.

CHAPTER 20

▼

"Ashes to ashes, dust to dust...." the priest intoned.

It was a beautiful day. Birds chirped, the sky was cloudless and blue, and the sun shone brightly, casting small shadows on the lush green grass. The air smelled of roses.

James stood next to Meridian and Shannon in a group mostly composed of Cameron Voice and Data employees. Vincent's mother stood nest to the casket, alone.

A large group of people stood behind the immediate friends and family on both sides of the casket. People from all over town had come to pay their respects.

James stared at the polished cedar casket covered by a white cloth. Flowers surrounded it.

James held a rose in his hand. He admired its vibrant redness, its pleasant scent, and he wondered how something so beautiful could so soon whither and die.

James met his father's eyes. Booby was standing on crutches a few feet away, fighting back tears.

The priest motioned for the group to pay their final respects. Vincent's mother went first. She placed her rose on the white cloth and rubbed her hand on the soft linen. Her mouth quivered. She lingered, then kneeled next to the casket. She wrapped her arms around the casket, giving her son one last hug. She began to sob uncontrollably.

"My baby...my baby...please forgive me...my baby, I'm so sorry...so sorry."

No one moved. Everyone allowed the woman her repentance. Finally, the priest helped her up and walked her away from the casket.

Next Meridian placed his rose on the casket. He tapped the lid with his fist. His face was puffy, and he clearly was struggling to hold back tears.

James stepped up to the casket and offered his rose.

The procession continued to move past.

James and Shannon had found a place near a tree, a little distance from the funeral. "It's nice to see so many people here," James said. "Vin would have appreciated that."

Shannon squeezed his hand. "I'm so sorry, James. I feel so bad for you."

James raised her hand to his lips and kissed it.

When the last person had paid final respects, James led Shannon to his car.

*   *   *   *

The Bell Lap Tavern was eerily quiet, considering the crowd.

Two long tables had been arranged along the wall, further narrowing the already narrow space between the bar and the wall. Tin trays had been placed on the tables; they rested on metal frames above the sternos.

Pitchers of beer and soda had been laid out along the bar.

Meridian worked behind the bar, bringing out beer glasses and plastic cups. He opened half a dozen bottles of wine and lined them on the counter.

James poured a pint of beer and offered it to Shannon. He saw his mother and father come through the door, and he nodded to them. He poured another beer and offered it to his father. Booby shifted his weight to his good leg and propped himself up on his crutch. He took the beer with his free hand; James' mother took a glass of wine.

James poured a pint of beer for himself, but it remained in his hand, untasted.

Meridian stood up on the counter and held up his pint of beer. "May I have your attention, please?" All eyes were on him. "I'm not very good with speeches, so please bear with me." Meridian looked around the room and locked eyes with several people. "I've known Vincent...Vin...since we were kids. As rough as his home life was at times, he never let it get to him. He never complained. And he always had a smile for you. He could always find something to laugh about. And if you needed help, it didn't matter with what, he was always there for you. I couldn't have asked for a better friend." Meridian choked as he tried to hold back tears. "Vin loved this bar. The Bell Lap Tavern was his life. He waited his whole life to have it, and at least he got to see his dream come true...if only for a little while." Tears streamed downed Meridian's face, and he held up his beer. "To Vincent."

"To Vincent," the room somberly repeated.

Meridian drank, and the room followed. "May he rest in peace," Meridian whispered. He climbed off the bar and was universally hugged and patted. He made it past a few people, and then he broke down and cried. The room was silent except for the plaintive sound of Meridian's crying.

James drank his beer quickly. "This is going to be a long day," he said to Shannon.

After several drinks, the atmosphere grew a little lighter. Tears gradually changed to solemn words of remembrance, which gradually changed again to fond remembrances and eventually, to jokes.

Plates of hot roast beef with gravy, chicken, and sausage and peppers floated around the room. Meridian and James took turns filling the pitchers of beer.

James stood with Shannon, and together they joined his parents. No one knew quite what to say. Finally, Mrs. Cameron attempted small talk.

"I want to thank you again for inviting us to dinner, Shannon," she said. "You were very pleasant company."

Shannon smiled. "It was my pleasure, Mrs. Cameron."

"Thank you for paying, too," Booby said. "As I told you, I would have been more than happy to pick up the tab."

"No, no, Mr. Cameron. My treat."

"You're young, booby. You need your money."

"Next time, I'll let you treat."

Booby grinned. "I'll buy you your first steak at the Mad Cow."

"How's the knee, Dad?" James asked.

"It's coming along. I'll probably have to wear the cast for another five or six weeks."

Mrs. Cameron jabbed him in the side, "And then, no more drunken parties. Do you hear me? You're getting too old to be horsing around like a teenager."

"Okay, honey. No more parties." He looked at James, and winked.

James laughed out loud.

Mrs. Cameron lowered her voice to a whisper. "Do they have any more information on that…that terrible man who killed Vincent?"

James lowered his head and shuffled his feet. "No. Nothing new."

The group fell silent.

Those who were not close friends of Vincent's began to leave the bar, singly and in pairs. Those who remained became a little drunk. Meridian moved around behind the bar again. People gathered in groups at various spots along the counter.

The door opened, and Mike Munro walked in. He looked around for Booby.

"What are you drinking?" Meridian asked.

"Water," Mike replied.

"Rehab is for quitters," Meridian teased.

Mike gave him a dirty look. Meridian poured a cold pint of water and handed it to Mike.

"Where have you been?" James asked.

"I knew there would be a lot of drinking here, so I figured it would be best just to stay away," Mike replied.

"There's more drinking now than before. And you missed Meridian's eulogy."

Mike nodded. "I know. James we never did get to talk—"

"Not today, Mike. C'mon, man. Not today." James shook his head in disbelief. James finished his beer, and Meridian poured him another. James ordered some shots. Meridian lined up a round of whiskey, and they lifted their shot glasses in a toast to their friend.

Booby reached for a shot, but Mrs. Cameron moved his hand away. "No. No liquor. Do you hear me? No liquor."

"C'mon, honey. This is in honor of Vincent."

"I don't care. No booze. Or you can give yourself a sponge bath until the cast comes off."

"Talk about kicking a man when he's down," Booby grumbled.

The group drank their shots, and Meridian filled the glasses again.

The two quick shots had their effect on James; he grew warm and flushed.

Mike came back over to stand next to him. "Don't you think it's morbid, having the repast in the place where Vincent was killed?"

James eyed Mike, a little drunkenly. "This was Vin's bar. This was his life. Look around you. Don't you see what he did to the place? I couldn't think of a more appropriate place to have his repast."

"I think it's sad that this bar was his whole life."

James turned on Mike. "It's not like he had a choice, Mike. This was the hand that he was dealt, and he made the most of it."

"He chose to be a bartender."

James sighed, calming himself. He stared at the liquor bottles arranged in neat rows on the shelf behind the counter. "He didn't choose the Bell Lap Tavern," he said quietly. "It chose him."

"That's a bunch of philosophical crap," Mike sneered.

James took a gulp of beer. "I don't even know why you're here. It's not like you were friends with Vin."

Mike became defensive. "Who are you to tell me who I can and can't pay my respects to?"

"It doesn't sound like you had much respect for him."

Mike shrugged. "He could have done better. That's all I'm saying."

"What the hell is that supposed to mean?"

"He never asked me for a job at Cameron. I would have given him a chance."

"He had no interest in working in telecommunications," James explained. "What Vin really wanted to be was an architect."

"Pfft. You still don't get it."

"What are you talking about? Like you're so perfect."

"Look at where you hang out," Mike spat at him. "Look at your friends. You associate with failures!"

"What?"

"You heard me!"

"My friend is dead, asshole," James said through clenched teeth. "He was not a failure. Take it back!"

"No."

Booby saw that the conversation between the two had become heated, and he moved to intercede. "Okay, guys. I know everyone is a little upset today—"

"Vincent was not a failure. Take it back, asshole!" James threatened.

Mike's face reddened, and his eyes bulged. "I came here today to apologize to you." Mike breathed heavily, and a vein pulsed along the side of his forehead. "But I see that I was just wasting my time. You're never going to change, James. You're always going to be a joke."

James threw himself at Mike, knocking him backwards onto the floor. Mike pushed himself up, nostrils flaring. Before Mike could raise his hands, James threw a hard right. He punched straight on and connected with Mike's nose and upper lip.

Mike's nose burst open, and blood spurted out. Mike fell back into one of the tables and knocked over a hot tin of pasta. Macaroni and pasta sauce flipped onto his back, running down his back and chest.

That suit is going to need some serious dry cleaning, James thought smugly.

Mike sat on the floor, holding his nose. Blood gushed out from between his nostrils and onto his shirt and tie. "You broke my nose!" he yelled. "I'm going to kill you!" Mike attempted to get up, but was held back by several people.

Meridian jumped over the counter and grabbed Mike's arm. "Fight's over, Munro. Time for you to go." Meridian roughly moved Mike to the door. Someone tossed a bar towel to Meridian, and he pushed the towel into Mike's face. The towel quickly turned red with blood.

Booby came hobbling over on his crutches. "Somebody needs to take him to the emergency room!"

Someone volunteered to give Mike a ride to the hospital.

Booby shifted his weight to his good leg and put his hand on Mike's shoulder. "I'm sorry, Mike. James didn't mean to break your nose. It was an accident, booby. Don't worry; we'll get your nose fixed up good as new."

Mike glared at Booby. He was led out of the Bell Lap Tavern, holding his nose.

"Ding-dong, the witch is dead!" Meridian yelled.

Most people laughed.

James stood in the middle of the bar, flexing his hand. Someone handed him a fresh beer.

Meridian approached James. "Did that asshole call me a loser?"

"Not in so many words," James replied.

"I have a good mind to break his nose again after it heals."

"Don't hold it against him, booby. Mike isn't a bad guy. He's just a little stressed out. He's been through a lot lately," Booby rationalized.

James and Meridian stared at Booby with raised eyebrows.

"There's never a dull moment in your life, is there?" Shannon asked.

James turned to her and smiled.

At the end of the night, all that remained were James, Meridian, and Shannon. They turned on the jukebox and played Vincent's favorite songs. Eventually, they left the bar, all very drunk.

The three stood outside of the Bell Lap Tavern. James and Shannon said good-bye to Meridian, and Meridian gave them both a long hug. James and Shannon stumbled up the street toward his apartment.

Meridian stood alone in the street. He locked the front door and placed his open palm on the new painted wood.

"Good-bye, Vin."

Meridian sighed and walked unsteadily away from the bar.

CHAPTER 21

▼

"Hello…ticket number?" Dennis said.

"For the love of God, Dennis; it's James."

"How can I help you, James?"

"Don't you ever look at your caller ID?"

"This is the technician line. Only technicians are supposed to call on this line."

"Do you know where Meridian is?"

"He's at Federated Wines and Liquors, installing the system that you sold them."

"No, he's not," James snapped. "I'm here now, and he's not here. And the customer is saying that he didn't show up yesterday."

Dennis frowned. "Let me check the computer. He called into the job yesterday, but never closed out. I assumed he forgot."

"And you didn't hear from him this morning?"

"No, not yet. However, I would have beeped him before lunch if he didn't call in."

"Okay, thanks, Dennis." James hung up the wall-mounted telephone and thought for a moment. He felt a chill, and then realized that the data center where he currently stood was permanently cooled to protect the collection of sensitive electronic and computer equipment it housed.

Mr. Anderson walked into the room. "Any word from your office as to the whereabouts of Mr. Meridian?"

"Yes, I just spoke to Dennis, our service manager. He said Meridian...called out sick the last couple of days. He should be back on the job tomorrow, or I would say Thursday at the latest," James lied.

"It would have been nice to notify your customer that your installation technician was not going to show up," Mr. Anderson complained.

"Yes, sir...I'm very sorry. I will make sure that in the future Dennis notifies you if one of our employees is not going to be here."

"That would be the professional thing to do." Mr. Anderson turned and left the room.

James picked up the receiver and dialed Meridian's number. After several rings, his answering machine picked up the call.

No Meridian. And no phone call. *This isn't like him*, James thought. James' concern for Meridian heightened as he reflected on the last few weeks. Meridian was already depressed, and Vincent's death had soured Meridian's mood even more. James prayed that Meridian hadn't done something foolish.

He headed for his car and sped off toward Meridian's apartment. Once there, James took the stairs three at a time. He banged on the door. "Meridian! Meridian, are you in there? Meridian!" James put his ear to the door and listened. He heard nothing. James contemplated kicking in the door, but first he gripped and turned the knob.

The door opened.

James stepped into Meridian's apartment.

"Meridian!" James called. He looked around the apartment but didn't see anything out of order. He searched each room, finally coming to the main bedroom. The door was half open. James held his breath and pushed opened the door. "Meridian?" he said. No response.

The bedroom was empty. The bed was unmade bed, but nothing seemed out of the ordinary.

Perplexed, James turned to leave. As he walked back through the kitchen, something caught his eye on the kitchen table. It was a letter, handwritten on yellow note paper. James began to read:

Dear Joe,

I'm sorry it's been so long. I've been meaning to write you or call you, but I didn't know what to say, and I knew you would be very angry. First, I want you to know that I'm okay. Second, I'm really sorry for taking our money like that, but I knew you wouldn't have given it to me voluntarily. I just couldn't live like that anymore. I had to leave. You didn't want to leave, but I had to. I needed to start a new life. Please don't write back or try to call me. It's over, Joe. I'm sorry. I will try to pay you back as soon as I can. I promise.

Kelly

James stared at the letter and slowly began to put the pieces together. He looked around the table for an envelope, found it, and checked the return address: Kendell, Florida. Right outside of Miami, his old stomping grounds.

James suddenly became alarmed. He ran back into Meridian's bedroom and looked under the bed. Nothing. He opened the sliding closet door and moved some clothes around, feeling along the wall. He slid open the adjacent door and checked that side of the closet. Still nothing. Meridian's shotgun was missing.

James ran to the telephone in the kitchen and dialed Shannon's cell phone number. "Shannon, I'm calling you from Meridian's apartment. Kelly, Meridian's girlfriend who stole all of his money, has contacted him."

"Oh? Where's Meridian?" Shannon asked.

"He's gone. He didn't show up for work yesterday or today. I think he's gone to go find Kelly."

"Well, maybe he needs to work things out with her."

"I don't think so, Shannon. He's taken his shotgun."

There was a long pause on the other end of the telephone. Then Shannon said, "Oh, that's not good."

"Shannon, I'm going to Newark Airport right now. I've got to catch a plane to Miami and get to Kelly before Meridian does."

"Wait…I'll go with you. Pick me up at the train station in an hour."

"All right. Just hurry up. I don't know how much time we have."

"You know, James, I really, really think way too much shit happens in your life."

"Tell me about it."

James took the letter and envelope off the table and stuck it in his pocket.

*   *   *   *

Meridian pulled off the highway somewhere in South Carolina.

He spotted a gas station about a quarter-mile down the access road and headed toward it. He pulled into the station and parked beside one of the gas pumps. A young man wearing greasy beige overalls came out from the open garage and approached the vehicle.

Meridian rolled down the window. "Fill it up," he said.

"Is that going to be cash or credit?" the attendant said in a heavy southern drawl.

"Cash."

The attendant opened the gas tank cover and inserted the nozzle. He pressed the release lever and locked it into place. He considered the vehicle. "Cameron Voice and Data? Is that where you work?"

"Yeah."

"You got a commercial vehicle. New Jersey? Are you from New Jersey?"

"That's what the license plate says."

"I don't see commercial vehicles all the way from New Jersey down here very often. You got business in South Carolina?"

"What? Are you writing a fucking book?"

"I'm just making conversation. No need to get rude." The attendant scowled.

"You want to know what I'm doing? Okay, I'll tell you what I'm doing. I'm driving down to Florida with my shotgun to kill my ex-girlfriend, who left me and stole all of my fucking money."

The attendant stared wide-eyed at Meridian.

"And then, if the mood hits me, I'll stick the shotgun in my mouth and blow my own fucking head off."

The attendant continued to stare at Meridian. "You Yankees sure have a funny sense of humor."

"Ain't that the truth."

The meter beeped indicating the tank was full. The attendant took the nozzle out and placed it back in its cradle. He walked over to the window. "That's thirty six-dollars."

Meridian threw him forty. "Keep the change, Gomer." Meridian hit the gas and screeched out of the station. He sped toward the highway and headed south.

*   *   *   *

James and Shannon landed in Miami International Airport about three o'clock. They sat in their seats, waiting for the jet to pull up to the gate. James tapped his feet.

"You tried calling her, right?"

James eyed Shannon. "Do I look that stupid? Besides, I don't think she even has a phone."

Shannon blushed. "Sorry."

James patted her hand in apology for snapping at her. "I even tried the police. They said they would send a car out to check on her, but who knows when that will be?"

"Relax, James. We're almost there," Shannon said.

After what seemed an eternity, the plane finally pulled up to the gate, and the giant air-conditioned arm swung over and latched onto the jet door. The captain made his standard announcement, indicated that the weather was eighty-three degrees and sunny. He wished everyone a pleasant stay in the Miami area.

James and Shannon grabbed their carry-on bags and moved up the line to the front of the plane. As soon as they disembarked, they ran toward the rental-car area.

"You know where you are going?" Shannon asked.

"Yeah, I used to go to school here. I've flown in and out of this airport a dozen times."

They navigated quickly through the crowds but managed to bump into several people along the way. They were given a few curses and once, a flagrant obscene gesture.

"These people act just like the people where we live," Shannon commented.

"Yeah. Miami is the place where old New Yorkers come to die."

Fortunately, there was only a small line at the Hertz counter. They waited for several minutes, then moved up to speak to the clerk.

"Welcome to Hertz! How may I help you?"

"I would like to rent a car," James stated.

"May I have your confirmation number?" the clerk asked expectantly.

"I don't have a confirmation number. I'm a walk-up."

"Oh." The clerk frowned. "Let me see…we don't have any cars. I'm sorry."

James looked at Shannon, exasperated, and then turned his attention back to the clerk. "You don't have *any* cars? Nothing?" He looked around the terminal and noticed that lines had formed at all of the other rental-car booths.

The clerk typed something in the computer, waited, and typed again. "Wait…I do have something. We also offer luxury and exotic rentals here. I have a Corvette convertible, midnight blue, with red seats." The clerk looked up. "It's expensive."

"I'll take it," James stated.

James completed the paperwork and charged the car to his credit card. The clerk also printed out a turn-by-turn list of directions to their destination and provided them a free map of the greater Miami area. James secured the maps and paperwork.

They exited the comfort of the air-conditioned terminal into the late-afternoon heat. The oppressive, humid air hit them instantly, and James began to sweat.

"Jesus, it's humid here," Shannon commented.

"And bright," James agreed, donning a pair of sunglasses.

"Let's go back inside and put on shorts."

They ran back into the terminal, went to the appropriate bathrooms, and quickly reemerged. James had also changed out of sneakers and into sandals.

They walked across the street toward the rental-car pick-up lot and searched for the sports car. After a few minutes, James found his Corvette.

"Nice car," Shannon said. "Just don't crash it."

"Don't worry. I took all of their insurance, and then some."

They gave the stylish car a cursory glance and got in. The wax fiberglass hull gleamed. The retracted roof exposed the leather interior, which smelled of polish. The windshield was wiped perfectly clean; not one smudge blemished the surface.

"Wow. I've never picked up a rental looking like this," Shannon commented.

"For the amount I just paid for it, it should come with a driver."

They stored their bags in the small trunk, and lowered themselves into the two-seater. James got acclimated with the various gauges. He felt very low to ground, a driving perspective he was not familiar with. James started the car, and the engine roared to life. He looked down at the shifter and realized that the car had a manual transmission, not an automatic.

"Shit. It's a stick shift. I'm a little rusty with a stick shift," James complained.

"Do you want me to drive?" Shannon offered.

"Drive? You don't even own a car!" James exclaimed. "Let's go." James put the car into gear, and it violently lurched forward and stalled. James tried it again with the same results. On the third attempt, he managed to get the car moving.

"Cross your fingers that Meridian isn't here yet."

Shannon squeezed his arm and nodded.

James pulled onto the access road and slid the car into second and then third gear. As the car picked up speed, the wind caught their hair, blowing it back. James moved his face into the wind, feeling the warm, humid breeze on his face. The long years since he had lived here quickly melted away, and the sights, sounds, and smells of South Florida were suddenly familiar again.

"I forgot how much I loved this place," James said.

"It must have been beautiful to live here."

"It was."

James pulled onto U.S. 1, heading east; palm trees lined the highway. Cruise ships slipped smoothly through Biscayne Bay on the way to the open sea.

James accelerated, shifting the car into fourth and then fifth gear. The white road lines raced by on the jet-black highway. A broad smile spread across his face.

"I could get used to this," he said.

Shannon nodded in agreement as she wiped away a lock of copper hair that had blown into her face.

CHAPTER 22

▼

The landscape on either side of the highway was green and flat, broken up by huge residential developments and strip malls. James had visited friends in Kendall several times during his years at the University of Miami, and he fondly remembered a dark-haired, white-skinned Cuban beauty he had dated off and on. The area was much more built up than he remembered it.

"We're getting close, keep a look out for Flamingo Ridge," James instructed.

James slowed down as they passed a series of developments. They saw their destination, announced by a pink and aqua-blue wooden sign that read "Flamingo Ridge," complete with a relief of a smiling flamingo.

They turned into the development. The houses here were small—two- and three-bedroom stucco ranch homes, definitely on the lower end of the spectrum. Most houses had a screened-in porch jutting off the rear that covered a patio, and many homes had a pool. The homes were set close together and practically identical. They were mostly dark beige, varied only by the shading: pinkish-beige, bluish-beige, and yellowish-beige.

James wound his way around the curved roads until he found his turn. He spotted the pinkish-beige home with an old Pontiac Grand Am in the driveway.

"That's Kelly's car," James pointed out. He drove down the block a few houses farther, then parked. As he and Shannon walked to Kelly's front door, James noticed that although the house had central air conditioning, the unit was silent. The front windows were open, letting in a slight breeze.

James rang the doorbell.

Half a minute later, the door opened.

Standing in the doorway was a tall, slender woman in her late twenties. Her short light brown hair was tucked behind her ears, and she was wearing a Mickey Mouse T-shirt and white shorts. She was barefoot. And very pregnant. She looked at James and then at Shannon. Her mouth dropped open a little, and her eyes widened. "James? What are you doing here?"

"Hiya, Kelly. Can we come in?" James pushed past her into the living room.

Kelly opened the door completely and let Shannon in.

"I don't know you," Kelly said to Shannon.

"I'm sorry. I'm Shannon O'Rourke. I'm James' girlfriend." Shannon gave James a wink. "And I'm a friend of Meridian's." Shannon extended her hand, and Kelly shook it.

Then Kelly turned to James, her hands on her hips. "James, what are you doing here?" she asked again.

James looked around the sparsely furnished living room. The only furniture was a cheap flower-print couch and a matching love seat. "When's the baby due?"

"Any day. You still didn't answer—"

"Why didn't you tell Meridian?"

"I couldn't. It was hard enough to leave. Telling Joe about the baby would have made it impossible. James, you don't understand. I couldn't live in that place anymore. It was killing me. I had to get away from it. All of it."

"You stole his money!" James accused her.

"I had no choice!" Kelly cried, tears forming in her eyes. "I had no choice. Do you know how many times I talked to Joe about leaving? About moving away? He would look at me like I was crazy. He likes it there. He lives for the bars and all that drinking. He *lives* for it."

Kelly paced back and forth across the tiled floor. Tears trickled down her cheeks. "I loved him; I really did. Maybe if we'd been married, things would have been different. We lived together for years, and I waited. I waited for him to do something, to propose or something. And he never did. I don't know—maybe he thought we would just live together for the rest of our lives."

"Kelly, Meridian loved you, too. He still loves you. You're all he thinks about," James said softly.

"Then why didn't he do something about it?" Kelly screamed. "He'd rather be out drinking at the Bell Lap Tavern with you and Vincent than with me!" Kelly dissolved in tears, and James put his arms around her. Tears welled in his eyes. He hugged her as she cried softly on his shoulder.

"Kelly…." James said slowly. "Vincent is dead. A few weeks ago, he…he was murdered. He was shot to death at the Bell Lap."

Kelly looked up into James' eyes, "Oh, my God! James, I'm so sorry."

James brought her up to speed on everything that had happened since she had left Meridian. Kelly listened to all he had to say, contemplating his words. Finally, she spoke. "Do you guys want something to drink?"

James wiped his perspiration-covered forehead. "How about a beer?"

"Can't help you there. The pregnancy, you know." Kelly patted her belly. "I have ice water or lemonade."

James and Shannon settled on lemonade.

Kelly disappeared into the kitchen and came back carrying two tall ice-filled glasses of lemonade. She handed the glasses to them.

"You still haven't told me why you're here," she said to James.

James sighed. "Kelly...we have reason to believe...that is, I think maybe...Meridian might be on his way here, right now."

Kelly gasped. "I knew it! I knew he would come here when he got that letter."

"I know about the letter," James said.

Kelly eyed James and Shannon suspiciously. "So why are you here?"

"To protect you," James said flatly.

"From...?"

"From Meridian. He's coming here to shoot you."

*   *   *   *

Meridian wolfed down the remainder of his Big Mac and washed it down with another long swig of beer. He finished the bottle and threw it into the back of the van with the dozen other bottles he had tossed there since this morning. A half-full case of beer sat on the front passenger seat. Meridian grabbed a fresh beer, now warm, and twisted off the top. He took a swig and placed the bottle between his legs.

He was drunk—and angry.

He grabbed a piece of paper off the passenger seat, a computer generated turn-by-turn list of directions to an address in Kendall, Florida. Meridian continued down Interstate 95 and read the highway sign on the side of the road: Miami—ten miles.

He pressed hard on the accelerator.

He recognized Kelly's car in her driveway. *Good*, he thought. *She's home.*

Meridian opened the driver's side door; a bottle rolled out onto the pavement. Meridian kicked it aside as he walked to the back of his van. His shotgun case was on the floor of the van. He unzipped the case and pulled out his shotgun. Then unzipped a side compartment and pulled out a box of shotgun shells. He studied the row of red cylinders before turning the shotgun over and loading it. He repeated the process five more times.

Meridian pumped the barrel. He heard a shell load in the chamber. He felt for the safety switch and moved it to the "off" position.

"Time to be terminated," he said, in his best Arnold Schwarzenegger voice. Meridian held the shotgun in one hand. He looked up and down the street; it was quiet and empty in the late afternoon. He spied a waxed and polished Corvette convertible parked down the street. *Now if I lived here,* he thought, *that's the kind of car I would drive.* Meridian marched purposefully to the front door and rang the doorbell.

He heard footsteps from inside the house. He steadied the shotgun at the door and waited. The door swung open.

James stood in the doorway, holding a glass of lemonade. He had a casual stance but there was no denying the seriousness of his tone. "Put the gun down, Meridian, and come in," James said evenly. "By the way, you're going to be a father in the next few hours. Kelly's pregnant, and her water just broke. She's going into labor."

Meridian stared at James, bewildered and confused. He lowered the gun, frowning. Slowly, Meridian began to absorb what James told him. The tension seemed to leave his body. "I'm...going to be a father?" he asked.

"You're going to be a father," James repeated.

"I'm going to be a *father!*" Meridian exclaimed. He threw the shotgun into the grass and ran past James into the house. He found Kelly sitting on the couch, breathing in and out deeply. Shannon stood over her, wiping her forehead with a wet cloth.

"We need to get her to the hospital," Shannon said. "Now."

"Kelly!" Meridian shouted. "Kelly, are you okay?"

Kelly breathed in and out rhythmically. She was sweating profusely. She saw Meridian and waggled her fingers at him. "Hi, Joe. I guess you got my letter." Kelly closed her eyes. "I'm really sorry about everything."

Meridian got down on his knees in front of her. He grabbed her hands. "Don't worry about any of that right now. Let's just get you to the hospital."

Kelly put a hand on Meridian's face. Tears were once again in her eyes. "I just heard about Vincent. I am so sorry, Joe. I know how much he meant to you."

Meridian's eyes welled up, and he choked back tears. "Kelly, why did you run away from me?"

Kelly reached for Meridian's hand and placed it on her protruding belly. "Do you feel that? That's our baby kicking? It wants to be born."

Tears ran down Meridian's cheeks.

Shannon tapped his shoulder. "I don't mean to break up your reunion, but we have to get this lady to the hospital."

Meridian stood up, suddenly alert. He gave Kelly a big kiss.

"Yuck," she said. "You smell like McDonald's and beer."

Meridian tried to take charge. "Go get her bag packed—"

"Joe, I'm already packed. The bag is sitting on the floor next to my bed in the bedroom."

James fetched the bag. Meridian and Shannon helped Kelly walk to the door. Kelly grabbed her car keys from the coffee table and handed them to Shannon.

"I think Joe's too drunk to drive," Kelly said.

"What do you mean?" Meridian asked. "I just drove all the way from New Jersey."

James came out of the bedroom with her bag, as well as another smaller bag containing her toiletries. He showed her the smaller bag. "I guessed you would be needing this stuff, too."

"Thanks, James. Today has been a little overwhelming."

Meridian helped Kelly into the passenger seat of her car. Shannon got in the driver's seat.

"I'll follow you to the hospital," James said.

James and Meridian ran down the street to the parked Corvette convertible.

"This is your car?" Meridian asked.

"Sweet, isn't it?" James grinned.

"It must be nice to have your money."

James started the car and smoothly turned it around. He was quickly getting the hang of the stick shift. Meridian snapped his fingers, remembering something; he asked James to pull up in front of the house. Meridian got out, picked up his shotgun off the grass, and turned the safety catch on. Then he stowed the shotgun in its case and locked his van. He ran back to the Corvette.

Shannon backed out of the driveway.

"What the hell were you thinking?" James said. "I can't believe you actually thought about shooting her."

Meridian stared at his hands. "Aw, I wasn't going to do anything. I was just going to scare her."

"Right," James said, giving Meridian a sideways glance.

"Just pay attention to your driving, huh?" Meridian said defensively. "Lady with a baby."

*   *   *   *

James, Meridian, and Shannon sat in the well-lit waiting area of the maternity ward; they didn't have long to wait. After arriving at the hospital, Kelly was in labor less than an hour before giving birth. A doctor came out and announced, "It's a girl!"

"A girl?" Meridian repeated. "I have a baby girl!"

Meridian had been offered the opportunity to watch the birth, but he declined. He was a little old-fashioned that way. Still, in the flurry of packing to come to Florida to shoot Kelly, it had not occurred to him to pack a camera. Meridian stood up, holding a disposable camera that he had purchased at a small gift shop located off the main lobby of the hospital.

James and Shannon hugged Meridian. Meridian took three cheap cigars out of his back pocket—also purchased at the hospital shop—and handed one each to James and Shannon.

"Congratulations, Meridian," James and Shannon said simultaneously.

The doctor, a thin Cuban woman, stood in the hallway. "Would you like to meet your daughter?" she asked with a smile.

James clapped Meridian on the back. "Let's go, Dad," he said.

Kelly was propped up in bed, holding her newly swaddled daughter. A nurse stood at her side, giving her instructions. Kelly's hair was a sweaty mop, but she radiated health. Her skin glowed, and her eyes shone. She gazed at her daughter in amazement and awe.

"That was the one of the quickest deliveries I've ever done," the doctor said. "That baby wanted to be born. And Kelly, you did really well." She turned to address Meridian. "Mommy and baby are healthy."

Meridian blew Kelly a kiss, snapped a dozen pictures, and then approached the bed. "Can I hold her?" Meridian asked.

Kelly nodded. The nurse gently picked up the baby and positioned Meridian's arms. Then she placed the baby in Meridian's cradling grasp.

"Put your other hand under her head," the nurse instructed, moving his hand. "Like this."

Meridian gazed into his daughter's face, and then into Kelly's.

"She looks just like you," he said softly.

"That's funny, because I think she looks just like you," Kelly responded.

The nurse took Meridian's camera, and snapped a few pictures of him holding his daughter.

"What should we name her?" Meridian asked.

"I have the biggest sunflowers growing in the backyard of that house I'm renting. How about Sunflower?"

Meridian frowned. "Isn't that kind of a hippie name?"

Kelly bargained. "Joe, I'll let you pick the middle name."

Meridian thought for a few minutes. "Well, if you're going to scar her for life by naming her Sunflower, I guess it wouldn't be the end of the world if I gave her Vincent as a middle name."

"How about Vincensa?" James offered. "At least that's female."

"Sunflower Vincensa Chippendale," Kelly said, rolling the name over her tongue. She beamed. "I think it has a nice ring to it.

James and Shannon looked at each other with raised eyebrows and chuckled.

Sunflower began to cry.

"I think Baby is hungry," the nurse said. She took the baby from Meridian, and helped Kelly get the infant attached to a nipple. It took a little work, but eventually the baby latched on and suckled softly.

"That feels a little weird," Kelly commented.

"Can Daddy go next?" Meridian joked.

Everyone cringed.

The doctor motioned James and Shannon to the door. "Let's give them a little time alone to bond with their baby," she suggested.

Meridian pulled up a rocking chair and sat next to Kelly, watching his daughter.

After a while, he cleared his throat, unsure how to begin. "What do we do now, Kelly?"

She sighed and looked away. "I'm not going back, Joe. I'm never going back there. I've been enrolled at Miami-Dade College since January, and I can get my bachelor's degree in about a year if I go straight through. I've got a good job, working nights as a cocktail waitress at Shooters on South Beach. Until I get my degree, I'll get by. Then if all goes well, I can get a job at a local bank, maybe even work my way up to branch manager."

"What about the baby?" Meridian asked.

"There are a lot of kids in my neighborhood and a lot of old ladies to watch them. I already have that taken care of."

Meridian frowned. "What about me?"

Kelly shrugged. "What about you? Joe, go back to New Jersey. Go back to your life. I love you, Joe, but I can't live with you anymore. I need to give my daughter something better."

"What if I married you, Kelly? Would you come back then?"

Kelly gave a short laugh, and her eyes welled up. "Joe, haven't you listened to a word I've said? I am not moving back there. Ever. I am done with that life."

Meridian's eyes filled with tears as well. "Okay, Kelly. I don't understand, but it's your life. You need to do what you think is right."

Kelly smiled. "It's going to be okay, Joe. We're going to be fine."

Meridian swiped at his eyes. "I'll send money for her. Every month. And I'm going to come visit every chance I get. I still want to be her father."

Kelly nodded. "That would be nice, Joe." They sat in silence, staring at their baby. Finally, Kelly spoke. "Joe, I'm feeling sleepy. I need a nap."

Meridian got up and kissed Kelly. He softly stroked the baby's head, then leaned over and kissed her, too. "Good-bye, Kelly," he whispered.

Kelly's eyes welled up again with tears. "Good-bye, Joe."

James and Shannon were reading magazines in the waiting area when Meridian joined them.

"What's going on?" James asked.

"I'm going home," he replied flatly.

"What? You're not going to stay—"

"I'm going home," Meridian said more forcibly. "That's what she wants." Meridian gave them both a hug. "Just take me back to my van, okay?"

"All right," James agreed, "but Shannon is going to have to sit on your lap."

Meridian forced a laugh. "Don't worry. I won't fondle her too much."

Shannon laughed. "Right. Not if you want to keep your hand."

They drove back to Kelly's house, and Meridian got into his van without another word. He started it up, and waved as he drove off.

"You know, Shannon," James said, "now that we're here, we might as well stay a few days. I can show you around, and we can bum on the beach."

Shannon rubbed her chin. "I don't know, James, I've got a lot going on at the office."

"You've always got a lot going on at the office. C'mon—live a little," he coaxed her.

She threw up her arms. "Why the hell not? Let's stay."

James smiled broadly. "That's my girl. Let's head down to Miami Beach and find ourselves a hotel."

James put the car into gear, and they drove off into the clear, warm Miami night.

CHAPTER 23

▼

James and Meridian untied the rear lines that held the *Ragin' Cajun* to the wooden dock, freeing the boat from the slip.

"All clear, Dad!" James yelled up to the command bridge. Booby waved, just barely hearing him above the roar of the twin-diesel engines. He put the boat into gear, and started for the exit to the marina.

James steadied himself on the deck, feeling the vibration of the engines through his boat shoes. He moved over to the large ice-filled chest that was secured against the rear of the boat; he flipped open the lid.

The chest was meant for fish, and the men were hoping for a good catch, but it also doubled as a beer cooler. James reached in and pulled out two cans of ice cold beer. As the beer came out, the fish would go in, or so the theory was.

James moved back across the deck and handed one of the beers to Meridian, who was reclining in the "fighting chair," a sturdy swivel job bolted to the boat in the middle of the rear deck.

"This is a gorgeous day!" Meridian yelled above the din.

James saluted Meridian, and grabbed on to the back of the chair for support. He took a small sip of his beer.

It was early, not yet nine o'clock, but it was already hot and sunny. By noon, it would be very hot and very sunny. It was the middle of July, and heat was usually what you could expect.

James adjusted his baseball cap and sunglasses. The air was still, the only breeze coming from the movement of the boat.

The *Ragin' Cajun* pulled around a dock and entered the channel that led to the Hudson River, which led past New York Bay, and eventually, to the Atlantic

Ocean. The destination today were the rocky shoals off of Sandy Hook, and the fish was fluke. And if that spot was dry, Booby had several others to try.

This was to be an easy day of fishing and beer drinking and a little swimming. Work had been slow for the last few weeks, as was to be expected during the dog days of summer. At the last minute, Booby asked James if he wanted to take a Friday day trip, and James was more than happy to oblige. He didn't have to twist Meridian's arm to go, either.

The trip didn't matter much to Booby, as during the summer months he spent more time on his boat than just about anywhere else. It also kept him out of Jane Cameron's hair, which suited both of them just fine.

The Jersey City marina was a community in and of itself, a community in which all boaters had a warm camaraderie. The boaters, as a group, spent more time on their boats docked at the marina than they did on the ocean. They loved to sit on their boats, talk about their boats, and talk about what they were going to add to their boats. And as a group, they loved to sit on their boats and sip cocktails. And grill. That suited Booby just fine, too.

The boating community was a friendly group. If one group went out and brought in a lot of fish, they would gladly share the fish with anyone within ear-shot. More often than not, a good fish catch was an excuse for an impromptu fish fry, which in boating terms meant party. The fish would get cooked up; some-body would appear with a pitcher of margaritas or a case of beer; somebody would crank up their custom five-hundred-watt, twenty-speaker, in-hull stereo system; and the party was on.

It was, very simply, a nice life.

James admired the long line of boats docked in well-maintained slips on each side of the channel. Pleasure craft came in all shapes and sizes, from small out-board single-engine models to several eighty- and ninety-foot yachts that were moored closer to the entrance of the river.

James and Meridian waved to the occasional people moving about their boats, and some waved back.

The *Ragin' Cajun* was an older boat but big, heavy, and sturdy. She could handle good-sized waves and could make decent headway, even in a storm. She was equipped with two powerful diesel engines and was built for fishing.

There are two types of pleasure boaters: people who like to cruise and people who like to fish. Booby was the latter, and the *Cajun* reflected it. She bristled with outriggers and electronics, and nets and poles were strapped to her sides.

If there was one thing that Booby liked as much as a martini, it was sports fish-ing. Every year he would go on three or four overnight trips, out to the edge of the continental shelf to a place called "the Canyon," where the bigger sports fish, like tuna and swordfish, rode the Gulf Stream all the way up from the equator. Those were the fish that required the use of the outriggers and the fighting chair. They fought, and fought hard. They were the fish that true fishermen dreamed of.

For some, fishing was a passion, an addiction. For some, struggling for an hour to reel in an eighty- or ninety-pound tuna was the most exhilarating thing they ever experienced. Booby had long ago tasted the sea life, and it had taken hold of him.

James placed his beer in a cup holder that was attached to the arm of the fighting chair. He told Meridian that he was going to stand up on the command bridge. Meridian gave him the thumb's up, and off James went.

James climbed the ladder that led to the command bridge and stood next to his father. Booby smiled and took a sip of coffee that was in a cup holder next to the steering wheel. The radio crackled with local chatter, mostly one boat trying to tell another boat, in some kind of cryptic code, where the fish were. There was a healthy respect, a silent code of honor, within the fishing community, but that didn't mean they went out of their way to tell each other where the fish were. The location and density of whatever fish happened to be running that day was a closely guarded secret.

Booby cleared the end of the channel and waved to a sharply dressed yacht captain in pressed whites, who was leaning against the rail on one the larger boats.

"Now that's a boat!" James said.

"Yeah, that's nice…but you can't fish off of it," Booby replied.

The *Cajun* reached open sea, and Booby throttled up the engines. A volume of white water bubbled up over the propeller, and as the engines were pushed harder, two plumes of spray jetted out behind the boat, creating a substantial wake. James could feel the boat rise a little in the water, and the wind whipped his face. James grabbed the back of Booby's chair with one hand, and with the other, held his hat on the top of his head.

They motored toward the Statue of Liberty and New York Bay. The *Cajun* bounced over the waves. They came up to a smaller, slower boat, a Bayliner, and passed it. Two girls sat on the front deck, dressed in bikinis. The men smiled and waved as they rode by. James noticed that the name of the boat was written in blue script across the rear: *Retirement Spent*. James laughed.

One boating custom was to give your boat a cute—or better yet, a cute and clever—name. The *Ragin' Cajun* was not named by Booby but by the original owner, who was a real-estate developer in the New Orleans area. The *Cajun* had spent the first twenty years of her existence enjoying the slow life in the Caribbean, meandering from one island to the next. Unfortunately, the owner contracted a rare form of cancer, and she put the boat up for sale.

Booby saw the boat advertised in the classifieds section of a boating magazine, and he immediately contacted the owner. They couldn't come to an agreement on price, but about a year later, the guy still hadn't sold the *Cajun*, and so he called Booby back. This time, the man was on his deathbed. Booby got the boat at less than his original offer, and the former owner even agreed to pay for the transportation expense of getting it to New Jersey. Talk about kicking a guy when he's down.

Booby took possession of the *Ragin' Cajun,* and everyone debated over what to rename her. After much deliberation, the SS *Booby* was the most popular choice. Just as he was about to make the change, Booby recanted, and left the original name, in honor of the original owner. Plus, Booby had decided that a name change would be bad luck. And he saved five hundred bucks on the repainting.

Meridian climbed up onto the command deck, carrying two open beers.

"You're beer is going to get warm," he scolded James, as he handed him the beverage.

James took the beer, smiled, and took a big gulp. "I guess I can't forget who I'm on this trip with today. The beer police."

James and Meridian sat on either side of Booby and enjoyed the ride out to the Atlantic Ocean. They passed Lower Manhattan, and then turned out to sea.

Meridian gazed at the Lower Manhattan skyline, making note of the obvious void. He turned to James. "Do you still think about that meeting you had on 9/11?"

James shrugged. "Sometimes. Not that often, anymore."

Meridian nodded. "I'll feel better when they finally put something back up there. That view seems empty without a big building there."

Booby, who had been concentrating on the driving, turned around and grinned. "And there's going to be a whole bunch of work when they do start construction on a new Trade Center, booby!" he yelled.

The three men laughed, and saluted each other.

Meridian finished his beer. "Who's ready for another round?"

"I could use a fresh beer," James said.

"None for me," Booby answered.

"What's wrong?" Meridian asked.

"I don't like to drink when I'm in charge of the boat. You have to be careful out here now, booby," Booby replied.

Meridian gave Booby a funny look. "You're getting old, Booby."

The *Ragin' Cajun* motored purposefully through the waves in New York Bay toward the Atlantic Ocean. Off in the distance, huge commercial transport ships formed a column heading to port. Gulls and other seabirds flew lazily over the boat, looking for leftover bait; they were early. Channel markers and buoys bobbed in the water, and Booby navigated through them. A light-gray navy cruiser passed in front of them, and Booby had to throttle back to ride over the massive wake the vessel left behind.

"It's busy out here," James commented.

"Always," Booby replied.

Meridian climbed back up with two fresh beers and took his seat. He tossed a beer to James, who opened it to a pop of fizzy foam.

The ride to Sandy Hook took about an hour, and Booby slowed and concentrated on the fish finder. They crisscrossed the rocky shoals for another half hour, until they got several solid sonar hits in a row. Booby slowed the boat even more, and looked at the water to see how the tides were moving. He turned the boat around and rode for a quarter-mile and then stopped. He shut the engine off.

"We'll drift back over the area where I just got the hit, and, I hope, catch some fish," he explained.

The three men moved back downstairs and worked together to rig up three rods; they cut up the bait squid into small pieces. Soon, three rods were in the water, lines weighted down and bouncing off the bottom. James and Booby sat in cushioned deck chairs situated on either side of the fighting chair, in which Meridian lounged, feet propped up on the cooler.

The silence was pleasant, and the small sounds of waves and birds were clear now that the engine noise was gone. The sun was rising, and James felt the rays intensify on his skin.

They sat quietly and sipped their beer, waiting.

Booby lit a cigarette, took a drag, and squinted across the water.

"How's the knee, Booby?" Meridian asked.

Booby continued to stare out across water and flexed his leg. "Feeling good. Still a little stiff at times, but it's going to be fine."

"I'm glad to see you bounced back so fast. You had me worried."

"Just got to keep a positive attitude, booby," he grinned. He blew a ring of smoke out over the back of the boat.

"So, are you still set on naming your steakhouse the Mad Cow?"

"Yeah, that's going to be the name."

"I still like 'A Taste of Booby,'" Meridian teased.

"What?" Booby asked.

"A Taste of Booby. That's the name I came up with for the restaurant."

Booby laughed. "That's funny. I hadn't heard that one before."

The three men grew relaxed by the gentle rocking of the boat. James took a sip of beer. "So, Meridian," he said, "have you talked to Kelly since you got back from our...our trip?"

Meridian took a big gulp of beer and belched. "Yeah, I've talked to her a bunch of times. Actually, I talk to her for a few minutes every day."

"Oh? About what?"

"Everything. The baby, of course. Kelly's school. Her job. She's been really nice on the phone."

"Yeah, now that you're more than a thousand miles away," Booby teased.

Meridian frowned and belched again. He took a huge pull on his beer, finished it, and crushed the can empty on his head. He reached into the cooler, pulled out another one, and popped the top. "I'm going to go back down and spend a week or two with her in August. She said it was all right. You know, help out with Sunflower—"

"Who?" Booby interrupted.

"Sunflower. That's my daughter's name."

"How—?"

"Don't ask!" Meridian finished. "I'm going to go down and spend some time with my daughter." Meridian stared at Booby to see if he had any further comments. "And I'll spend some time with Kelly, too. I'll help out around the house, buy the kid some stuff—you know, try to make myself seem useful."

James slapped Meridian on the back. "Who knows, Meridian? Maybe there's hope for you two after all."

Meridian shrugged. "I don't know, James. Kelly and I have been together for so long, and we have been through so much, that I'm not sure we can put it back together. We have different views on a lot of things. We always did. When we were younger, those things weren't that big a deal. But as you get older...." Meridian's thoughts trailed off, and he looked out over the water, watching the sunshine glint off the surface of the ocean. He refocused his thoughts. "At the very least, I'm going to be there for Sunflower. I'm not going to give her up. Maybe if I show Kelly I'm committed to our daughter...maybe things will get better for us, too."

"How are you feeling about all of this?" James asked.

Meridian gave him a dirty look. "What are you? My goddamn shrink?" He took a drink of beer. "I'm actually feeling a lot better, thank you. What was killing me was the not knowing. That's what bothered me. Not knowing where she was…why she left. But now that I know where she is, and I know she's okay…I feel okay, too. Okay?"

James smiled. "Okay, therapy is over."

At that moment, James' line started to bounce. James turned and gripped his reel and yanked the tip up. He felt the familiar tug, and he pulled up the rod and turned the reel. "Fish on!" he yelled.

Simultaneously, Booby and Meridian hooked onto fish, too.

The conversation stopped, and for the next thirty minutes, the three men reeled in fish. Each time they pulled up a fish, someone was there with the net or pliers to free the fish, measure it, and either toss it in the cooler or throw it back in the ocean. They would quickly rebait the pole and drop it back into the water. James' first fish was a keeper, a big one, about twenty-five inches long. Each man pulled in half a dozen fish, with a couple of good-sized keepers apiece.

After the initial activity died down, Booby climbed back up onto the command bridge. He started the engines and headed back up-tide. He drove for about a quarter-mile and then stopped the boat again.

The *Ragin' Cajun* made another pass, but this time they only caught two fish each, with one keeper. The school had moved on, and now it was time to find the fish again.

The men were in no hurry, and all three lounged on the back deck, now stinking of fish, basking in the sun.

"That was a good run!" Booby said, as he eyed the cooler. "Maybe it *is* time for a beer."

"That's the Booby I know and love!" Meridian cheered. Meridian opened the cooler, and a gray-green fluke flopped up and hit the top of the lid.

"Down boy!" Meridian commanded, as he reached in and rummaged around the fish for a cold beer. He pulled one out and flipped it to Booby.

Booby popped the beer, saluted Meridian, and took a long pull. He lit another cigarette and sat back in his chair.

"You know," Meridian said pensively, "I wouldn't complain if Kelly and I did get back together someday."

"Look on the bright side, Meridian. Life is long, and we are young. I'm optimistic that things are going to turn out fine for you," James replied.

"You are starting to sound like your father."

"Nothing wrong with being an optimist, booby!" Booby grinned.

The three men sat on the boat, enjoying the perfect summer afternoon.

They returned to the dock about five o'clock, after fishing and swimming for the rest of the afternoon. The catch was good, almost two dozen keepers. The men felt fine, tanned, and relaxed.

Booby backed the *Ragin' Cajun* into its slip, and James and Meridian threw the dock lines to a couple of Booby's dock mates. They secured the boat to the dock and tied off the bow to the forward post.

A tall, muscular Jamaican named Ben, who had a boat down at the end of the dock, came over. Ben was a true lover of the sea and of boats. In fact, he lived on his. He was an expert filet man, the fastest in the marina. He would take care of your catch, as long as you took care of him.

"Hey, Booby, how'd you do out there today, man? I heard the fish were a jumpin'!"

"We caught some nice keepers, booby!"

Ben jumped up onto boat and opened the top of the ice chest. "You did catch some nice fish! Want me to take care of them, man?"

"Be my guest, Ben," Booby replied.

Ben grabbed the chest, and Meridian helped carry it off the boat to one of the few filleting stations on the docks. Ben took out the first fish and deftly removed the head and tail. He sliced open the fish and quickly cut two perfect filets.

A few other people who James recognized came over, but he made his introductions again anyway.

"Fish fry?" one asked.

"How about a martini, Booby?" another offered.

James looked at Meridian. "I guess we're not going anywhere."

"Fine by me," Meridian replied. "I'm starving."

Someone rolled out a grill and started it up.

A pitcher of margaritas appeared. James poured himself one and handed one to Meridian.

"Should be a fun evening!" James exclaimed, taking a big sip of his margarita.

*   *   *   *

James awoke with a start. He heard a splash and muffled noises coming from outside. His head pounded. He squinted at his watch. It was after three in the morning. James tried to remember where he was.

He was sitting at the center table in the main cabin. He forced open his eyes and surveyed his surroundings. Bright moonlight streamed through the small rectangular windows, casting the cabin in a colorless gray-white pall. An empty bottle of scotch whiskey sat on the table. Beside that sat a half-empty bottle of tequila. James remembered those bottles being new when the night had started.

Slowly, James began to remember. Fish fry. They'd had a fish fry. And margaritas. Lots of margaritas. Then the sun went down, and they'd made their way up and down the dock, hanging out on one boat after another. They drank more. A lot more. The hours melted away.

Finally, they found themselves back on the *Ragin' Cajun*, drinking scotch, laughing drunkenly, too drunk to even converse, but still drinking. That's the last thing James remembered. Now that the alcohol was wearing off, he was left with a huge headache and an intense feeling of nausea.

James tried to get up, lost balance, and sat back down. He heard splashing and yelling. He slowly realized it was Booby. Booby was outside—and in the water.

James forced himself up and staggered out of the cabin, onto the back deck. The moonlight shone brightly, which to James felt like sunlight. He squinted to ease the pounding in his head.

"Dad, where are you?" he yelled.

James looked over the side of the boat into the water. Just in front of the boat, swimming in the water, Booby floundered and splashed. Booby dived under the water. James had no idea what he was doing.

James climbed off the boat and ran down the thin wood-planked decking that separated the slips until he reached the end of the dock. He waited for his father to surface. Booby broke the water and gulped for air.

"Dad! What the hell are you doing?"

"Meridian fell in! Meridian fell in!"

"Oh, shit!" James yelled. He kicked off his sandals and dove into the water.

Booby and James swam around the dock for several minutes, trying to find Meridian. In the moonlight, the water was ink-black, and finding anything meant physically swimming into it.

James dove under and swam a few dozen yards. He surfaced. He dove under again and swam back toward the dock. He hit his head on the pier, underwater, and swore to himself. He came up for air. He dove a few more times, crisscrossing the area in front of the *Cajun*.

Meridian was nowhere to be found. James began to tire, and he looked for his father. Booby had gone under but had still not surfaced. James began treading water, listening for Booby. Thirty seconds went by. Nothing.

James began to panic. He swam out into the middle of the channel and dove under the water, arms outstretched, feeling for anything. His head slammed right into his father's, coming up from the bottom. James saw a blinding white flash and felt a sharp pain. Then he felt nothing, and he lost awareness of everything.

Don't black out, he commanded himself.

James forced himself back to consciousness and grabbed his father's arm, which was strangely limp. James looked for the surface but had lost direction. The water all around him was black. James tried to relax and let out some air. He grabbed his father, picked a direction, and kicked hard.

James broke water and gasped for air. He pulled on his father, making sure that Booby's nose had cleared the surface. Bone tired, James swam for the dock. He grabbed hold of one of the planks with one arm. He held onto Booby for dear life with the other.

"Help!" he yelled. "Somebody help!"

James yelled and yelled. Soon, he felt himself slipping. He was grabbed by two strong arms. Ben!

"Don't worry, man, I got you!" Ben assured him.

Ben pulled James up onto the deck and helped get Booby out of the water. James lay flat on his back on the dock, dazed and hugging his father. Booby slowly came back to consciousness.

"What is goin' on, man? What are you doin' in the water?" Ben asked.

Booby choked and spit up some water. His eyelids fluttered, and he rolled over onto his knees.

"Booby said Meridian…fell into the water," James gasped. "We need to find him."

Ben frowned. "We better be callin' the police…."

CHAPTER 24

▼

Searchlights beamed up and down each side of the pier, along the docks and slips, and across the channel that separated them. A Coast Guard cutter moved slowly, and a dozen eyes were on the water.

James stood with Booby off the back of the *Ragin' Cajun*, sipping coffee and speaking to a police officer. Several more officers stood around, speaking to the other boaters who had now awakened and either sat on the backs of their boats or stood on the docks.

The officer, a New Jersey state police officer—as the marina was technically on state park property—shone a pen flashlight into Booby's eyes and then James'. He refocused his attention on Booby.

"And how much did you drink, tonight, sir?"

"A lot…I don't know…I had a good amount," Booby slurred.

"And what was the nature of your relationship with the missing man?"

"Employee…he works for me."

"And he just fell overboard?"

"No…I don't know…I heard a noise."

"What happened then?"

"I heard a noise…I thought he fell in the water…and I went in after him."

The officer studied Booby and James. He walked away from them, conferred with some other officers, and then returned. He looked at his notepad. "Were you and…Mr. Meridian involved in any kind of disagreement or altercation tonight?"

Booby looked confused. "No ossifer…I mean, officer, I told you. He works for me."

"He's your employee, and you socialize with him?"

"He's…my son's friend."

"What kind of employee is he?"

"Technician…union. He's our shop steward."

"He's the union representative for all the union employees in your company?"

"Yes, but it's not what you think…we're a family business."

"Have you been having labor difficulties lately?"

Booby rolled his eyes. "Well, yeah, sure, booby. We always have labor issues."

James listened to the conversation and cringed.

"And you claim that Mr. Meridian just fell into the water?"

"Yeah…I'm not sure."

"Why aren't you sure?" the officer asked quickly.

James stepped in front of his father, a little too close to the officer. "Look, sir, I don't know what you think happened here tonight, but Meridian is one of our—"

The officer stepped back and shone his light in James' eyes. "I am not directing my questions to you at the moment, Mr. Cameron. You need to step back, or I will have you restrained."

"Yes, sir," James said meekly.

"Both of you gentlemen, wait right here."

The officer stepped away and conferred again with several other officers. The searchlight from the Coast Guard ship swept across the dock. Radios crackled in the still night air.

The officer came back. "Mr. Cameron—" He indicated Booby and then pointed at James. "And Mr. Cameron, I am going to have to ask you to come with me for questioning. If you would, please come this way." The officer turned to leave, and two other officers moved close to Booby and James to help escort them to the waiting car.

"What the hell is going on!" a familiar voice boomed from the end of the dock. Walking down the wood planking, dressed only in shorts, was Meridian. "It's loud as the hounds of hell out here!" he complained.

"Meridian!" Booby and James exclaimed. They ran up to him and hugged him.

"Okay, okay. What is going on?" Meridian asked.

"Where were you?" Booby asked.

"You were snoring too loud, so I went to sleep in the back of my van."

James rolled his eyes.

Meridian looked around and noticed the cadre of Jersey City police, New Jersey state police, and—sitting out in the water next to the *Ragin' Cajun*—a Coast Guard cutter. "Did somebody start a war?" Meridian asked.

"We thought you fell in the water," James explained.

The officer in charge identified Meridian and called off the search. The Coast Guard left, as did the Jersey City police.

The officer angrily approached Booby. "Mr. Cameron, next time you decide to call the police, please check to make sure the person that you claim is missing is actually missing. You created a big mess here tonight." He shone his penlight in Booby's drunken eyes. "I promise you, there will be fines."

"Yes, ossifer…officer," Booby replied.

"I suggest the lot of you go to bed…and sleep it off."

"Yes, officer."

"And if I have to come back here tonight, I'm going to arrest you, and you can sleep it off in jail."

"Yes, officer."

The officer scratched his chin. "Well, have a good night, then."

James glared at his father. "You know, Dad, I have been on the ass end of a police flashlight way too much lately. And I'm really getting sick of it. In fact, I'm just about sick of everything around here."

Booby looked drunkenly at his son and shrugged.

James continued. "Do you have any idea how screwed up our lives are? Do you think this is how normal people live, Dad? Do you? Every direction I turn in I'm looking at either somebody getting drunk, somebody getting high, somebody getting arrested, or somebody getting dead. And I am fucking sick of it."

There was silence. The dock made a creaking noise, and water lapped up against its side.

Meridian burped. "I don't know what time it is, but I sure could go for a Freddy pie."

*   *   *   *

"Hello?" Shannon answered the phone. She had just gotten out of the shower, and water dripped from her arms and legs.

"It's James."

Shannon rubbed a towel over her hair with one hand as she spoke. "Are you coming in tonight, or do you want me to come out there?"

"Shannon, did you have a good time with me in Florida?" James' voice was tense, and his speech was sharp. He was holding his head in his hands, trying to ease the throbbing.

Shannon stopped drying her hair and sat down. "What's wrong, James?"

"Did you have a good time with me in Florida?" he repeated.

"Sure…yeah, of course I did. James, what's happened now?"

James gave her a brief overview of the previous night's debacle.

Shannon sighed. "You know, James, I would like to feel sorry for you, but you bring a lot of this stuff down on yourself. Nobody told you to drink until you were blind drunk, and nobody told you to dive in after your father."

There was a long pause on the other end of the phone before James spoke again. "I know, Shannon. I know. But—and you have to believe me when I tell you this—I am ready to change. I'm finally ready to make a change. Last night was the last straw. Maybe Kelly is right. Maybe there are certain people who were born for this place…my father…Meridian. And maybe there are certain people who weren't. I was never meant for a life here, Shannon. I know that now."

The line was quiet.

"Shannon? Are you listening?"

"I'm still here James," Shannon said gently.

"Shannon, my father and Meridian, these…situations, events, problems, whatever you want to call them…this shit does not faze them. This life rolls off of them like water off of a duck. I almost died, Shannon. I could have died. My father could have died. But today, life is going to go on like nothing ever happened."

"It is pretty strange, the things that happen to the people in your life."

"You know, Booby could die tragically tomorrow, or live until he's one hundred. And I have no idea which way it's going to go, but I wouldn't be surprised by either outcome."

"I know what you mean. What do you want to do, James?"

"Did you like Florida? Did you like Miami?"

"What are you asking me, James?"

"Come to Florida with me, Shannon. Move with me to Florida. Let's start over."

"James…I don't know. Are you sure? You're probably really tired, and really hung over right now. And I can tell you're upset. Are you sure you should be making these kinds of decisions today?"

"I've never been more sure of anything in my entire life."

Shannon considered the conversation. "What are you going to do in Miami, James? What do you have in mind?"

"I still have some friends from school who live in the area. And Kelly is there. I can look in on her from time to time for Meridian. And I want to get back to doing what I always loved. Working with words. I was a journalism major before I switched to business, you know."

"I remember your telling me."

"Well, I was thinking about trying to get a job with the *Miami Herald* or the *Fort Lauderdale Star Telegram*. I can go back to school and take some more classes, if I have to. And doesn't your company have an office in Miami?"

"They have a sales office. It's not big. I guess I could try to relocate...I really need to think about this, James."

"There's one problem, though."

"Only one?" Shannon chided.

"I'm not going to make a lot of money as a newspaper reporter. Not that I make a ton of money now, but I would probably take a big pay cut to work for a paper. At least, at the beginning."

Shannon laughed. "James, I've told you a hundred times: I don't need anyone to take care of me. I make pretty good money for myself."

"I know you do," James agreed.

"Don't worry; I wouldn't let you turn into a freeloader. I would make you find something worthwhile to do."

"Shannon, the Mad Cow is having its big grand opening in two weeks. Saturday night. I was planning on telling my father at the end of the night that I'm leaving. I would really like it if you decided to come with me."

"James, I really need to think about this. I can't promise you anything right now."

"Shannon...you need to know...that either way...*I'm* going to Florida."

"I understand."

"Do you still want me to come over tonight?" James asked.

"No. Not tonight, James. I really need to think about this."

"All right then. I'll call you tomorrow."

"Okay, James. Call me tomorrow."

Shannon curled up on her couch and looked out her window at the Hudson River and the Jersey City skyline. She wrapped her towels around her, and she began to cry.

CHAPTER 25

▼

James and Shannon parked in the newly paved lot, where the strong smell of tar was still in the air.

"Will you look at that," James said as they walked toward the front door.

Booby had redone the outside of the restaurant in white stucco, and mounted around the top perimeter of the building was a thick wood molding, painted green. A new rich-looking oak door, also painted green, stood open. Sitting on a platform above the door was a statue of a cow: It was sitting up, tongue hanging out to one side, and it was wrapped in a straightjacket. Large block letters above the statue spelled out "The Mad Cow."

Shannon laughed and pointed at the statue. "That is too funny."

"My father never ceases to surprise me," James said.

James had dressed in his best suit for the occasion. Shannon was wearing a new dark-green summer dress, high heels, and the jewelry that James had bought her. Her copper hair gleamed in the fading light.

Standing just inside the door was Russell, dressed in a tuxedo. His face beamed.

"Russell, you are looking fabulous!"

Russell held out his hand, and James and Shannon shook it. "Welcome to opening night. You are going to be impressed."

"I'm already impressed," James replied. "Hey, where did you guys get that cow?"

Russell put his finger up to his lips and made a shushing sound. "That's a trade secret."

The interior temperature of the Mad Cow was cool, even a little cold, in stark contrast to the heat and humidity outside. A new, waxed wood floor gleamed from the light that emanated from a large crystal chandelier hanging in the center of the room, as well as candlelight from the crystal holders sitting on each of the twenty-plus white-linen-covered tables. Each table was surrounded by four or six overstuffed red-leather chairs.

The walls were newly plastered, painted stark white. Prints of various French-themed artists encased in thick frames were placed in appropriate spots. Framing the walls was a dark wainscoting. Against one wall was a massive fireplace with a marble hearth and mantle. Even though it was summer, a fire roared.

Against the other wall, a new bar had been built and was richly finished, with a thick mahogany ridge and detailed cornice. The bar, also newly waxed, gleamed. Standing at the bar, dressed in a tuxedo, was Booby. A fresh three-olive martini sat on the counter.

"James! Shannon! Come on in. Welcome to opening night!" He motioned for them to join him at the bar.

"Are we early?" James asked.

"Right on time, booby. You know how people are. Everyone is coming tonight. It's going to be great!" Booby smiled. Booby took a small sip of his martini. "James, I have to show you this." He got up and walked behind the bar and flicked a switch, and it was then that James noticed the counter was not wood but a dark Plexiglass. James watched at the glass glowed a deep red.

"That is cool!" James exclaimed.

"Keep watching," Booby instructed.

The counter slowly turned from red to yellow to green and back to red again.

"Now that is too cool."

"Can I get you drink?" Booby offered.

James and Shannon each ordered a glass of Cabernet.

Booby pulled out two wide-rimmed wine glasses from a suspended glass cabinet. He poured two glasses of Cabernet, handed one first to Shannon, and then to James. Booby picked up his martini and made a toast. "To the Mad Cow!" he saluted.

"To the Mad Cow" they echoed.

They sipped their drinks.

"Dad, I have to say, this place is fantastic. It turned out better than I ever would have expected."

Booby winked. "Just wait until you taste the steak."

Booby looked at his watch. "I'm sorry, but you need to excuse me. I have to check on the kitchen and make sure everything is ready."

Booby disappeared through swinging doors into the kitchen, which James could see was bustling with activity.

James and Shannon sat at the bar. James gazed into Shannon's eyes and took her hand, giving it a light squeeze. "So…what have you decided, then?"

"I was going to wait until the end of dinner to give you my answer," she replied coyly.

"Well, maybe this will speed things up." James reached into his pocket and pulled out a small black box. He placed it on the bar in front of Shannon.

"Is that what I think it is?" she asked.

"Go ahead and open it."

Shannon tentatively picked up the box and held it in her hands. She slowly lifted the lid. Inside rested a magnificent diamond ring. Shannon opened the lid fully and stared at the ring. Light danced off the diamond, and it sparkled in the candlelight.

"Shannon, will you marry me?"

Shannon was silent for a moment, as she stared at the ring. She locked eyes with James. "Wow, James. You're hitting me with a lot lately."

James moved in closer and kissed Shannon lightly on the lips. He put his arms around her. "Marry me, Shannon," he whispered in her ear.

"I love you, James," she said softly. "I would love to marry you." Shannon sat up in her seat. "Yes, James," she said confidently. "I will marry you."

James smiled broadly, took the ring out of the box, and placed it on her finger.

"Now, we don't have to actually get married tomorrow," he said. "We can wait a year or two to plan the wedding. You know, so we can do it right."

Shannon kissed him. "I love you James," she said.

"So does this mean that you've agreed to move with me to Miami?"

Shannon smiled and pinched his cheek.

Booby came out from the kitchen. "Everything is all set!" he told them.

James held up Shannon's hand, presenting the diamond ring to his father. "Shannon and I are getting married."

Booby stopped, frozen in his place. He stared at the ring, seemingly dumbstruck. "James," he said slowly, "you're getting married?"

"Dad, we're going to get married!"

Booby gave them both a shower of hugs and kisses. "That's great! Welcome to the family!" Booby said to Shannon.

Russell heard all the commotion. He was told the news, and James and Shannon were given another wave of congratulations. They picked up their glasses and toasted to the occasion.

"This calls for champagne!" Booby went behind the bar and pulled a chilled bottle of Moet out of a wine refrigerator. He opened the bottle and popped the cork, which made a familiar sound. He poured the bubbly and handed everyone a glass. They toasted to the marriage again. Russell excused himself, and moved back to his station at the door to greet the customers.

After the initial excitement died down, James grew serious. Booby looked at his son.

"What's wrong, James?"

James took a deep breath. "Dad, I was going to wait until after dinner tonight, but I figure I might as well tell you now."

"Tell me what, James?"

"Dad…I'm moving to Florida. To Miami. Shannon and I. We're going to move to Florida. I'm just…I don't know…I'm just burnt out on this job…and this life here. I need to try to find myself. I need to try to finally figure out who I am."

Booby smiled. "Miami? I know all about that. I was just waiting for you to tell me. It's okay, booby. I understand. You need to follow your heart, James."

James looked at his father, startled. "You knew?" James stammered. He gulped his Champagne. "How did you know?"

"James, you've been walking around the office the last couple of weeks saying your good-byes to just about everyone. You've been parceling out your proposals, delegating your work. And I overheard you talking to a moving company. It doesn't take a rocket scientist to figure out was going on."

"Oh…and here I thought I was being so secretive about it!"

"We work at a small company, James. It's hard to keep secrets." Booby winked.

"And you're okay with this?"

"I was in business for fifteen years before you showed up. I'm sure we'll manage."

James thought a minute. "Brian is a good kid, you know. He's a little young, but I think he can handle being the sales manager. He could do a good job for you."

Booby grinned, and grabbed his son's shoulder. "James, we'll manage. Go to Miami. Go do what you have to do." Booby took a sip of his martini. "Besides, if it doesn't work out, you can always come back. I happen to know the owner."

James and Shannon laughed, and Booby joined them.

Booby reached into his vest pocket and pulled out an envelope. "And *I* was going to wait until after dinner tonight to give you this. It's for you James. Your commission for Federated Wines and Liquors."

James' eyes lit up. "I've been waiting for that!" James opened the envelope and glanced at the check. James studied the amount, frowned, and looked again. He grinned, but looked at his father with a puzzled expression. "Dad, what's this?"

"That's your commission check…plus something extra."

James showed the check to Shannon.

Her eyes popped open wide. "James, that's six figures. That's your commission? How do I get a job at your company?"

"Actually, about a third of that is my commission. The rest is…" James turned to his father.

"I can't take it with me, booby!" Booby said. He grew serious. "James, I know things haven't always been easy for you here. I understand that. Look, that money…you deserve it. You've earned it. Go to Florida, and use that money to get a good start on things. Just remember to treat me nice when I visit."

"You're welcome any time, Dad," James said, hugging his father.

Booby's face lit up. "There's really good fishing in the Keys, booby. Maybe I'll take my boat down."

"That would be great, Dad."

Russell turned toward the door to greet the next guest; in walked Jane Cameron.

Mrs. Cameron was dressed very elegantly in a black evening gown. "It's too cold in here!" she said to Booby.

Booby turned to his son, smiled, and winked. Then he greeted Mrs. Cameron. "You look lovely tonight, my dear," Booby said, giving his wife a big kiss.

Shannon showed her future mother-in-law her engagement ring, and Mrs. Cameron nearly fainted. When she recovered, there were more kisses and hugs all around, followed by another toast.

More people started to trickle in, and soon the restaurant was packed. Most of the Cameron office staff showed up, as well as the Cameron's extended family.

Everyone made their greetings, and James and Shannon were subjected to a few dozen more rounds of hugs and toasts.

"One more toast, and I'm going to be looped," Shannon giggled.

Mike Munro entered the restaurant, perfectly dressed. He made his way around the room, and finally stopped in front of James. "James, I know we haven't talked since…since our fight…."

"That's because I've been avoiding you," James said coldly.

Mike sighed. "Look, James, I don't want to argue. I just want to apologize, okay? I just wanted to say I'm sorry."

James stared at Mike. "Your nose looks good."

Mike spoke gruffly. "You're a good kid. You've got a good heart. I know I haven't been easy on you over the years...and I've had my own problems. I just wanted to apologize and wish you luck in Miami." Mike offered his hand, and James shook it. They both nodded.

"If things don't work out," Mike said, "you know you can always—"

James held up his hand. "I've already gotten the 'Feel free to run home with your tail between your legs' speech."

Mike nodded. "Well, I just wanted to say good luck."

"He's such a pleasant fellow," Shannon commented as Mike moved on to another group of people.

The room had filled, and Booby asked everyone to find their seats. James took a table with his mother and Shannon. A chair sat empty. Booby was too busy working the room to sit and eat.

When everyone was settled, Meridian burst in through the front door.

"Sorry I'm late!" he yelled. "I couldn't find my goddamn tie!"

James waved to Meridian, who came over and sat down.

"I don't know how you wear suits all the time, James. They're a real pain in the ass."

Mrs. Cameron gently slapped his face. "The mouth on you," she chided.

Meridian was shown the ring, and James and Shannon suffered through another series of hugs and kisses, and one last toast. James also told Meridian the news that he was leaving, at which Meridian frowned.

"First Vincent...now you. What the hell is going on around here?"

"Don't worry, Meridian," James comforted him. "We'll still see each other. I have a funny feeling it'll be more than you think."

Meridian sulked. "It's goddamn hot in Florida."

"It sure is," James agreed.

A few waiters appeared and worked their way around the room, taking drink orders, then dinner orders, which, to a person, consisted of steak.

Sooner than expected, the dinners were served. The waiters brought out large trays of creamed spinach, scalloped potatoes, and macaroni and cheese. The steaks and the side dishes smelled great. Mouths watered in anticipation.

"Now that's what I'm talking about!" Meridian exclaimed, and dove into his food.

James and Shannon watched Meridian eat with gusto.

"Do you think he's going to be all right without you?" Shannon whispered to James.

James nodded. "He's going to be just fine. In fact, I think we're all going to be just fine." James gazed once again into Shannon's eyes. "Thank you for marrying me," he said.

"You're welcome!"

"I love you, Shannon." James took her hand and kissed it.

"I love you, too," she whispered.

Booby stood in front of the fireplace. "How's the food?" he yelled to the crowd.

Everyone in the room cheered.

"Can I get another steak?" Two-Boy yelled out.

"Only if you pay for it," Booby responded, pointing at him and smiling expansively.

The room toasted Booby, and saluted with their drinks.

"God bless A Taste of Booby!" Meridian yelled.

The restaurant erupted in laughter.

James and Shannon laughed along with them.

THE END

978-0-595-38952-0
0-595-38952-X

Printed in the United States
113667LV00013B/93/A